The Hunt for Jack Reacher Series

Don't Know Jack
Jack in the Box
Jack and Kill
Get Back Jack
Jack in the Green
Jack and Joe
Deep Cover Jack
Jack the Reaper
Black Jack
Ten Two Jack
Jack of Spades
Prepper Jack
Full Metal Jack
Jack Frost
Jack of Hearts
Straight Jack
Jack Knife
Lone Star Jack
Bulletproof Jack
Bet On Jack
Jack on a Wire

The Michael Flint Series

Blood Trails
Trace Evidence
Ground Truth
Hard Money

The Jess Kimball Thrillers

Fatal Enemy
Fatal Distraction
Fatal Demand
Fatal Error
Fatal Fall
Fatal Edge
Fatal Game
Fatal Bond
Fatal Past
Fatal Heat
Fatal Dawn
Fatal Shot

The Hunt for Justice Series

Due Justice
Twisted Justice
Secret Justice
Wasted Justice
Raw Justice
Mistaken Justice
Cold Justice
False Justice
Fair Justice
True Justice
Night Justice

Diane Capri

Lone Star Jack

Copyright © 2022 Diane Capri, LLC

All Rights Reserved

Excerpt from **Echo Burning** © 2001 Lee Child

All rights reserved as permitted under the U.S. Copyright Act of 1976. No part of the publication may be reproduced, distributed, or transmitted in any form or by any means, or stored in a database or retrieval system, without the prior permission of the publisher. The only exception is brief quotation in printed reviews.

Published by: AugustBooks

http://www.AugustBooks.com

ISBN: 978-1-962769-27-3

Original cover design by: Cory Clubb

Lone Star Jack is a work of fiction. Names, characters, places, and incidents either are the product of the author's imagination or are used fictitiously, and any resemblance to actual persons, living or dead, business establishments, events, or locales is entirely coincidental.

Published in the United States of America.

Visit the author website:

http://www.DianeCapri.com

Dedication

Perpetually, to Lee Child,
with unrelenting gratitude.

Lone Star Jack

Cast of Primary Characters

Kim Otto
Carlos Gaspar
Charles Cooper
Michael Flint
Kathryn Scarlett
Martin Weber
Carmen Greer
Alice Aaron
Bobby Greer
Rusty Greer
Cesar Baez
Pilar Inez Mendoza

and
Jack Reacher

ECHO BURNING

By Lee Child

"They had a choice. They could have been upstanding human beings. But they chose not to be. Then they chose to mess with me, which was the final straw, and they got what they got. ..."

"You're a hard man, Reacher," Alice said.

"I think I'm a realistic man," he said. "And a decent enough guy, all told."

"You may find normal people don't agree."

He nodded.

"A lot of you don't," he said.

Chapter 1

Saturday, May 21
Remote Southwest Texas

Mateo Lopez hid in the trees, watching the house, willing the woman to turn off the lights and go to bed. He saw her silhouette cross the light from the window as she moved around inside her bedroom.

He had no idea what she looked like. How old she was. Whether she had friends and family. None of that mattered to him. He didn't even know her name.

She was the target. This was a job he'd been forced to do. He didn't need to know anything else.

When Mateo completed the work, his family would be safe. Nothing mattered more.

Even in the darkness, without the unrelenting sun overhead he'd endured all day, the outside temperature was uncomfortably hot for late May.

Mateo had lived in Mexico his whole life. He was used to the heat and the hot breezes and the dust. So much dirt. He shook his head.

But this was spring in Texas, the rainiest month. He'd dressed in warm clothes, expecting cooler temperatures and even a bit of rain so far north. Now he was sweating like mid-August back home and fighting to breathe.

3 Lone Star Jack

Briefly, he considered stripping off his clothes. He didn't.

He inhaled the warm air and held it in his lungs, like a drag on a cigarette. Good thing he'd quit smoking before he'd set off with his family from Mexico. If the artist happened to glance outside while he was grabbing a smoke, she might have seen him. One less worry.

The artist would die, as he'd promised. But she would die in her sleep. She wouldn't suffer. Which mattered to him. He would kill her. That should be enough. He drew the line at torture.

He'd walked miles from where he'd parked the old sedan on the dirt road south and west of here, lugging enough gasoline to create and feed a raging hot fire. The closest neighbors were miles away, too. Farther away than the car.

He wondered why she'd chosen to live in such a hell hole. Whatever her reasons, the location made his job easier. The old dry wood-framed house, filled with the woman's painting supplies, should burn fast and hot long before anyone noticed the fire. No firefighters would reach this place to prevent total destruction.

The gas cans were heavy and awkward, and he could only carry two at once. Progress was slow. Sweating, breathing hard, watching his step in the gathering darkness.

5 Lone Star Jack

The last thing he needed was to trip and fall and spill the gasoline.

Finally, he'd managed to bring eight full cans to the edge of the clearing.

Only nocturnal animals had noticed him. He was sure of that.

He squatted and sat on the dirt in the shadows to rest, wiping the sweat from his face with his shirt. He wasn't a young man anymore. He had a wife, two children. Soon, they would join him here. José had promised.

"Work hard, Mateo. Do this one thing. Do it well. Your family will be okay. You have my word," José had said.

Mateo believed the comforting words because he was desperate. He could do this terrible thing, and then his family's new life could begin.

This woman was nothing to him. She lived alone, here in the dusty nowhere. She probably didn't even have a family. Not like Mateo's, anyway.

He'd been a laborer all his life, like his father before him. Mateo was no stranger to hard work. He was familiar with fire, too.

His young son had been badly burned when he fell into a fire pit near their home in Mexico years ago. Mateo had pulled the boy from the fire and burned his own hand, which was now scarred and painful.

7 Lone Star Jack

He'd been too slow to react. His boy had died. Mateo and his wife were devastated.

Even now, Mateo's hand burned and ached as if the wound were fresh. He had lost one child. He couldn't lose the others. He'd do anything to give them a better life. **Anything.**

Mateo knew what to do and he knew how to do it. Even as he knew murder was wrong, he also knew his family was worth it.

He frowned when the thought surfaced that his wife would be appalled by his actions. He shrugged. Sofia would never know.

While he waited, Mateo went over the plan in his head again. First, he'd break into the house. Which would be easy, José said, because the woman never locked the doors.

She lived a solitary life, remote from people. She'd implemented no security measures, probably because she didn't expect trouble.

José told Mateo to enter through the kitchen door in the back of the house because it was closest to the stairs. Her bedroom was one flight up, directly above the kitchen.

"She doesn't close her bedroom door," José had said. "No reason to. You won't even need to use the doorknob. But wear your gloves, just in case."

Mateo had raised his eyebrows in question. "In case of what?"

9 Lone Star Jack

"You don't want to leave fingerprints. Forensics men are smarter in Texas. They might be able to identify you. You don't want that, amigo," José replied.

Mateo nodded. He intended to destroy the house and reduce it to charred rubble. He didn't believe there would be any way to gather evidence against him from the ashes, even if he made a mistake.

But José was the boss here. Mateo had already pulled on the latex gloves, as instructed.

"You just walk into the bedroom. Be careful not to shine a light or wake her up," José had instructed. "Put the pillow over her face and smother her. Then burn down the house. That's it. Simple, no?"

Mateo had nodded again, throughout the instructions. Things were almost never as simple in the execution as they sounded during planning. Mateo knew that much.

So did José.

But it didn't matter. The plan was as good as they could make it, under the circumstances.

"See you when you're done, amigo," José said, patting him on the shoulder. "We'll go to pick up your family together. I'll drive you to California personally. Get you settled into your new home. New job. We've already set up your banking and the cash payout we promised. You'll be all set."

They shook hands.

11 Lone Star Jack

José went back into the bar.

Mateo headed out to the middle of nowhere. To kill a woman he didn't know so that his family could live in peace and prosperity.

How had his life come to this?

Mateo shook his head and glanced upward again.

The light in her bedroom on the second floor finally shut off, snuffing the last ambient illumination from the black night.

He'd been staring into the light when it disappeared. A ghostly image lingered on his retina for a moment.

He closed his eyes and when he opened them again, he saw only the blocky shadow of the building across the short distance from his position under the trees.

Mateo waited to give the woman time to fall asleep. He didn't have a watch. He guessed the time was about two thirty in the morning and judged he'd waited long enough.

He stood and knocked the dust off his clothes. He grabbed two of the gasoline cans and humped them into the backyard, dropping them close to the door so he could grab them easily.

Four trips, hustling back and forth, to move all eight cans to his staging area.

Mateo patted his pockets again to be sure he had the disposable butane lighters within easy reach. He took a deep breath of the hot air and exhaled again to steady his hands.

Sweat ran down his face and from his armpits. He wiped his face with his sleeve, closing his eyes against the stinging wetness.

“Now,” he said quietly under his breath.

He turned the knob silently and pulled the back door open. He stepped inside, waiting a moment for his eyes to adjust to the even darker interior of the kitchen.

The staircase was exactly where José had told him it would be, which seemed like an affirmation of José’s word, somehow. Maybe the other things José had said about saving his family were also true.

Mateo climbed the stairs as quietly as he could, given his heavy work boots. At the second floor, he turned toward the open bedroom door.

She had a nightlight turned on in the bathroom in the hallway. It provided weak illumination, but enough to see her silent body lying on the bed under a thin sheet. He paused to focus his vision. Her chest rose and fell gently in regular rhythm. Her curly yellow hair was splashed across her pillow like a fluffy halo.

As if he were approaching a sleeping rattler, Mateo approached the woman with as much stealth as he could muster.

15 Lone Star Jack

He grabbed a pillow and pushed it down over her face, applying all of his weight through his heavily muscled arms.

She thrashed her body and grabbed at his wrists, trying to free herself. Mateo kept his force even and steady and strong.

Until she stopped struggling.

He held the pillow another full minute. To be certain the job was done.

When he finally pulled the pillow away, her eyes were open and as lifeless as the chickens he'd beheaded for special dinners back home.

He checked her carotid pulse, like José had shown him to do. He felt nothing. No beating. No breathing. No seeing.

"It's done." He nodded once. She was as dead as he could make her.

He glanced upward, as if he could see her spirit rising from her body. Softly, he said, "Thank you for your gift of life to my children."

Mateo turned and hurried downstairs to collect the gasoline.

He splashed the first two cans over her bed, soaking the body and the bedding. Four more cans to cover the bedroom floor, the hallway, and the staircase. The gas fumes irritated his eyes and his nose and made him cough.

17 Lone Star Jack

He used the seventh can liberally in the kitchen. Then he opened the eighth can and pulled three hand towels from his pocket. He stuffed one of the hand towels into the top of the eighth can.

Mateo looked at his handiwork, satisfied that the towels would do the job.

He ran back upstairs, lit the first towel, and tossed it onto the bed. The whoosh flashed the fumes pulsing up from the gasoline-soaked bedding and began to burn hot and bright.

He turned and ran toward the staircase. He dropped the second towel onto the wet carpet before he hurried down the steps. He felt the heat on his back all the way to the bottom and into the kitchen.

Mateo bent over the eighth gas can and ignited the towel sticking up from its neck. He believed he had a full minute. Maybe two to reach safety outside.

He was wrong.

He turned to dash out the still open back door.

The strong, hot wind blew into the back door and caught the fire exactly the wrong way.

Mateo heard the gas fumes ignite behind him.

The explosion blasted into the night air, hard, high, and hot.

19 Lone Star Jack

Pressure threw Mateo across the room and dropped him on the floor, six feet from the exit.

His last prayer was that Sofia would be comforted to know that he didn't feel a thing.

He didn't suffer.

He wasn't tortured by the flames that consumed him.

Chapter 2

Sunday, May 29 (one week later)
Ojinaga, Mexico

Cesar Baez stood, master of all he surveyed, admiring the sunset from the veranda of his villa. The distant rolling hills led to the dusty pasture surrounding the ranch buildings in a single, cohesive whole.

He owned it all. He'd worked for it. His father had left him nothing.

Cesar had fought to acquire every square inch of what he owned, and he held on with a tight-fisted fierceness few men would care to master. Even fewer made the attempt.

He was still dressed in his expensive riding clothes, holding his third tall glass of sparkling water. He looked more like an Englishman back from the hunt than a ruthless **Capo**.

Diego Baez, Cesar's father, had embodied the **Capo** depicted by every Hollywood cliché. Diego came up off the streets. He was vicious. Cruel. Effective.

Diego had built the family business from Durango. For two decades, the Baez Cartel had inspired fear and obedience and enjoyed massive prosperity throughout Mexico.

Cesar came from that world.

But unlike his brothers, Cesar no longer lived there, in body or soul.

Cesar left Durango and the old ways of the family business behind before the old man died.

His brothers ran the original illegal activities of the Baez Cartel now, including the bigger and better legitimate enterprises the family had transitioned into these past two decades.

As the youngest, Cesar had been cast aside, assigned to mind the smaller branches of the family business in the hinterlands of Ojinaga.

Cesar had no regrets. He had created an empire of his own, better in every way than the old Baez Cartel.

Cesar's carefully cultivated public façade resembled film roles played by the young Ricardo Montalbán. He was clean shaven. Well trimmed curly hair swept back. Always well dressed, always a gentleman whenever he appeared in public.

Grace under pressure, Cesar reminded himself often.

As a child, Cesar had watched hours of old films starring Montalbán, the handsome Mexican actor. He'd learned to mimic Montalbán's body movements. Their common Mexican heritage informed not only Cesar's appearance, but his speech and mannerisms as well.

Cesar's desire to move from the shadowy criminal underworld he grew up in fueled the persona he'd adopted completely when he left Durango for college.

The transformation was accepted now by all who knew him.

Diego Baez had been a street thug and a smuggler and a killer. Both of Cesar's brothers were carbon copies of the old man.

Cesar Baez was not.

Or so his savvy colleagues professed to believe. Those who publicly declared otherwise had been removed.

A current observer would see Cesar admiring his property and waiting patiently for his business manager to appear, exhibiting control and class. As Montalbán would have done.

Yet, Cesar's nostrils flared and the heat of his Latin temper threatened to erupt without warning. He controlled himself with the same iron will he applied to life in general.

José Del Campo was late.

Tardiness was a character flaw Cesar rarely tolerated.

He expected employees to wait for him, not to keep him waiting.

As with so many other innate characteristics, Cesar Baez was his father's son.

Had any employee dared to keep the old man waiting for even five minutes, retribution came swift and hard and sure.

The old man had a sadistic streak, too.

Life was cheap in Durango when Cesar was a boy. Employees were little more than chattel. His father had disciplined them harshly every day of the week for relatively minor infractions.

Secretly, Cesar believed the old man enjoyed torturing them, because he fought those impulses in himself.

For tardiness, his father's response was swift and crude amputation.

Five minutes waiting time and one of Diego's **sicarios** would lop off the miscreant's finger with a dirty machete brought in from the fields. Fifteen minutes tardy would cost a hand. And so on.

What would Diego do when a worker simply didn't show up at all?

Cesar didn't know. Employees never missed an entire day of work. They didn't have the nerve.

Cesar shook his head. At fifteen, Cesar had rebelled against his father's ways. They had argued.

Knowing too well his father's cold heart, Cesar had skipped emotional appeals. Instead, he said maiming employees was impractical because it interfered with their job performance.

“Just the opposite,” Diego had replied, without a trace of humor. “The penalty for poor performance is death. Solves the problem every time.”

Cesar had controlled the shudder the old man’s unwavering ruthlessness inspired.

Even so, the peasants lined up, hat in hand, for Diego Baez’s next available job. They didn’t care what the job was because they had no alternatives.

Everyone who worked in the village near Durango was employed by the old man or they were not employed at all.

Which meant they were as good as dead anyway.

29 Lone Star Jack

At eighteen, like his brothers before him, Cesar left Mexico and attended Harvard. He stayed for business school afterward. By the time he came back to Durango, the old man remained the same, but the world had changed.

His father passed the business on to Cesar and his two older brothers. The company was divided. Each brother received a territory and the operations located there.

Cesar inherited Ojinaga, the smallest and least successful drug smuggling division of the Baez Cartel.

That was ten years ago.

Cesar had applied the lessons he'd learned in business school to triple the Ojinaga drugs division's revenues and profits. The operation was thriving, providing more than ample wealth for the family.

But Cesar also wanted to build something of his own. He'd started a construction company and devoted his skill to developing that business as well.

His brothers were jealous. They watched and waited for the chance to steal what Cesar had created.

Which was why he developed another operation. One his brothers knew nothing about. A business much more lucrative and easier to manage.

Like his father before him, Cesar proved to be a successful **Capo**. He smiled. It was impossible to change one's DNA.

Inspired during his studies at Harvard, the old enterprise known as Murder, Inc. had fascinated him.

Murder, Inc., acted as the enforcement arm of the Mafia and other closely related criminal organizations. Believed to have been responsible for more than four hundred contract killings. Maybe as many as a thousand murders between 1929 and 1941, some reports claimed.

Four hundred kills in twelve years was an ambitious number. More than thirty each year. More than one per month. If the death toll was closer to one thousand, the company served as a prolific and efficient killing machine, indeed.

Ultimately, Murder, Inc., became too brazen. Made too many mistakes.

Lessons Cesar took seriously as he developed his own operations.

He heard footsteps. He drained the last of the sparkling water from his glass and placed it carefully on the table beside him.

Cesar turned his back to the setting sun and folded his hands behind. He was backlit, his face in shadow.

He narrowed his eyes and watched José approach.

Chapter 3

Sunday, May 29
Ojinaga, Mexico

"Sorry to keep you waiting, Cesar," José said boldly, as if punctuality rules did not apply to him. **Tenientes**.

José was lucky he didn't work for Cesar's father. The old man would have cut off José's arm for that insolence. His position as a lieutenant would have meant nothing to Diego.

José said, "The call came later than expected. I tried to reach you from the car, but your phone went to voicemail."

Cesar nodded. Once. Curtly.

The excuse was better than most excuses. But not good enough.

José cleared his throat. "Mateo Lopez completed his task, as required."

"The target?"

José nodded. "Results were confirmed. I saw the ashes myself."

"And Lopez?" Cesar asked, still annoyed, but calming a bit.

José shook his head. "Didn't make it."

"Good," Cesar said, his mood improving incrementally. "His family?"

José shook his head again. "No survivors, I'm afraid. Sofia Lopez and her children perished in the desert on the way to their new home. Dehydration. Nothing could be done."

Cesar pursed his lips. The news was good but expected. The fee Cesar had demanded from the client in exchange for sacrificing the Lopez family was substantial. Cesar was satisfied.

José had been right to wait for the confirmation call. Cesar would let his tardiness go this time.

"And the two cases in Texas are on track?" Cesar said, chewing his lower lip.

José nodded. "A bit of scrambling because the old senator died and the target's plans changed."

"Rescheduled?" Cesar asked.

José nodded again.

"And the woman?"

"Both jobs will be completed when I see you next," José assured with a single curt nod.

"We'll talk more tomorrow. I don't want to keep my guests waiting," Cesar said on his way into the house.

He heard José's long exhale as he passed. José had narrowly escaped Cesar's wrath this time.

José was no fool. He wouldn't be late again unless he was prepared to pay the price.

37 Lone Star Jack

Cesar went directly to his study to verify the arson to his client. He located the dedicated number he'd engaged for this purpose. He sent the one-word message: **Terminado**. Which meant finished, completed.

Briefly, as he waited for confirmation, he wondered why the client had wanted the woman killed. She lived alone, bothered no one. Killing her seemed unnecessary.

Cesar shrugged. The reason mattered not to him. Murder was a mere business transaction.

If he started asking about motives, his clients would stop calling, stop referring new business. Which was not acceptable.

When the return message pinged, he saw he'd received the appropriate one-word response: **Pagado**. Paid in full.

Cesar checked his offshore account created specifically for this purpose. With a few quick keystrokes he verified the wire transfer deposit.

Excelente, he murmured.

He locked his study and dropped the key into his pocket on his way to shower and change for dinner with the ambassador and his wife.

The shower washed away the last of his annoyance with José.

These jobs were tricky. Cesar was pleased to close another one successfully.

39 Lone Star Jack

When he joined his wife in her dressing room, she was ready and waiting.

Gabriella reminded him of the American actress, Grace Kelly, when she was still fresh-faced, young, beautiful, and compliant. Not too smart. Eager to please. Delectable arm candy.

He'd known she was the perfect choice when he first laid eyes on her at a reception in Cambridge. Which was why he wooed her. And married her. And brought her here.

Cesar noticed when other men coveted her. Gabriella served as further evidence that Cesar Baez was not his father. The knowledge pleased him.

He kissed her neck. “You look beautiful, as always.”

“Thank you.” She smiled and glided toward the limo as he walked beside her into the night air perfumed with the scent of jasmine, her favorite.

Which was why jasmine was planted in all the gardens. It was a small thing, easy enough to give, and it made her happy.

Briefly, his thoughts returned to the dead Lopez family. Sofia Lopez had been a handsome woman. Similar in size to Cesar’s wife.

Which made him wonder how long Gabriella would last were she forced to trek across the hot desert with her children and nothing but the clothes on their backs and the possessions she could carry.

Gabriella and the children wouldn't last long, he suspected. Not long at all.

Cesar smiled. Good to know.

Chapter 4

Sunday, May 29
Braun, Michigan

FBI Special Agent Kim Otto leaned back in the driver's seat, one hand on the steering wheel, enjoying the nostalgic spring drive.

Dinner at her parent's home in Braun, north of Detroit, had been a regular Sunday event when she had a regular government job. Before she'd been assigned to the Reacher file.

She slipped easily into the old habit, feeling normal for the first time in a good, long while.

43 Lone Star Jack

Unlike last year when winter had lingered way too long, the change of seasons was well established. Even the dirty snow piles alongside the parking lots had melted. The grass was greening up nicely in the parks and lawns surrounding the familiar middle-class homes.

Forsythia, tulips, daffodils, and hyacinths were already long past their prime. Lilacs were just beginning to bloom now.

Kim loved lilacs. With luck, she'd still be here and able to enjoy them when the blooms exploded and filled the air with their pleasantly sweet fragrance.

She smiled as the familiar and comfortable engulfed her. After weeks of running on what she called her standard triple As—adrenaline, ambition, and anxiety—she felt her body relax.

Braun was a small town populated mostly by German Americans when her parents had located here decades ago. Growing up, Kim never met a stranger. Her family knew the neighbors, the kids at school, and the members of their Lutheran church.

Which amounted to just about everybody living in Braun back then.

Through the years, the area had changed.

It seemed the mayor must have been working overtime to raise property values since Kim left home for college years ago. Braun had become so gentrified that Kim hardly recognized the place these days.

Two-lane roads had been widened to boulevards. The centuries old downtown had been toned up. Two upscale shopping malls anchored either end of town, and strip malls galore lined the main streets on all sides. Franchises had replaced the small independent businesses she'd grown up with.

"Still, no place like home, as they say," she muttered aloud.

Kim drove through to the north side of town and turned right onto what had been a local farm road when she'd lived here. The farmer died and his family had sold the land to developers a few years back. McMansions built on one-acre parcels seemed to spring up overnight on both sides of the now smoothly paved throughway.

When she passed the last of the oversized homes, she crossed her family's property line and fell backward in time. Nothing much had changed here since her parents moved in all those years ago.

Grandpa Otto had bought the decrepit farm for them after the war, when her parents were newlyweds.

Dad was never a farmer, either before the war or after. He was an engineer and he worked at the local automotive design center. He'd fixed up the house for their new family as best he could.

Mom was the one who loved to grow things. The rich soil and flat farmland had seemed an unimaginable luxury to the young Vietnamese war bride.

The old farmhouse still sat at the end of the road, where it had always been. The house could have been used for a 1930s movie set. Dad had updated the interior a couple of times over the years, but the white clapboard house itself reflected the era when it was originally built.

The house had grown by fits and starts with gables and angles added as needed. A good-sized porch on the front was part of the original construction. The garage had been added about 1970 or so, long before her parents moved here. A black shingled roof tied it all together.

This town and this house had been as good a place as any to grow up, Kim supposed. Constant physical activities were necessary to keep her three brothers out of trouble, her parents believed.

Plenty of room in the backyard for an ice-skating rink in the winter and a baseball diamond in the summer. Close enough to the public schools and the town shops.

The bottom line was that the Otto kids were raised like their dad and his siblings had been. A close-knit family in a close-knit community of similar people having mostly the same experiences. They watched broadcast television, talked on landline phones, drove used cars that burned cheap gas, and grew their own vegetables.

Not exactly **The Waltons**, but close enough.

After she left home for college, Kim finally realized that her childhood was common to an earlier generation. She'd led an old-fashioned life unlike the ones her college classmates had experienced.

Which was just one more reason she felt different from her peers.

During her time at college, and the years that followed, Kim came to understand how difficult life had been for her mother. Moving across the world to raise her family in a foreign land and another culture must have been overwhelming.

Sure, Mom had a better life now than she ever would have had in Vietnam. But that didn't mean the new life had been easy for her. Quite the opposite.

Kim shook her thoughts from her past when she pulled the SUV into her parents' long driveway. She parked in the turnout beside the garage.

Her vehicle slipped into her spot like a homing pigeon returning to its roost.

Dad had built the turnout when the kids had started driving and had their own rides. Five kids required five parking spaces. The spaces were still there, even though the whole family rarely gathered now.

Kim's brothers wouldn't be here today, either. All three worked in the tech industry and lived in California. Except for occasional video calls or family weddings and funerals, she saw them rarely.

Kim frowned as her SUV settled next to the sporty yellow two-seater that belonged to her sister Mỹ.

The whole family had called her younger sister Sunny since childhood. Ironically. Because her disposition was anything but bright and cheerful.

Kim sighed. She hadn't spent a pleasant hour with her sister in years. Come to think of it, maybe never.

The prospect of an enjoyable Sunday afternoon with her parents disappeared. Some of the tension returned to Kim's body, raising her personal danger meter out of the green zone.

Briefly, Kim's mind considered her sister's sour personality.

Dad had named the boys. He'd chosen German names from the Otto family tree for her three brothers. Albert, Ernst, and Wilhelm. They looked like every Otto in the family tree, like they belonged.

53 Lone Star Jack

Kim felt tall and blonde and German on the inside. But she and Sunny both resembled her mother. Hard to fight genetics. Both Kim and Mỹ definitely stood out among the German Americans in the town, the school, the church. They looked like strangers in a world that was as much their own as anyone else who lived in Braun.

Mom, perhaps in some misguided sense of honoring her ancestors, chose Vietnamese names for the two girls, Kim and Mỹ. Her sister's name was more than apt.

Mỹ meant "beautiful" in Vietnamese, and Sunny certainly was. Much more beautiful than Kim.

Her name was pronounced “me,” which was appropriate. Sunny was always all about Sunny, for sure.

Mỹ hated her name and her nickname. But then, she’d have been unhappy no matter what name their parents had chosen. Sunny was grim and dour about everything. She’d been born that way. Her beauty seemed to be of little comfort to her.

Kim shook off the old thoughts, took a deep breath, grabbed the flowers she’d brought for Mom and the chocolates for Dad, and climbed out of her SUV.

She was here now. Sunny was here, too. Nothing she could do but make the best of the circumstances.

55 Lone Star Jack

No sooner had she set both feet on the driveway than The Boss's burner phone began to vibrate in her pocket.

She set the chocolates down on the front seat and fished the phone out.

"Otto," she answered, as if there were dozens of people who might have responded to his call on the dedicated line. "What's up?"

"I need to see you," Charles Cooper said politely, as if she really had a choice. Which she didn't.

They both knew the score here.

He held all the power in their relationship.

But that didn't mean she was his slave. He should have figured that out long before now.

She was entitled to an evening off.

Charles Cooper had moved from his career as an army general to the unofficial top of the food chain at the FBI. He wasn't the director. Not yet. The Director's job was mostly a figurehead position, anyway.

Cooper was the man in charge, the one who got things done.

He was her boss.

He could throw her under the bus in a hot second if he felt like it, and her career would be over. Nothing to be gained by denying that reality.

There had been a time when Kim would have dropped everything to respond to Cooper's whims instantly.

Those days were long gone.

Chapter 5

Sunday, May 29
Braun, Michigan

During the course of her Reacher assignment, Cooper had abused Kim's trust too many times. She no longer afforded him blind loyalty or obedience.

Kim didn't bother to ask why Cooper wanted to see her. No point. He wouldn't tell her anyway.

"I'm having dinner with my parents. I can fly to DC tomorrow."

"I'll meet you in your apartment tonight."

He disconnected before she had a chance to argue, and she wouldn't have objected anyway. She'd already planned to go back home after dinner tonight. But there was no reason to tell him that.

She shrugged. Whatever Cooper wanted could wait a few hours.

Otherwise, he'd have landed on her parents' driveway in a helicopter and scooped her up. He'd done it before.

She dropped the phone into her pocket and made her way to the front door, which was never locked despite her attempts to bring her parent's security systems into the twenty-first century.

Kim turned the knob, let herself in, and followed her nose to the kitchen where her mother was preparing traditional Vietnamese dishes along with the German style food the rest of her family loved.

The combined aromas didn't mix well, but they smelled like home and churned Kim's stomach in the way she remembered.

She pulled an antacid from her pocket and plopped it in her mouth before she smiled and greeted her parents with hugs and gifts and the suggestion that they sit outside to enjoy the fresh spring breeze.

"Where's Sunny?" Kim asked when they were settled on the patio, Vietnamese iced coffee in hand.

Kim loved the sweet concoction and always had. Family lore claimed that

Mom had given Kim Vietnamese iced coffee within minutes of her birth, establishing her love affair for coffee as the most enduring relationship of her life.

“I saw her car out front. Isn’t she joining us?”

“Don’t sound so hopeful,” Sunny said as she came outside and plopped onto a chair, looking as stunningly gorgeous as always. “Why wouldn’t I be joining you? I live here, remember? You’re the one who plops in from the sky and jumps out like hot popcorn.”

Kim had seen too much death and mayhem these past few weeks to spend what little precious down time she had arguing with her sister.

"Nice to see you, too," Kim replied as pleasantly as possible, taking the high road. "Mom said you were sick last week. I hope you're feeling better."

But her sister wasn't mollified. Sunny frowned, tossed off a surly "Thanks," and then refused to engage any further.

Dad, ever the peacemaker, picked up the conversational ball and changed the subject.

After ten minutes or so, Sunny stood and went back inside without so much as a middle-finger salute.

"What's wrong with her?" Kim asked, genuinely peeved. Sunny should be more mature by now. Would she never grow up?

"I'm not really sure," Dad replied. "She's been like that for a while now. Since Martin deployed to the border."

"Who's Martin? What border? Deployed by whom?" Kim asked, raising both eyebrows.

Over the years, Sunny had had more boyfriends than Kim could count. Kim had always been the studious one. Sunny was beautiful and could display an infectiously sparkling personality when she was so inclined.

But Kim didn't remember a guy named Martin.

Mom shook her head, as if Kim should already know the answers to these questions. Which she probably should.

Dad chuckled and sipped his coffee. "You can take the girl out of the FBI, but…"

Kim shrugged.

"Martin Weber. They've been dating about a year. He's in the National Guard. Got deployed to the US southern border in Texas for a short stint," Dad said, draining his glass.

Kim's eyes widened. "Mỹ has been dating him for a **year**? And I'm just hearing his name for the first time?"

Mom tsked and shook her head and flashed a disapproving frown. "It's not like we've seen much of you lately. If you came around more, you'd have met Martin already."

"You know I've been on assignment, Mom. It's not like I've been avoiding you," Kim said, holding onto her patience. "Is Sunny serious about him?"

Kim made a mental note to check up on Martin Weber as soon as she had a chance. As annoying as Sunny could be, she was Kim's younger sister, and she didn't want Sunny hurt.

Maybe the guy was good enough for her sister.

And maybe not.

Dad shrugged. "As serious as Sunny ever is about a guy, I guess."

"That's not fair, Albert," Mom scolded gently. "Martin is a good man. He's good to Mỹ. She says she loves him. Surely you remember what it was like to be fighting a war when your girl was stuck back home. I certainly remember what those years were like for us."

Dad reached over and patted Mom's hand. He didn't say more about Sunny's current fling, but conflicting emotions washed across his face.

A whole year was a long, long time for Sunny to stay with any one guy. Maybe this relationship wasn't a fling. Perhaps she was serious about Martin Weber. Maybe Sunny was genuinely worried for him.

Even so, whatever was going on with Sunny, it was nothing like the hell her parents had endured.

Albert Otto and Sin Ye had braved more than bullets to be together at the tail end of the Vietnam War. They'd fought the US Army, the Vietnamese government, both sets of parents, and the racial prejudices of the time to be together.

The struggle had bonded them like plating adheres gold to base metal.

Kim could only imagine the hardships.

None of those conditions existed in Sunny's life.

She'd been born and grew up in Middle America, like the rest of the family. The Ottos weren't wealthy, but they weren't poor, either.

67 Lone Star Jack

Sunny should have been a lot more grateful than she ever seemed to be, in Kim's view.

But Dad didn't want to upset Mom or the pleasant evening she'd planned, so he didn't argue.

"So what is Martin Weber doing down at the border, exactly?" Kim asked, moving the conversation to a slightly less personal topic. "Last I heard, National Guard troops deployed down there had been called back due to budgetary issues."

"He's posted at Presidio, south of Pecos, Texas. Says it's dry and unseasonably hot. The situation is grueling for everyone involved. His unit has already picked up hundreds of people crossing the border at night," Dad explained, shaking his head. "Terrible situation."

Kim nodded. "Yes, it's dangerous for the migrants and enforcement personnel, too."

"It's more than dangerous." Dad lowered his gaze and his voice. "Martin says they've found people dead in the desert. Dehydration, mostly."

Kim nodded. She'd seen the reports.

"And some die due to foul play. Disputes among themselves or with the locals, usually," Dad said. "Whole families are impacted. It's heartbreaking. Martin's worried. Which means we're all worried."

"Does Sunny think Martin's involved in something he shouldn't be?" Kim asked tentatively, because of the vibe she'd picked up from her sister.

Dad gave her a knowing look but didn't have a chance to say more before Mom interrupted. If Weber wasn't as solid as Sunny claimed, he wouldn't be the first of her boyfriends with a less than stellar moral code. She had always been attracted to the bad boys.

"Enough of this talk." Mom was upset by the turn the conversation had taken, perhaps remembering a time she'd rather forget. Or simply worried for her daughter. "Kim, come help me finish dinner."

"Sure. I'm starving. Let's do that," she replied, setting her glass on the tray.

She gave her father a long look and then followed her mother inside, leaving him alone on the patio.

Whatever Martin Weber's situation in Texas, it wasn't something they could solve with a bit of conversation before dinner. The border was a complicated situation. Too complicated for easy solutions.

The border agents were overwhelmed.

The honest migrants were exploited by their own people and endured way too much for a chance at a better life.

Dishonest agents and migrants were devious and often avoided arrest.

And those were only the obvious problems. There was more serious trouble active below the surface. Countries south of the border had significant criminal elements, too. Just as the United States and every other country on the planet did.

Kim's FBI Detroit Field Office received regular reports of potential terrorist activity around the country and the world.

Which meant she got regular briefings about the violence and unrest at both borders, even though the FBI wasn't generally charged with protecting the peace there.

From her office window, she could see across to Canada. The country was beautiful and the people friendly. Americans felt safe with Canada next door.

But the Canadian border was also more dangerous than ordinary citizens suspected.

In Detroit, the two countries were separated by the Detroit River. A bridge and a tunnel provided the only crossing points.

Despite the best efforts of law enforcement on both sides of the border, some terrorists had been thwarted in their efforts to pass through while other terrorists had succeeded.

And the Canadian border in Detroit was much easier to monitor than the southern border.

Because the Mexican border was long and much of it just a line in the dirt or a navigable river, defending it was exponentially more difficult. Federal, state, and local agents of all kinds were putting their lives on the line. Migrant families were, too.

The situation was a powder keg. The body count was tragic and rising.

Martin Weber could easily find himself in real trouble very quickly.

Sunny had every right to be terrified, especially if she cared about the guy.

Kim's sister was flighty and annoying as hell, but if she was serious about Weber, then he'd better be worthy.

Which meant, at a minimum, doing his job within the bounds of the law.

Easier said than done.

The border was chaotic and unpredictable. There were not many bright lines to define the right side of the law down there. Some border agents had crossed that line, to be sure. Every group everywhere had its bad apples.

Martin Weber simply could not be one of the bad ones.

Kim hoped.

First things first, though.

If Sunny loved him, Martin Weber needed to stay alive. No easy task, under the circumstances.

Kim's thoughts on the matter churned along with her stomach as she made every effort to enjoy the precious family time she so rarely managed these days. She had no idea when she'd be able to return.

Chapter 6

Sunday, May 29
Presidio, Texas

Pilar Inez Mendoza slumped into the front passenger seat of the van, toes tapping nervously inside the dirty sneakers she'd stolen from her sister before she ran away from home.

She kept to herself. The last thing she wanted was to encourage bold advances from the men.

She'd been wearing the same filthy clothes for twelve days. Jeans and a loose-fitting shirt. Nothing remotely provocative.

Which meant she smelled as rank as the male passengers.

The van driver, Miguel, was the only one who had bathed recently and the pungent body odor wafting toward her suggested that his last shower was a while ago.

Pilar had pulled her curly black hair into a ponytail and anchored it with a rubber band. She'd wrapped the ponytail into a bun, tucked it neatly inside the hole in the back of her baseball cap and then lowered the bill to shield her face from the traffic cams.

Pilar was twenty-three years old, but she looked fifteen, which was an asset to her family's prostitution business. She'd learned to exploit her appearance long ago. Without makeup, wearing the jeans and the cap, stinking as much as the others, she should pass for a boy. She hoped.

As the van moved north toward the border, Pilar scanned everything she could see through the dirty windows. Taking it all in. Locating escape routes amid the unfamiliar landscape and anchoring them to memory.

Just in case something went wrong.

Because things always went wrong in her world.

Pilar had never been to Ojinaga before, and she was only passing through. With luck, she'd never come this way again. She didn't need to remember much of it. Just enough to keep herself safe.

She'd been born in a dusty Mexican village too inconsequential to require a tiny dot on the map. She'd never traveled more than ten miles from her home in all those years.

She'd still be there now if her life had unfolded as expected.

As it was, Pilar could never go back home. Not as long as that bastard was still alive.

Revulsion coursed through her body, making her skin crawl every time his cruelty crossed her mind.

Too bad Pilar hadn't killed him when he'd tried to choke her last breath from her throat.

She'd stabbed him with the dagger she kept under the edge of the mattress for emergencies.

The doctor patched him up and let him go the next day.

He was angry and more dangerous than ever.

Pilar's only chance of survival was to escape Mexico and never return.

If the bastard saw her again, he'd surely kill her, Pilar's mother agreed.

And even if he didn't kill her, another man would. She had no illusions about that.

Pilar was like a dog on the road.

81 Lone Star Jack

It was only a matter of time before another violent bastard came along to finish the job.

She'd lost two sisters and four cousins to abusive men who thought paying for sex gave them permission to behave like savages. Which was sadly true in her village.

Pilar's fate would have been the same if she'd stayed, her mother said when she sent her youngest daughter to Cesar Baez.

"You have only one choice, Pilar," her tearful mother had said as she pressed a few pesos into her hands. "Cross the border and disappear. No matter what you have to do to take care of yourself, just do it. Never come back here. Never."

Pilar didn't cry or argue because objecting was pointless. Her mother was right. They both knew how the world worked for women like them.

She nodded and gave her mother a tight hug.

"Go!" She released her daughter and gave Pilar a hard shove in the right direction.

Pilar had stumbled across the gravel, shoving the pesos into her pocket, and scrambled into the bed of a waiting pickup truck headed out.

That seemed a lifetime ago.

Now, the van driver approached the border crossing at Presidio, Texas. As illegal crossings went, this one would be safer than most. She hadn't been forced to swim across the Rio Grande or trudge through the hot, dry land on both sides.

Pilar had begun to hope that she might actually survive.

Because of her business arrangement with Cesar Baez.

Miguel pulled up slowly behind the big SUV already in line. He reached into the console, pulled out the documents, and passed them to Pilar low across the seat in the dark, where the cameras couldn't see.

"The guard will ask for our passports and visas. Simply hand them over," Miguel repeated the instructions she'd been given several times already. He must think she was stupid. "Don't talk. Just hand him the papers."

There were eight in the van. Four of her traveling companions had legitimate Mexican passports and work visas. The other four were forgeries.

To Pilar's untrained eye, all eight were indistinguishable.

She nodded. "And then what?"

Miguel pulled a fat envelope from the console and placed it on her lap.

Before he closed the console cover again, Pilar spied the pistol resting inside.

She recognized the handgun instantly.

85 Lone Star Jack

She had learned to shoot before she'd learned to drive. Her family owned a couple of pistols exactly like Miguel's Glock 17. Traveling across the border with guns in the van was illegal as hell and made the trip much riskier.

The counterfeit documents might pass inspection undetected. A loaded gun most certainly would not.

But still, good to know the pistol was there.

Miguel said, "He'll give you the documents back. You give him the envelope. Then he'll wave us through."

Pilar nodded, as if the procedure weren't dangerous as hell. "Why me?"

"Because you look young enough. Innocent enough," Miguel replied gruffly. "And because Baez said so."

Pilar nodded again. She trusted Baez because she had no options. She knew that. Miguel knew that. Hell, everyone in the van knew it because they were all under Baez's protection, one way or another.

Surely he wouldn't callously throw them under the bus. He'd done everything within his power to get them all across without incident.

Still, if the crossing got screwed up, she'd be dead soon enough. Along with the other three illegals inside the van.

They'd been warned.

Miguel had orders to execute them before they fell into the hands of skilled border patrol agents who might persuade them to reveal things Baez didn't want law enforcement to know.

No reason to discuss it further.

Pilar noticed her left leg was bouncing along the floor as it often did when she was stressed. She had no idea how long it had been knocking around like that.

"Relax." Miguel reached across and placed his big hand near her knee to stop the nervous habit. "Act like you've done this a million times before. We'll be through here and on the other side within twenty minutes. Can you keep it together that long?"

Pilar nodded, her mouth too dry to utter words.

There were two guards up ahead. One stood inside the booth. The other was talking to the SUV passenger in front of Miguel's van.

A man's hand extended through the passenger side window of the SUV, holding papers for the guard.

A tall, blond man in uniform, took the papers and glanced at them before he leaned forward to look inside the vehicle.

He nodded, handed the papers back, and said something across the hood of the SUV to the guard in the booth.

The guard raised the orange restraining arm in front of the vehicle.

89 Lone Star Jack

The driver put the SUV into gear and rolled slowly forward, past the booth, and accelerated onto the road ahead.

The whole process was smooth and easy for the SUV. Just like Miguel said it would be for Pilar and the others in the van.

Chapter 7

Sunday, May 29
Presidio, Texas

Pilar felt the sweat rolling from her armpits down her sides, although the air conditioning blasted through the vents directly onto her body, raising gooseflesh on her arms.

She'd been told that Texas was cooler than Mexico. May was one of the wettest months, too. Perhaps, if her luck changed, Pilar might travel through a bit of rain to cool things off and hydrate her body.

Was that too much to hope for?

91 Lone Star Jack

Miguel rolled into the first position and stopped.

She lowered the window as the tall guard moved toward them. A warm breeze flowed into the van through open window.

“Mierda!” Miguel whispered angrily under his breath as the guard approached. He rested his right hand on the console, ready to raise the lid and grab the pistol.

His reaction alarmed her, but Pilar had no time to ask why Miguel was pissed off.

“Good evening,” the guard said, pleasantly enough.

Up close, Pilar was startled to see that he had blue eyes to go with the blond hair and fair complexion. She'd seen gringos before. But this one's eyes pierced like a wolf's.

"Where are you headed this evening?" he said.

Already, they were off script.

She glanced at the guard's name tape on his uniform above his breast pocket. **M. Weber**.

"Dallas," Pilar said the first Texas city that popped into her head. She heard the tremor in her voice and cleared her throat.

"That's a long drive. What's the purpose of your visit?" M. Weber asked, nodding as if she'd answered the first question correctly.

“Work. Road construction,” Pilar said, waving toward the sign on the side of the van proclaiming **Ojinaga Construction.**

“Young for construction work, aren’t you?” Weber asked, arching his eyebrows. “Can I see your papers, please?”

“Of course.” Pilar croaked from her parched throat. She was moving her hand toward the passports and visas when she heard the second guard call out from the booth.

“Weber! Hold up!” he shouted over the noise of the van’s engine, heading toward the van.

He must have pushed the button to raise the gate security arm before he left the booth. Pilar wondered how far they'd get if Miguel simply floored the accelerator and sped into the darkness.

Weber glanced toward the approaching guard.

Pilar relaxed a bit when she saw the second guard's familiar Mexican features. He looked like a man who could be on Baez's payroll, which was what she'd expected to see.

"What do you need, Gomez?" Weber asked, his hand still extended, waiting for the papers.

"Boss wants to see you," Gomez replied, a little breathlessly, his Mexican accent heavy and pronounced.

Weber shook his head. “I’m almost done here. I’ll head over after this van.”

Miguel’s hand pushed the button to unlock the console. The cover clicked open.

“He sounds angry, amigo. **Now. No excuses**.” Gomez mimicked the boss’s tone as he nodded toward an office across the parking lot where both a Mexican and a US flag were flying. “I’ll finish up here. You go.”

“What the hell?” Weber shook his head.

“I dunno, man. You know how he can be. Tell me when you get back,” Gomez replied, turning to Pilar and extending his hand. “Can I see your papers, please?”

After another scowl, Weber turned on his heel and stomped off toward the office. Pilar released her pent-up breath and handed the papers to Gomez.

He glanced at them briefly, making a show for the camera of looking at each of the eight passports and the eight visas. Then he handed them all back to her.

Behind the cover of the papers held in his extended right arm, he lifted his left hand to collect the fat envelope Pilar passed through the open window.

Gomez lowered the envelope to his side, outside of the camera's eye. Then he stepped back and nodded to Pilar.

“You are free to go,” he said, waving Miguel through the open gate.

Pilar nodded, pushed the button to raise the window, and clasped her hands in her lap to stop them from shaking.

“Gracias, gracias,” Miguel whispered quietly.

He removed his hand from the console and his breathing returned to normal as he rolled the van slowly, carefully through the crossing and into the dark Texas night.

The six men in the back of the panel van laughed and whooped, joyously high-fiving each other as if they were all children, making Miguel laugh with them despite the tense moments back at the border crossing.

Pilar took a moment to join in the revelry and welcome her new freedom.

"Why did you say we were going to Dallas? Our papers say Pecos," Miguel said quietly, for her ears only.

Pilar shrugged.

"Anyone else asks you where you're going, say Pecos," Miguel admonished.

Pilar nodded and offered a weak smile. "Are we going to Pecos?"

Miguel frowned. "We are. You're not."

He said nothing else, but his words made Pilar even more wary.

She resolved to steal the Glock in the van’s console as soon as she had the chance.

Pilar didn’t know what was coming next. But she knew she wouldn’t be safe until she’d completed Cesar Baez’s assignment.

She was more likely to succeed if the pistol was within easy reach.

Chapter 8

Sunday, May 29
Detroit, Michigan

It was late when Kim finally pulled into the underground garage and parked in her reserved spot. She should have felt uneasy about meeting Cooper inside her apartment, but she was too annoyed.

Why the hell couldn't he just schedule a meeting at the FBI Field Office in the morning like a normal supervisor? And why hadn't she insisted he follow protocol?

She needed boundaries. Especially between herself and Cooper.

From the outset, with her very first call out at four o'clock in the morning back in November, every interaction she'd had with Cooper's covert operations had pulled her deeper into the morass of all things Reacher.

She'd agreed to do a routine background investigation and now found herself in the middle of a deadly game with faceless enemies and higher body counts than she'd ever expected to encounter.

If her covert mission was officially discovered, she'd be on her own. The government would not come in to rescue her. Cooper had made that plain more than once.

Which was not what she'd signed up for when she'd joined the bureau.

She knew her strengths and her weaknesses. She'd expected to be a part of an elite FBI team with plenty of back up.

But the Reacher case quickly became a solo mission when her partner, Carlos Gaspar, retired.

Yet, Kim felt drawn to the Reacher assignment like a gawker to a train wreck. She couldn't pull herself away from the danger. Or the challenge.

Reacher had proven to be an enigma. One she was determined to solve for herself, even in the face of ruthless opponents and faithless friends.

Like Cooper.

Whose side was he on, anyway?

Kim stuffed her hands into her pockets and left the SUV, pressing the door lock button on the fob as she walked toward the high-speed elevator.

She rode upstairs alone in the quiet building.

Her neighbors would have retired for the night. Tomorrow was a workday.

The elevator car zipped up and stopped softly. The doors slid silently open half a moment later.

On her way to her front door, she saw nothing amiss.

She spent no time wondering how Cooper had infiltrated her secure world. He'd been here before.
It seemed he had contacts and

methods that allowed him free access to everything in life. Nothing she could do about it.

Kim placed her palm on the reader and her front door lock released with a satisfying click. She pushed the door open and stepped into the aroma of freshly brewed coffee.

Cooper had been here awhile and made himself comfortable. Too comfortable.

“Finally,” he said by way of greeting, from his seat at her kitchen table, holding a steaming mug of coffee.

She nodded but said nothing.

No point in complaining. He would do whatever he wanted, whenever he wanted, regardless of how she felt about it.

Cooper was an attractive man, given his age and mileage.

He might have been a dapper film star costumed as a Fortune 500 CEO at a weekend retreat. Expensive casual, the fashionistas would call his attire. The charcoal grey cashmere sport coat alone must have set him back five thousand dollars. Maybe more.

Kim spent no time wondering where he got the money to pay for his expensive wardrobe. Cooper's financial situation was one of the items on a long, long list of things she didn't want to know.

She slipped her jacket off her shoulders and dropped it on the sofa before she made her way to her favorite coffee mug. Poured the steaming brew into the thermal cup and leaned against the sink, ankles crossed, facing Cooper.

"How can I help you?" she asked, getting straight to the point and choosing not to voice the annoyance she felt.

Engaging him on ancillary matters was a waste of energy.

"Reacher's fallen off my radar," Cooper muttered, as if the admission pained him. Which it probably did.

"You're admitting that Reacher was **on** your radar now?" Kim sipped the steamy coffee and waited for him to come to the point.

“He knows I’m looking for him. Or at least, he knows you’re looking. He’s a smart guy. He’s deduced that you’re reporting to me.” Cooper frowned at her impertinence and gripped his cup with both hands as if he might squeeze the liquid through the top like a ketchup bottle. “Which is why you’ve failed. Reacher wants you to fail. So you shall. Until he decides otherwise.”

Kim smirked. “I appreciate your vote of confidence.”

Cooper didn’t bother to respond.

Her mind wandered as they drank coffee in silence.

She'd come to accept her role in the hunt for Reacher. She was the pawn Cooper was more than willing to sacrifice while he moved Heaven and earth to capture the opposing king.

Kim had believed the mission was a righteous one at first.

Cooper had been her mentor for a long time. He'd plucked her from bureau obscurity. She'd trusted him. Idolized him. He'd said Reacher was a ruthless killer and she'd believed him.

Why wouldn't she?

"Are you disputing the facts, Otto?" Cooper asked after a pause, sipping his coffee as if he were chatting with an uninformed fool. "Shall I refresh your recollection?"

He kept talking, but Kim barely listened. He rarely said anything trustworthy. Every word out of his mouth supported his own agenda. Whatever that was.

Kim had discussed Cooper with Gaspar more than once. In the early days of their assignment, Kim believed in Cooper's loyalty. Gaspar didn't.

"Cooper warned us against Reacher, as if he was genuinely concerned. He didn't want Reacher to ambush us," Kim had argued.

"Manipulation, Sunshine. Pure and simple," Gaspar had replied lazily, eyes closed, ankles crossed, hands folded across his flat belly. He always seemed relaxed.

"Cooper supplied Reacher's entire army file. Backs up Reacher's supreme expertise and ruthless methods," Kim had argued.

"No argument here. The guy's a psycho, for sure." Gaspar remained unpersuaded. "Nothing in the official records suggests Reacher can be tamed or captured, either."

Kim nodded. "Not by anyone."

"For any reason," Gaspar agreed. "He's killed too many times. We'd be foolish to believe otherwise."

While feeding drips of information and frightening background to her over the next few months, Cooper had given Kim every reason to believe that Reacher would kill her without a moment's hesitation, if she gave him the chance.

Her mission was simply stated. Find Reacher. Stay alive.

It had taken her a while to acknowledge that Cooper assumed Reacher would win the battle with Kim.

Because Reacher always won.

Cooper was simply biding his time. He viewed victory as certain. All he had to do was to put the players in close proximity and wait for the inevitable to happen.

He thought his plan would unfold smoothly.

At some point, Reacher would kill Otto.

When that happened, Cooper would scoop Reacher up and charge him with Kim's murder.

Killing a cop was always a bad thing to do. Murdering an FBI agent was exponentially worse.

Reacher would be drawn and quartered. Figuratively.

Actually, he'd go to prison for a long, long time. Probably forever.

Kim couldn't fathom why Cooper wanted Reacher off the board so badly. She still didn't know. Not exactly.

But Cooper wanted power over Reacher that he didn't have now.

She'd worked all of that out in bits and pieces as the hunt for Reacher forged ahead.

Perhaps the most important thing she'd learned was the intel that emboldened her now.

Reacher was as wary of Cooper as she was.

Which was even more curious since Reacher could take Cooper out without breaking a sweat. He'd killed a man inside the Pentagon once and escaped without notice. He could easily manage Cooper.

Why was Reacher wary?

Chapter 9

Sunday, May 29
Detroit, Michigan

Reacher would eventually win the war with Cooper. At this point, Kim was sure of it.

How would it happen?

Would Reacher take Cooper's bait? Kill Kim and wait to be arrested?

She shook her head. Reacher was too smart for that.

Besides, if he wanted to, he could have brought the game to a close long before now.

In the past seven months, Reacher had had more than one chance to eliminate Kim from the playing field.

He'd done the opposite.

He'd saved her life at least twice.

He'd helped her defeat enemies along the way, too.

If Reacher were the stone-cold killer Cooper claimed, why was he toying with her?

Here and there, she'd discovered witnesses who swore that Reacher could be a loyal friend as well as a lethal enemy.

But which was he to her?

Not a question she or anyone else could answer.

Whether he was friend or enemy was totally up to Reacher to decide.

And Kim had no idea what criteria he used to make that decision.

Which meant there was no way she could game it.

The evidence was conflicting. At this point, Kim truly could not answer the question. Not even in her own head.

Reacher rarely did the expected thing.

One of his great strengths was anticipating disaster. He went straight at his enemies, hard and fast. Surprise tactics deployed with accuracy and extreme prejudice.

117 Lone Star Jack

A trail of bodies followed Reacher across the country and around the world to prove his competence.

After everything she'd been through on the hunt for Reacher, Kim now believed he had anticipated Cooper's plan.

He wouldn't fall into Cooper's trap.

Instead, he'd mount a counter offensive, on his own terms and at a time of his own choosing.

No way for Kim to prepare for that.

She simply had to wait for it. And to be as ready as possible to survive when Reacher dropped the hammer.

And while Reacher avoided Cooper's trap, Kim would stay alive.

For Cooper and Reacher, that meant stalemate.

For Kim, it meant she still had a chance to win this contest.

Sure, Reacher had a lot of advantages. Theirs was nowhere close to a fair match.

For starters, Reacher was exponentially bigger than Kim. She was tiny. Barely five feet tall and weighed less than one hundred pounds.

At six-feet-five inches and two-hundred-fifty pounds, he could crush her in his turkey-sized hands in a hot New York minute.

He could toss her off a roof without breaking a sweat.

He could kick her aside like a footballer with a kitten.

The ease with which Reacher could dispatch her and end the game was terrifying.

She couldn't even appeal to his sense of fairness, whatever that was.

He wasn't amoral. Not exactly. Not totally.

Reacher possessed a convenient moral compass that allowed him to ignore the law and do whatever he damned well pleased. Which was anathema to her.

Kim carried a gun and a badge and had taken several oaths to uphold the law.

Reacher acted as judge, jury, and executioner.

How could she compete with that?

In the end, Kim was just a cop. A damned good one. But still, a by-the-book hunter who played by the rules like she was wearing a straitjacket. Which she was.

Bottom line, Reacher versus Otto was not a fair match. Not even close.

But she still believed she could win.

Because she had no choice.

She would never, ever give up.

Which left her with win or die.

As her mother always said, when there's only one choice, it's the right choice.

She had to win. Simple as that.

"Here's all the details." Cooper was winding up his soliloquy. He pulled a small, padded envelope from his pocket and pushed it across the table toward her.

She left it untouched. "Details about what?"

"I told you. Reacher's off my radar. I'm working on that," Cooper said, one forearm on the table as he sipped the coffee. "Until we can find him again, we'll take a slightly different approach."

"Which is?"

"After Reacher left the army, he became embroiled in a domestic dispute in Texas," Cooper said. "Wife shot and killed her husband. Motive was money and custody of their kid. A girl. About six years old at the time. Curiously, Reacher tried to keep the wife out of prison for the husband's murder."

"Was she attractive?"

Cooper smiled as if Kim were a particularly apt pupil. "Dazzling was the word for her then. Still is."

"Of course she is." Kim nodded, narrowed her eyes. "How long after Reacher left the army did all this happen?"

Cooper replied. "Fifty-one months or 4.25 years, to be exact."

Kim did the math quickly. "Ten years ago."

Cooper nodded. “Give or take.”

“Doesn’t sound like the kind of thing Reacher would mess with, does it? Sleeping with another man’s wife? Why? He’s got a lot of choices. Women throw themselves at him all the time,” Kim said, trying on the idea and rejecting it. Made no sense unless the facts were a lot more complicated. Which they probably were. “What kind of domestic dispute was it?”

“Not sure. The records are spotty.” Cooper shook his head. “Back in the army, Reacher was a lot of things, but not the kind of guy to sleep with another man’s wife. Like you said, he never had to. There were always plenty of single women who were willing. And he has never displayed the slightest interest in raising his own kid, let alone raising another man's child. Just the opposite. When he was an MP, he busted a few heads when guys got themselves involved in messes like that."

"So why was this situation different enough for Reacher to get involved?" Kim asked, cocking her head, glancing toward the envelope.

Her curiosity was aroused, no doubt just as Cooper intended.

"I'm not sure it was **different** enough. But the case is an anomaly and it's tied to Reacher. It's also the only lead we've got at the moment. Like I said," Cooper drained the coffee and pushed the cup away. "Until something better comes along, we'll chase this lead down. Might get us somewhere."

Kim thought about what he'd said for a few moments and then shook her head. "There's more to the story. Must be."

"Such as?"

"Reacher's rescued damsels in distress a few times, for sure. But this woman had a gun and she used it to kill her husband. Not even a hint of distress in that scenario." Kim paused, turning the facts over in her head. "What did she need Reacher for? And why do we care about all this ancient history now? And more to the point, why would Reacher care about any of it after all this time?"

"Why, indeed? You always have had a firm grasp of the obvious." Cooper smirked, stood up, and deliberately pushed his chair in closer to the table. He stuffed his hands in his pockets. "Everything we know is on the flash drive in that envelope. You can read the files in flight. You tell me." He paused. "We're running late. Grab your bags. Helo's waiting."

"Late for what? Go where?" Kim said, but he'd already left the apartment.

She scrambled into her bedroom to collect her travel bag and her laptop case, which were always packed. She slid her cell phone into her pocket.

The burner phone that was a direct line to her former partner rested on the bedside table. She snagged it, sent Gaspar a quick text. **Headed out with Cooper. No clue where**.

Kim slipped Gaspar's phone into another pocket. Just in case.

She took a quick look around the room to confirm she'd left nothing she might need. Then she hustled to meet Cooper at the elevator.

Chapter 10

Monday, May 30
Red House Ranch, Texas

Pilar had dozed off during the mind-numbing ride from the border. Even in the daylight there would have been nothing to see except miles and miles of empty land. Every now and then, windmills and oil rigs. That was it. Certainly nothing to stay awake for.

When Miguel slowed the van as if he were preparing to turn off the main road, she opened her eyes just enough to see more darkness and not much else.

"Where are we?" she asked, blinking herself awake. In the weak wash of moonlight, she could make out the ghostly shadows of windmills and oil pumps in the distance.

"About sixty miles south of Pecos," Miguel replied, leaning over the steering wheel and peering through the windshield as if getting closer to the headlights might help him find whatever he was looking for.

"Can I help?" Pilar said, straightening up in her seat, willing herself to emerge from her stupor. She took a couple of sips from a water bottle.

A fairly new barbed wire fence ran along the property line ahead. It looked like it had been installed maybe ten or fifteen years ago.

Newer than the ones she'd seen before she nodded off an hour ago. As if the landowner might be more prosperous than his neighbors.

About half a mile further along the barbed wire changed to a picket fence. Pilar had only seen absurd fences like that in old movies when she was lucky enough to have the price of a theater ticket admission back home. Which was rarely.

When the van's headlights hit the picket fence, Pilar saw it was painted dull red. The paint seemed reasonably fresh and new in the moonlight.

The picket fence ran about half a mile to a wooden ranch gate, which was also painted dull red, arched over the entrance. The fence picked up again on the other side of the arch and ran beyond until the headlight beams failed and she could see the fence no more.

Miguel slowed the van to a crawl as they approached a well groomed gravel drive running beneath the red gate. He turned in.

There was a name painted on a sign high above their heads at the top of the gate's archway. Red paint on red wood.

Pilar twisted her neck to see it.

Red House.

Why paint everything red? Why make the words so difficult to read? Failure of imagination or did they simply get a great deal on a supply of red paint?

She shook her head. Gringos were loco sometimes, her mother always said. Pilar had certainly witnessed such crazy behavior before, and she was certain she would see it again.

The van's headlights pointed straight ahead. After a short while, they revealed a big house with a two-story core and a tall chimney and several one-story additions. The shadows of low barns and sheds clustered near the oddly shaped house were all painted the same dull red.

As near as she could tell, the whole ramshackle affair was not too old and reasonably well maintained. It felt especially strange to see a place so nice perched in the middle of nowhere, Texas.

Miguel drove up to the front of the main building, which was even more impressive up close.

It had a wide planked porch with wooden columns and a swinging seat hung from chains. The porch and the columns and the seat were all painted the same dull red.

A cement sidewalk ran from the steps to the circular drive-in front of the house where Miguel had stopped the van.

He slipped the transmission into park.

"Come on, Pilar," he said as he opened his door and slid out into the night. He walked around to the back of the van, opened the door, and pulled her duffel from the cargo hold. He closed the door and checked the handle to be sure the lock held.

When Miguel came around to the passenger side, Pilar had not moved from her seat. He opened her door and let the warm air rush in, flooding the cabin with the smell of hot dirt.

“Let’s go. End of the line for you,” Miguel said, waving his arm toward the house.

“What are you talking about?” Pilar said, widening her eyes, suddenly terrified.

She’d grabbed Miguel’s pistol from the console and stuffed it into her pocket, but the gun didn’t make her feel any more secure than her dagger right at the moment.

Pilar whipped her head around, looking in every direction. “You can’t leave me here. I don’t have a car or money or anything. I don’t even know where we are. This is crazy.”

“I told you. We’re south of Pecos. About sixty miles. Echo County, it’s called. We’ve left others like you here.” Miguel grabbed her arm and pulled her out of the van. “You’ll be fine. Come on.”

She stumbled on the gravel but managed to get her footing before falling on her ass.

The porch light turned on and the front door opened. A big man stood in the doorway holding the inside door handle. He spent a few seconds sizing up the situation and then headed down the steps toward the van.

He looked to be in his mid- to late thirties, give or take a decade, Pilar guessed. He had a big square face lined by experience and wild yellow hair. His body was big, too. Blocky. Like he worked out daily. There was probably a gym somewhere in that sprawling house.

Pilar was outmanned. She swallowed her fury. Miguel would leave her here. Nothing she could do about it. Not tonight, anyway.

She reached for her duffel. Miguel handed it over with no fanfare.

The big man landed on the sidewalk at the bottom of the steps and stopped five feet away. He smiled and extended a big, hairy paw in Pilar's direction.

"I'm Bobby Greer," he said and paused expectantly, as if the name should mean something to her. It didn't.

She didn't take his hand, either.

"Pilar Inez Mendoza."

His hand flopped to his side.

"Thanks for dropping her off. We'll take it from here," he said to Miguel.

Miguel nodded and returned to the van. Pilar stood rooted to the spot and watched as he drove around the circle and headed out along the same gravel drive toward the road.

Pilar said nothing as she watched the headlights reach, and then turn, onto the main road. She stared at the taillights growing dimmer in the distance until she could see them no more. Still, she stood rooted to the spot, as if she could will Miguel to return for her.

Bobby Greer had been standing with his hands stuffed into his jeans.

After a while, he said, “Are you hungry? Let’s get you a bite to eat and then I’ll show you your room.”

Pilar nodded once and followed him up the steps and inside the house, still seething.

Her mind was made up. If she ever saw Miguel again, she would kill him for leaving her here.

Chapter 11

Monday, May 30
En route to Dallas, Texas

Kim had followed Cooper into the elevator, up to the roof, and boarded the helicopter waiting on the helipad. She ducked her head against the rotor wash and plowed through the wind to the open door, praying silently for clear weather.

The copilot took her bags and stashed them in the cargo hold. A brief glance told her they were safely stowed.

She climbed into the cabin and settled into her seat. Cooper was already inside, as relaxed as an exhausted puppy.

Kim hated helicopters. They crashed at an even higher rate than planes. Proponents liked to claim helos were safer transportation than automobiles, but she had her doubts. They had to admit that too many crashes were caused by pilot error, a notoriously difficult thing to prevent.

And helicopter speeds were only marginally faster than road vehicles, particularly when traffic was light.

Helos were never a good choice as far as she was concerned.

Not at all.

Not that Cooper had asked. Or cared about her opinions.

Conversation was impossible in the noisy bird, which was another strike against them. She kept a tight grip on the armrests and said nothing during the short flight to the executive terminal near Detroit Metro Airport.

The pilot set the helo down near a private jet with its engines already running, ready to depart.

Quickly, Cooper exited the helo and strode across the tarmac. Kim followed, pulling her bags along behind her.

"Your security detail is already aboard," advised the copilot, waiting at the bottom of the jet stairs.

Cooper hustled up and inside. Kim trudged along behind him.

Two FBI agents were already seated in the second row's roomy seats. Two men. Average looking. Caucasian. Brown hair, brown eyes, boring haircuts, dark suits and ties.

Cooper acknowledged them with a curt, "Johnson, Miller. This is Special Agent Kim Otto."

"Sir," they responded in turn, offering Kim a quick nod.

The copilot followed up the stairs behind Kim. "We've been cleared for takeoff and we're running late. Grab a seat. We want to get ahead of the weather."

He sealed the door and joined the pilot in the cockpit.

Kim stowed her bags and plopped into a window seat, popping an antacid into her mouth to calm her stomach.

The pilot started to taxi before she had a chance to fasten her seatbelt.

“Where are we going?” she asked, watching the low clouds in the night sky as the jet lined up and then increased speed until it lifted off. Turbulence buffeted the jet as it climbed.

“Dallas,” Cooper replied easily.

“Why?”

This situation was definitely not normal.

Cooper ruled his kingdom from his office in DC. He never went into the field for any reason. He had minions like Kim and those two agents sitting in the cabin to handle the ground game.

"Senator Edward Redstone's funeral," Cooper said, relaxing deeper into his seat as the jet gained altitude. "Ed was one of my oldest friends. We were at West Point together. Finer man never walked the earth. We lost him much too soon."

Kim had heard the sad news when it happened.

Senator Edward Redstone was a legend. He'd died suddenly last week after a protracted battle with Parkinson's disease. Arrangements for his elaborate funeral had been days in the making.

He'd been a senator for decades, well regarded by his political colleagues at all levels. Some called him a beloved politician, which was surely an oxymoron if ever there was one.

Redstone ran for president once and lost in a huge upset election. His friends and many of his enemies believed the opponent's campaign was corrupt and stole the election. Redstone did the honorable thing and conceded, which endeared him to the whole country. He'd been encouraged to run again, and he probably would have won the second time.

His death was premature, certainly. Parkinson's disease defeated him in a way his political opponents could not.

A long list of Redstone's friends and colleagues were expected to pay respects at the church service in Dallas. Security was tighter than a State dinner at the White House.

The news accounts said Senator Redstone had prepared his wishes and entrusted the execution to his only surviving son, Edward. The one they called Teddy. A silly moniker for a grown man. But it was more dignified than calling him Junior or Deuce or some other nonsense, Kim supposed.

She hated funerals and made every excuse in the book to avoid them whenever possible.

"I didn't take you for the sentimental type," Kim said to Cooper, in a gross bit of understatement.

"Don't assume that you know me, Otto," he replied sternly.

She nodded. He was right. She didn't know him. Everything she knew about him suggested his heart was icy cold, though. He'd certainly never engendered warm fuzzies from anyone, anywhere, any time. Not that Kim was aware of, anyway.

Flying across the country to attend the funeral of an old friend was definitely out of character for him.

"The church will be crowded. Security tight," Kim said. "I'm sure I'm not on the approved attendee list. I never even met Senator Redstone."

Cooper gave her a brief smile as he pulled his cell phone from his pocket.

"You can be my plus one," he said before he released the buckle on his seat belt and moved to the back of the plane for a longer conversation.

Kim flashed a scowl toward his receding back. Johnson and Miller exchanged a grin at her expense, which deepened her annoyance.

Focusing on work could distract her from constantly cataloguing the perils of small jet travel for a while. One of her superpowers was intense focus.

Something she was born with, her mother said. She'd perfected the skill through college and law school and a brief but intense and stormy marriage.

All of which meant she could simply stop thinking about Cooper if she tried.

She opened her laptop and inserted the flash drive Cooper had delivered back in her kitchen. As soon as the list of contents appeared on her screen, she fell down the rabbit hole that hunting Jack Reacher had become.

The flash drive contained five files.

One was labeled Jack Reacher.

The other four were labeled Carmen Greer, Alice Amanda Aaron, Bobby and Meredith “Rusty” Greer, and Maria Greer.

Kim read through the files quickly the first time and more carefully the second time. The third time through, she focused on the specific details and made notes of her questions.

Back then, Alice Aaron was a pro bono lawyer in Pecos, Texas. Carmen and Rusty Greer lived at the Red House Ranch, south of a place called Echo, Texas. Rusty’s son, Bobby, lived there, too. Reacher had been involved with all three of them.

Maria Greer’s file was the thinnest and Kim buzzed through it. Maria had been the Greer’s maid.

Presumably, Reacher had known her, too.

Maria Greer perished recently when her house burned to the ground. The fire was an obvious arson, according to the report. The arsonist had also died in the blaze. Some evidence existed to suggest that the arsonist had killed Maria Greer before he set the fire. Motive was unknown.

Kim shrugged. Of course, Cooper had included only the intel he wanted her to know. On the first pass, she'd found nothing remarkable or even particularly useful in the materials he'd provided.

What had she missed?

Chapter 12

Monday, May 30
En route to Dallas, Texas

Kim studied the photos.

Carmen Greer was a petite beauty, for sure. But not Reacher's usual type. He liked strong women, often law enforcement. It seemed to be a thing with him. Which, Kim had long suspected, was one reason Cooper had given Kim this assignment in the first place. To attract Reacher.

But Carmen Greer was nothing like Reacher's other women that Kim had met on this assignment so far. Why had he become involved with her?

153 Lone Star Jack

The Reacher file included on the flash drive contained a brief summary of the known events that had occurred while he spent time in and around Pecos, and Echo, Texas. Ten years ago.

The summary reflected the usual sort of trouble Reacher attracted like honey drew ants. As always, there were few records and those that existed contained only sketchy details.

Reacher had been hitchhiking along a dusty Texas road when Carmen Greer offered him a ride. Then she offered him a job and took him back to the Red House Ranch in Echo.

Things went south from there.

At some point, like Cooper had said, Carmen Greer's husband ended up dead.

Briefly, Kim wondered if Reacher had killed the man.

Seemed he hadn't, according to the file. Reacher had a solid alibi. He'd been in custody at the time the murder occurred.

Carmen Greer was arrested and charged with her husband's murder.

Alice Aaron was Carmen's pro bono lawyer.

Which was curious.

The Greers had money. The dead man was worth millions. Why Carmen Greer needed a free lawyer wasn't explained in the file.

Which was only one of the myriad questions Kim would have when she met Alice Aaron, if she got the chance to ask.

The murder and mayhem didn't stop with the dead husband. Kim would have been surprised if it had.

Reacher's methods predictably resulted in multiple homicides and a few cracked bones for the survivors. His brief stint in Echo, Texas, was no exception.

After the dust finally cleared, Rusty Greer, the dead man's mother, was also arrested. Formal charges against her were a little vague but accounted for at least one of the deaths on the score card.

Rusty Greer had been in prison for the past ten years and was released a few weeks ago. Available intel on that was sketchy, too.

According to the file, it was believed Rusty had returned to the Red House Ranch when she was released from prison. The ranch was currently occupied by her younger son. Robert Greer. The one they called Bobby.

Reacher, of course, had walked away from Echo and Carmen Greer unscathed.

No charges filed against him. No records to prove he was involved. Hell, nothing much to prove he was ever present at all.

Same as always.

Kim shook her head as she closed the laptop, leaned her head back, and dropped her eyelids to think.

Too bad Gaspar wasn't here. Gaspar thought like Reacher. She missed his insight.

She knew a lot more about Reacher now than when she'd first caught this assignment. At that point, she didn't know Jack Reacher at all. She was smarter now.

The hard-won knowledge she'd acquired over the past seven months said the Greer situation didn't pass the smell test. Not even remotely.

Back in November, she'd been assigned to complete a background check. She was told that Reacher could be dead. Or hiding. Or maybe just living deep off the grid like some wacko, holed up with canned food and enough ammo to defeat marauders of all sorts.

Cooper had told her Reacher was a dangerous killer and warned her to be exceptionally wary. She took his advice to heart. He was her boss and she owed him. Simple as that.

Cooper hadn't lied, exactly.

But he hadn't revealed the whole truth, either.

Lies of omission could be just as fatal as intentional deceit. She'd learned that the hard way, too.

Bottom line of her hard-won experience was that Cooper couldn't be trusted.

And Reacher?

Was he the stone-cold killer Cooper had warned her about?

Partly.

As the case had progressed from a background check into a full-on manhunt, she'd had several close personal encounters with Reacher.

She'd also interviewed witnesses who had known Reacher for short periods of time under intense, dangerous conditions.

Kim had survived the kind of hot, hard, constant pressure that makes diamonds out of coal.

Which meant she'd learned an unthinkable lesson.

A lesson she'd resisted for way too long.

A lesson she'd never have believed if she hadn't lived it herself.

Simply put, the FBI couldn't be trusted.

Reacher was a killing machine as good as any the US Army had ever produced. One of the best. Didn't make him a psycho. At least, not totally.

She'd also come to believe Reacher was a fundamentally good person, down deep.

Depending on the situation, Reacher could be either saint or sinner.

The choice was always and solely his and his alone.

He made his decisions without consulting his target, sometimes without exchanging a single word or experience between them. He chose up sides based on his own criteria, and then he set out to destroy the opposition.

For Reacher, there were never two sides to any story. There was Reacher's view and only Reacher's view.

Reacher's methods and his hubris were anathema to Kim.

She was a lawyer by training and experience, as well as an FBI agent. Experience and the law admitted that there were always multiple sides to every story.

The good guys and the bad guys were sometimes impossible to identify.

They didn't actually wear team jerseys or fly flags during Reacher-style combat.

Reacher had received some of the same training Kim did. He was a military cop for thirteen years. He knew the rules.

He was a good cop, too. Everything in his army files said so.

Even though he too often ignored the law he was sworn to uphold simply because he wanted to.

When Reacher walked away from the army, he'd walked away from **all** the rules. Which was what made him so dangerous.

Well, that, and his bulk and his no-holds-barred fighting skills.

All of that had been in play during the time Reacher was in Echo, Texas. What the hell happened down there?

Kim felt a slight shift in the jet's cabin. The small jet had been flying through turbulence since they left Detroit, but this was different. She shuddered and opened her eyes.

Cooper had returned carrying two cups of black coffee. He offered one to her and took his seat. "Well? See anything in those files that suggests we might catch up with Reacher in Dallas?"

"Sadly, no." she replied, accepted the coffee and sipped as if it contained the elixir of life. Which, of course, it did.

"Let me rephrase." Cooper smiled. "Assume Reacher is in Texas. Where will we find him?"

"Why do you think he's there at all?" she replied.

"We'll get to that," he said.

Chapter 13

Monday, May 30
Dallas, Texas

Before sunrise on Javier Garcia's third day in Dallas, his entire body vibrated with anticipation. He was as ready as he'd ever be. He wanted to move on from the relentless and oppressive pressure of his life in limbo.

It was time to turn the page. He had a good woman now. A baby on the way. Due any day now. A boy, he felt sure.

Javier's life was on the verge of great things. He and Elana were excited. Only this one thing left to do before they settled down together.

The van had dropped him off on the outskirts of town two days ago, on Friday night. He had the clothes on his back and a paper shopping bag. Inside the bag was the disguise they'd given him, and the gun.

In his pockets he'd carried five hundred dollars in cash. Nothing else. No wallet. No identification.

He'd spent some of the cash for two night's rent at the no-tell motel and food at the diner. Eggs in the morning and burgers later.

He'd nursed a couple of beers for an hour, to avoid suspicion in the bars. Everybody else was drinking from brown long-neck bottles.

Javier wasn't much of a beer drinker. He preferred tequila. But he wasn't drinking until after the job was done. He'd promised Elana. Too much risk, they'd both agreed.

On the first day, he'd wandered the area around the outdoor site for the political rally, listening, watching, getting a feel for the place. Which didn't take long.

He was only interested in the park and the neighborhood around it. Which was larger than his village back in Mexico but smaller than the whole of Dallas. Javier had never seen such a big city and he hoped he never would see Dallas again.

But he'd worked diligently, and he was ready. Monday afternoon, he'd complete the kill. José would collect him Monday night and he would move on with his life.

Javier smiled. That promise of a new and better life drew him like a child drawn to free candy.

Everything was in place for Monday. Soon, he'd be finished here and on his way. Very soon.

He'd been watching television in the bar Sunday night when his well-organized plans went completely off the rails.

Trejo's face had filled the oversized screen. The news reporter said Monday's political rally was canceled. Trejo would be attending the funeral of Senator Edward Redstone instead.

In an instant, Javier's new life was destroyed by the whims of a politician.

Anger boiled his blood. If he'd known where Trejo was right that minute, Javier would have marched to his home and killed him, his family, and anyone else standing nearby.

He'd fumed and drank and worried and watched the news for another hour before he'd decided what to do.

The answer, once it came, was simple.

Javier's work could be done as well in a church as in a park.

Trejo had canceled the rally, but he was still here in Dallas. He would show up in a public place.

Trejo could die as easily in one place as the other. More easily, actually, as Javier thought about it.

Javier had paid close attention to the recycled news story to learn the name of the church where the funeral would be held. The reporter stood out front, giving Javier a good long look at the entrance.

Javier had attended church every Sunday for his entire life. He pictured the big, open interior of the building. One church was the same as another, surely.

He imagined pews filled with seated mourners. Eyes closed as their prayers were offered.

The more Javier thought about it, the easier it seemed.

Trejo would be seated. Shooting a stationary target would be simpler than killing the man as he walked through a crowd shaking hands with supporters. Much simpler.

After another hour of persuading himself, Javier was feeling good about things again. He'd have called José to report his change of plans. José had repeatedly stressed the importance of following directions. He was likely to be angry.

But Javier had no way to reach José. There was nothing he could do.

No matter.

He would do the job and go to the meeting point to wait.

José would pick him up Monday night, as planned. He might be angry that Javier had changed the plan. But he'd be happy the job was done.

Until then, Javier was on his own.

He'd left the bar and returned to the motel as excited as a schoolboy before a big championship football game.

Javier had slept soundly and left the motel this morning early, as he'd planned. Ominous clouds filled the sky, which was better than the relentless sun and heat he'd dealt with since he'd crossed the border.

He located the huge church where the funeral was scheduled to be held a few hours later.

The church wasn't difficult to find. It was near the center of the city. At this early hour, the streets were deserted. Javier had an unobstructed view.

Parking was not allowed on the street near the front entrance. There were parking garages nearby.

But Javier didn't have access to a car, so the parking didn't matter. The only thing he wanted to confirm was that he could easily get in and out of the big church when the time came.

Javier carefully staked out several concealed spots near the entrance and waited.

People began to arrive before seven o'clock making the church ready for the funeral. Huge arrangements of flowers were delivered. Blockades were placed across the street from the entrance.

He'd had a chance to sneak inside, carrying one of the big flower stands. He was able to get familiar with the interior layout and find good places to hide until he had the opportunity to do the job he came for.

As he'd imagined, the interior of the church was one big open space. There were aisles between the pews. Doors in the back as well as the front.

He located the perfect waiting spot. He could establish his line of sight, approach the target easily enough, and get away by at least three different escape routes.

He'd prefer to kill Trejo outside.

But he could do the job inside the church as well.

Javier followed the workers outside again. He sat on a bench across from the church's entrance and closed his eyes to visualize his plan, over and over, until he could perform without thinking.

The casket would be placed near the alter. The family would stand nearby to accept condolences. Javier would make his move after the service, when the mourners were filing out.

Javier was not that familiar with American political activities, but politicians were the same everywhere. Even at funerals, they'd shake everyone's hand.

There would be a line of people waiting to meet Trejo. Javier would join the line, and when Trejo reached to shake Javier's hand, he'd shoot at close range.

No chance he could miss.

Also no chance the candidate could shoot back.

It wasn't a perfect plan. But it should work well enough.

The candidate was nothing special.

Luis Trejo was a small-time hustler with big ambitions. Javier thought he should have started with a run for local judge or mayor or dog catcher.

Anything to get name recognition with voters and some work experience under his belt before he took on the big political machines.

Instead, Trejo had jumped into the race for US Senate right off the bat.

Even Javier could see that he didn't stand a chance.

Which probably meant Trejo was angling for something other than the actual Senate seat. Something he could negotiate in exchange for endorsing the likely winner.

Something someone didn't want Trejo to have.

Javier wondered again why that someone wanted Trejo dead.

Chapter 14

Monday, May 30
Dallas, Texas

Javier had tried to puzzle it out in his head.

But no matter how he looked at the political race, Trejo wasn't likely to win, and Javier could think of no good reason to kill him.

Still, Javier had been sent to kill Trejo and that's what he would do.

He had no choice.

He'd accepted support of his immigration from Mexico from Cesar

Baez in exchange for this one simple task.

Kill the guy and run.

Which Javier could surely do, even though he'd never done such a thing before.

He'd shot wild boar though.

From Javier's point of view, politicians and feral pigs were not that far apart.

Javier swept his gaze over the setup again, confirming his tactics. Man, it was hot.

He raised his heavy hat and wiped away perspiration with his sleeve. The damned thing was polyester and held body heat like a solar panel atop his head.

Once he finished the job, he would toss the hat, with its fake hair glued to the band.

He'd shaved his head before he reached Dallas. His shoulder length black hair normally flowed over his shoulders and would have made him easily identifiable.

When he thought about his long, silky locks filling the plastic trash bag, he shrugged.

He'd have years and years of freedom. His beautiful hair would grow back.

Javier had heard people talking in the diners and the bars as he wandered the town. The local people didn't care that much about what went on in Washington, DC. But the dead senator had been in office a long time. Quite a few mourners were likely to show up today.

Which was good. The more screaming, fainting, crying mourners after Javier shot Trejo, the better.

Trejo would want to do his grip and grin and get the hell out.

Which meant Javier wouldn't have much time.

He needed to move fast.

The element of surprise was his only advantage.

Tactics were simple.

Rush forward, shoot Trejo, and run like hell before the security team had a chance to shoot back.

He'd been warned.

José said, "Make no mistake, reaction time from security staff will be short and the response swift. No question about that."

Javier nodded. He'd expect no less.

José said, "They might try to capture you alive. If they do, don't worry. You'll be deported and we'll pick you up back in Mexico."

Javier shook his head. He would kill himself before he'd let that happen.

He was never going back to Mexico. His very life and the lives of his entire family depended on that.

Simply put, if Javier could do the deed, he'd live to collect the reward his patron had promised.

Otherwise, he'd be killed. By the guards or by his own hand.

Either way, this waiting would end today.

He shrugged. The stakes were worth it.

He'd been as good as dead most of his miserable life in Mexico anyway. The men he was running from now would kill him if he went back.

Killing Trejo was Javier's last chance to change his life for the better.

Anyone in his circumstances would have agreed to try.

He'd practiced his plan again last night while all of Dallas was sleeping. He'd had several hours to rehearse in the moonlight.

Taking long strides, Javier could cover the distance in seconds. He was no sharpshooter. He had to get close enough. He couldn't miss.

He marked the spot with a visual cue and embedded it firmly into his senses.

He practiced again in his head. He stepped quickly away from the cover of the imaginary mourners.

Ran to his chosen location.

Stop.

Aimed his pistol.

Shot.

Hit the target.

Stuffed the gun into the pocket of his camo hoodie and ran like hell while confusion and chaos distracted the mourners and the bodyguards.

The street was off limits. It would be closed and guarded.

Which left a headlong run toward the back and into the alley.

Shed his bulky camo and the itchy hat into a dumpster along with the gun.

Then a period of hiding in one of the decrepit buildings he'd found nearby until it was safe to go.

He only had to survive until the darkness rolled around again on Monday night. José was scheduled to collect him at midnight at the drop-off point where he'd left him on Friday.

Tomorrow, he'd be living a whole new life in a new place. Elana would be there. Their baby would be born in the United States, and they'd live here in peace. Forever.

Javier let his mind wallow there for a few more minutes, savoring the promise at the end of this very long nightmare.

And then he turned his mind to the work at hand again.

A growing crowd began to gather beyond the barricades. At first, Javier thought they were mourners here to show support to the Redstone family.

Until he saw the signs they were carrying and noticed their rowdy demeanor.

Javier glanced at the big clock atop the brick hotel across the street.

A few more hours left to wait. More people approached and the shouting began.

The wind picked up, gusting across the crowd. A wide slash of lightning flashed across the sky, followed by a deafening blast of thunder.

Javier hunched down in his camo.

And then it began to rain.

Chapter 15

Monday, May 30
Echo, Texas

Amazing aromas drifted upstairs while Pilar Inez Mendoza was still asleep. The scent of bacon frying and coffee brewing filtered into her unconscious, awakening her more effectively than any alarm clock.

She hadn't eaten since she'd left Mexico and the gnawing in her stomach roused her from emotional and physical exhaustion.

Before she opened her eyes, she stretched broadly, feeling the soreness within her body. She had been stuffed into small spaces far too long. The tension of escaping Mexico to her new life had taken its toll, too.

Her muscles were cramped and short and achy and fairly screamed to be released. Nothing three hours of yoga wouldn't fix. Or even a good stretch followed by a five-mile run might do the trick.

Problem was, she would have neither.

Pilar patted her pillow to be sure the Glock was where she'd hidden it last night. Then she threw back the covers and sat naked on the edge of the bed.

Her eyes were still closed, but her nose and her stomach were fully awake.

When she finally looked, she saw her clothes were tossed into a careless pile on the floor near the bed. Her nose wrinkled of its own volition when she realized she'd need to wear them again today.

She had left home with a small duffel bag half-filled with mostly sentimental possessions. She barely owned any clothes, and she shared them with her sisters. Her mother had sent her away with only the clothes she was wearing and one more set of jeans, T-shirt, and underwear.

The pile on the floor was the spare set. The ones in her bag were dirty and in worse condition.

Pilar had intended to buy jeans and a shirt at a thrift store in the first town she came to. But Miguel had dropped her off at this godforsaken place sixty miles from Pecos and no way to get there.

She'd promised herself she'd kill him last night for his part in stranding her here. She'd meant the threat literally then and she hadn't changed her mind.

The bacon and coffee aromas tempted her. She felt the urgency to pee. She reached for the dirty jeans and pulled them on. Slipped her arms into the stinky T-shirt and walked barefoot across the cool wood floor.

When she grabbed the doorknob and attempted to turn it, the door was locked.

Which meant Pilar had been locked in after she fell asleep. She grimaced. Probably that man who had led her up here after Miguel dropped her off.

Bobby Greer, he'd said. He'd offered to feed her. She was so angry, she'd refused. He'd shrugged. "Suit yourself."

Act in haste, repent at leisure, as her mother often said.

Pilar leaned back against the door, flipped the light on, and looked more closely at her prison. As prisons went, this one was spartan but definitely upscale.

There was a window directly across from the door. The window was closed by plantation shutters.

Pilar padded across the room in her bare feet and opened the shutters. She stood for a moment at the window and looked outside.

She was on the front side of the house. The window offered a view of several outbuildings painted the same brick red as everything else. She saw the circular driveway that became the long dirt road that ran under the painted gate and to the paved road out front.

The road that led to Pecos. Sixty miles away.

Briefly, she considered hitchhiking to Pecos. Sixty miles wouldn't take that long, if she caught a ride. Even a slow-moving farm truck would get there in a couple of hours.

She didn't see a single vehicle on the road. But if a road existed, that meant there would be traffic of some sort. Surely.

She adjusted the shutter slats to allow a bit of sunlight into the room and returned to her search for a toilet. Which was when she saw a closed door on the right side of the bed near the corner.

When she opened the door Pilar found a small, tiled bathroom. White pedestal sink, white toilet, and a white tiled shower stall with a clear glass door. White ceramic tile covered the floor.

There were white towels, a white bar of soap, and on a freestanding holder waiting beside the toilet, the whitest toilet paper she'd ever seen.

Pilar smiled with pleasure. It was the first time she'd smiled since forever. The smile and the pleasure felt strangely grotesque. What did she have to smile about?

She turned on the shower, used the toilet while the water heated up, and then stepped into the shower completely dressed.

It was a ridiculous plan, of course. But washing her clothes and her body at the same time seemed like an efficient way to do things. At least, until she could execute a better plan.

Besides, it was so hot and dry outside that the air would suck the moisture right out of them. They'd be stiff as new canvas, but they'd soften up after a bit.

Pilar stayed under the spray until her growling stomach snagged her attention again. She should have joined Bobby Greer for a meal last night when he'd offered. But she was too angry at Miguel to eat then.

Anger wears off. Hunger lingers much longer.

She turned the water off and patted herself dry with the towel. Her clothes were soaked. But she'd seen enough dirt swirling down the drain to hope that they were cleaner now than before.

She removed her jeans and her T-shirt and her underwear. She twisted them as hard as she could to squeeze the water out before she put them back on again. An hour in the sun and they'd be dry. Probably.

Pilar finger combed her long, black, wavy hair. She pulled it into a ponytail, low on her neck, and secured it with a rubber band.

When she looked into the mirror, she was almost surprised to see how young and clear-eyed and fresh-faced she seemed.

A hard knock sounded on the bedroom door.

“Pilar? Are you ready for breakfast?”

She recognized Bobby Greer’s voice. “Coming.”

She reached under her pillow, grabbed her dagger and slid it into the side zip pocket of her jeans. She stuffed the pistol into her waistband at the small of her back and pulled the loose T-shirt down to cover it.

She slipped her arms into her denim jacket and took a quick look in the mirror. The gun wasn't obvious. Which was the best she could do for now.

Pilar slipped her feet into her shoes and covered the short distance to the door. She tried to turn the doorknob again, and this time, the door opened.

Bobby Greer was standing in the hallway, waiting. He looked her over. His lips twitched and then he said, "Come on. You're late. Bring your bag. Follow me."

He turned and walked toward the stairs. Pilar grabbed her duffel and trudged behind him, shivering in the artificially cold air.

At the bottom of the stairs, he veered right down a long corridor and kept striding toward the back of the house. Framed photographs were hung on the walls on both sides above a built-in bookcase crammed full of well-thumbed paperbacks.

Pilar only had time for a brief glance as she followed. The photos might have been shot here at the ranch. She thought she recognized a couple of the ugly red barns. The paperbacks were old westerns and detective novels. Not that it mattered. Pilar's ability to read English was too limited to enjoy novels, anyway. She'd learned English by watching American television.

She realized soon enough that she was following her nose as much as Greer's broad back. The scent of bacon and coffee grew stronger with every step she took. Her stomach growled with hunger.

Chapter 16

Monday, May 30
Echo, Texas

After a few more long strides, the corridor opened into the oversized, brightly lit kitchen. Large windows along one side offered a different, more expansive view of the ranch. From here, Pilar could see a pasture with horses near another barn painted dull red.

Ranch personnel were exercising the horses. She watched a few moments, mesmerized. Pilar's knowledge of horses and ranch work in general was limited. She hadn't known anyone in Mexico rich enough to have horses or enough land to keep them.

A long table was laden with dirty dishes, suggesting that the ranch hands had already had breakfast and headed out to work. An older woman with bright red hair was seated at the head of the table. And one clean plate was left nearby.

“Pilar Mendoza, this is my mother, Rusty Greer,” he said, introducing them as if they might one day be friends. Which was preposterous.

Pilar nodded. “Senora.”

Greer gestured toward the clean place setting with an open palm, clearly inviting Pilar to sit.

"Sit, sit. Let's talk a little," Rusty Greer suggested. Her voice was raw, raspy. Not like a smoker. Like a weak old soul. She was thin and pale, and a strong wind could easily blow her over. She lifted her coffee and sipped while Pilar made up her mind.

"Ms. Mendoza," the woman cooking at the big stove said with a firm smile and a quick nod. "I'm Isabella."

She was Mexican. Maybe fifty years old. Comfortable both in her role and in her skin. She seemed healthy and well fed. Like Pilar's mother might have looked under better circumstances.

"We have eggs, bacon, biscuits, and coffee. Will that suit you?" Isabella asked.

Pilar looked from the cook to both Greers and back, twice. She didn't know these people. Didn't trust them. But she was hungry and the food smelled better than anything she'd eaten in a long time.

"Have a seat," Greer said again. "You've got enough time to eat before your ride gets here."

Pilar didn't need to be asked again. She plopped her duffel onto the floor and sat at the table. Half a moment later, the cook brought an overflowing plate of food and a big mug full of hot coffee.

"Cream and sugar on the table," Isabella said with a smile. "Plenty more food on the stove, if you want more after you eat this."

“Gracias,” Pilar tilted her head and offered her appreciation. Isabella patted her shoulder for comfort before she started cleaning up.

Greer continued to watch her as if she was a science project.

After a few bites, Pilar’s hungry stomach quieted down. She said, “Do you know why I’m here?”

Greer nodded. “Don’t you?”

“Not really. No one told me we’d be making this stop.” Pilar said, after swallowing a mouthful of the best scrambled eggs she’d ever tasted. “When will Miguel be back?”

“A week? Maybe two?” Greer said. “But your ride is coming this morning. Should be here in another hour. Give or take.”

"He won't come any faster just because you want to get away," Rusty spoke up again.

"Why isn't Miguel coming back?" Pilar asked after chewing and swallowing more of the delicious eggs.

"He wasn't going your way, I guess," Rusty shrugged. "Besides, it's better if you don't stay in one place or with one group too long."

She put the fork down and stared at Rusty. "Why not?"

Pilar heard the diesel engine of a big pickup truck as it drove up and stopped outside the open kitchen door. The driver's side door opened and a pair of heavy work boots hit the ground when he jumped down from the seat.

The boots clumped heavily up the wooden steps to the porch and stopped at the screen door. A deep baritone voice said, “Morning Ms. Greer. Mr. Greer. They ready to go?”

“Morning, Felipe,” Bobby Greer nodded and replied. “Four men out in the barn. And this one here, Ms. Mendoza.”

Felipe opened the screen door. “Come on, Ms. Mendoza. We’re running late.”

Pilar widened her eyes and looked at Rusty Greer. “Me, alone, trapped with five men I don’t know? Going to a place I don’t know? Does that seem like a smart idea?”

Rusty shook her head. “Not to me. But orders is orders. And it’s kinda late for you to be worrying about that, isn’t it?”

“What do you mean?” Pilar’s breakfast was churning in her stomach. She worried it might come back up.

She took another sip of the coffee, hoping to keep everything where it should be.

“Look, honey, you’re illegal. You’ve been on a collision course with trouble since long before you left Mexico. You wouldn’t be here otherwise. Surely you know that,” Rusty said flatly.

Pilar narrowed her eyes to glare at the old witch. Rusty laughed.

Bobby Greer stood up and pushed his chair under the table. “You’ve got nothing to worry about from these guys, Pilar. Until you finish the job you came here to do, you’re still under your patron’s protection. No one will lay a finger on you.”

“That’s right.” Rusty cackled, “And if they do try anything, honey, just shoot ’em!”

Pilar’s blood ran cold as Bobby Greer and the driver laughed along with the old witch.

Isabella gave Pilar a stare that straightened her spine. The kind of look her mother gave her to get Pilar moving when she refused to perform as she’d been told.

Pilar nodded toward Isabella. She rose from the chair.

“Thank you for the breakfast,” she said to Isabella. She picked up her duffel and headed toward the screen door. “I’m ready.”

She walked past Felipe and went outside.

Chapter 17

Monday, May 30
Dallas, Texas

Cooper had nodded off for the remainder of the flight to Dallas, refusing to answer any of Kim's questions about Echo, Texas, and Reacher and the files he'd provided.

Johnson and Miller were sleeping, too.

She could hear her former partner's voice in her head. **Sleep when you can,** Gaspar always said. Good advice. Impossible to follow.

Kim never slept on airplanes, no matter how tired she might be. She envied anyone who could sleep while riding in a steel tube traveling faster than any human was meant to move.

She spent the time evaluating the Texas files again, pouring over the words on the screen as if they might contain secrets she didn't find before.

When the pilot announced preparation for landing and lowered the landing gear, Cooper's eyelids opened. He straightened his body into the seat and fastened his seatbelt.

The aircraft had been riding the turbulence like a cowboy on a bronco for the past half hour. Cooper had slept soundly through the jolting ride.

"Approaching Dallas?" he asked, as if they might have been diverted due to the bad weather.

"More or less. DFW Corporate Aviation," Johnson or Miller replied from the row behind her. Kim couldn't see which one was talking and she couldn't distinguish their voices yet.

"Even better," Cooper said. "Any coffee left?"

"No. But we'll be on the ground in fifteen. We can get coffee in the terminal," Johnson or Miller replied.

Looking at the laptop screen while riding the turbulence was making Kim queasy. She closed the laptop and stashed it under her seat. She pulled an antacid from her pocket and slipped it into her mouth.

She didn't need to fasten her seatbelt. She'd never unbuckled it since she stepped on board.

The entire flight had been rough. But they'd been bouncing especially hard for the past hour. She knew all too well that clear air turbulence could be dangerous. Safer to stay buckled in her seat, just as the commercial carriers recommended.

Cooper turned his head toward her. "Oh, come on. You're not afraid of flying, are you?"

"Not afraid at all." She squared her shoulders. "I simply have a healthy respect for the limits of human behavior, the realities of mechanical equipment tolerances, and the whims of Mother Nature."

Cooper laughed out loud, shaking his head. “That’s absurd. Flying is the safest way to travel. Safer than any other form of transportation. I’m surprised you don’t know that.”

“Statistically, perhaps,” Kim replied. “But it doesn’t matter what the odds are if this flight is the unlucky one.”

“If you flew every single day for the rest of your life, statistical probability indicates it would take you nineteen thousand years before you’d succumb to a fatal accident,” Cooper said, warming to his subject.

“I know the facts,” she responded, tilting her head as if she had to search her memory for the math she’d stored somewhere on her internal hard drive.

She recited by rote. “One hundred and thirty people a day are killed in car accidents in this country. A 727 would need to crash every day of the year, with no survivors, to hit those numbers. You’ve got a one-in-a-million chance of dying on a trans-continental railroad accident. Flying coast to coast is ten times safer. Flying is nineteen times safer than riding in a car. And so on. And so on.”

“None of that is persuasive to you?” Cooper asked, shaking his head. “You’re more likely to die in a tornado or a lightning strike or by accidental gunfire or even a bee sting than you are to die in a commercial flight.”

“We’re not on a commercial flight, though, are we?” Kim nodded. “Small private planes suffer five accidents **per day** in the US alone. More than five hundred lives are lost annually."

"But those are citizen pilots mostly, not well trained military pilots like ours," Cooper replied reasonably.

Kim raised her hand and lifted one finger for each point. "More pilot error, fewer redundancies to protect from likely causes such as lightning strikes and electrical faults and computer failures, wake turbulence, weather, pressurization failures, wildlife strikes. Shall I go on?"

"Don't worry. Passengers who die in plane crashes are only conscious for a moment or two." Cooper shook his head and flashed a grin. "You won't even know it happened."

Kim frowned deeply and replied with heavy sarcasm. "Well that's comforting."

"Death will be swift and certain," he teased. "Pain free, too. Almost."

She gave him a solid nod and then added with finality, "And don't even get me started on the crash statistics for helicopters."

Cooper grinned. "Wouldn't dream of it."

The pilot lowered the landing gear.

"And then there's the tires hitting the runway at extreme speeds under pressure," Kim said. "If we're lucky, the tires won't explode."

"Oh, come on. You know that's not at all likely," Cooper replied sternly.

“We’re not discussing what’s likely. We’re talking about what’s actually happened, way more than once,” Kim said, watching the fast-approaching pavement through the window as the jet descended.

After the pilot managed to level the wings and executed a perfect landing on the tarmac, Kim relaxed her grip on the arm rests. But she didn’t let go. The plane wasn’t safely stopped yet.

She said nothing more as they taxied toward the gate. When the jet finally came to rest, the pilot powered down. The copilot entered the cabin, opened the exterior door, and lowered the jet stairs.

"Welcome to Dallas, folks. You'll want to hustle inside. Storm's headed this way fast. Strong winds and driving rain are already upon us," the copilot said, standing aside to allow the passengers to leave. "We were just ahead of it all the way in. I'm sure you noticed the bouncy ride."

Kim gave Cooper a pointed glance before she gathered her bags and lugged them down the wet, slippery jet stairs in the blowing rain.

Johnson and Miller followed, heads lowered, plowing forward, sliding across the rain slicked pavement wearing leather-soled shoes.

Kim forced her body forward as the warm wind pushed back. Hard rain pelted her face. Moments later, she was soaked to the skin.

They dashed toward the terminal's entrance and hurried inside just as the bottom fell out of the dark clouds, pouring rain like a fire hose.

The air conditioning inside chilled her wet body as if she'd jumped into a freezer. Her teeth began chattering and her hands turned blue. But she kept going, striving to keep up with the long-legged men.

When they peeled off to the men's room, Kim entered the women's restroom. She turned on the hand dryer and stood in front of the warm air to chase the chill from her skin.

While she was away from the others, she fished Gaspar's phone from her pocket and dashed off a quick text to let him know where she was. He could locate her anywhere on the planet. But it could take him a while if he had to search the whole damned globe.

A few minutes later, Kim emerged with a slightly less bedraggled appearance. Cooper and Johnson were standing in the corridor. Cooper was on the phone.

"Miller went to get the SUV," Johnson said as she approached. He extended his hand, palm forward and began to walk toward the exit. Kim joined him. Cooper trailed behind, still holding his phone to his ear.

"Where is this funeral?" Kim asked.

"First Methodist Church. Downtown. One of the oldest churches in

Dallas," Johnson replied. "You should stay close to us. There will be plenty of security there, but still."

Kim cast him a side-eye. "Why? Are you expecting trouble?"

"Early warning signs are suggesting problems, yes. We're not on the security team for the funeral. But we'll get caught up in whatever happens," Johnson replied as they neared the exit. "Our priority is Cooper. You'll be on your own. So stick closely with us."

"I can take care of myself," Kim said with conviction.

Johnson gave her a quick look and a stiff nod. "Good to know."

The driving rain was still coming down in sheets. A small crowd of arriving passengers had gathered near the terminal exit. A few vehicles pulled up out front, close to the awnings, to collect them. In groups of ones and twos, the passengers scurried out into the storm to catch their rides.

Johnson peered through the foggy glass looking for Miller.

Chapter 18

Monday, May 30
Miami, Florida

Carlos Gaspar was settled into the sidewalk café in South Beach with his guava Danish and second cup of Cuban coffee waiting for Katie Scarlett to arrive. He'd arrived early, which gave him time to reconsider what he'd come to ask.

Gaspar had not relocated his offices to Houston when he'd recently retired from the FBI.

One reason he'd retired was to spend more time with his family after his only son was born. Which meant continuing to live in Miami.

When the offer too good to refuse came from Scarlett Investigations, the timing seemed wrong, but it wasn't.

He'd left Kim Otto in the lurch right in the middle of their Reacher assignment. She'd been understandably upset because he'd left her without a replacement.

He didn't tell her why he'd made the choice, but she had to know.

As much as he hated to accept reality, he simply couldn't handle the demanding acrobatics of being Otto's number two anymore. He realized his failures could have easily cost them both their lives, and almost had.

More than once.

He knew it. She knew it. He knew she knew it.

Even worse, Cooper knew it, too.

Gaspar had been more hinderance than help to Otto right from the start of their partnership, although she was too loyal to complain.

He'd had to go.

It was long past time.

Whether she liked it or not.

All of which meant that he'd only met with Katie Scarlett in person once. Before he'd accepted her offer, he'd flown to Houston to see her operation.

And to meet Michael Flint, the operative she jokingly called her "secret weapon."

Several things about that visit cemented his intention to join Scarlett's team.

Her operation was well funded. In his business, money definitely mattered. Money could buy assets and guns and travel and all sorts of weapons, real and virtual.

Some thought the government's total control of the application of the law was the biggest advantage the FBI had over private operatives. They were wrong.

Laws were for the law-abiding. Crooks and criminals and killers of all sorts gave not one fig for what citizens called justice.

No, available cash was the single biggest advantage the FBI and other government agencies had over independent operatives, in Gaspar's opinion.

Scarlett not only had the money, she'd offered a sizable chunk of it to Gaspar for his services. Way more than his government salary had ever been or ever would be.

Gaspar had seven hungry mouths to feed and five college educations to pay for. At least twenty years before he could retire. Money mattered.

But salary and benefits weren't the only things.

Scarlett Investigations had other qualities that made the offer attractive to Gaspar.

Autonomy. No smothering supervision. No worries about performance reviews or promotions or pensions or backstabbing ladder climbers chasing him on the way to the brass ring.

Scarlett's operation had more toys and gadgets and means and methods to deploy than anything Gaspar could legally obtain through the FBI. And she had access well beyond everything the FBI had, too.

To all of which she gave Gaspar open access.

As Otto's number two hunting Reacher, the effort felt like swimming up Niagara Falls in a straitjacket. Hard to avoid drowning.

Working with Scarlett was more like hunting an angry, rabid whale with full use of all available satellites to locate it and the means to capture it alive.

The final sweetener Scarlett had dangled to entice Gaspar when he was still on the fence? Michael Flint.

Scarlett promised two things.

Gaspar could use Flint to help Otto whenever he was needed.

And Flint would do the work on Scarlett's dime.

Subject to Flint's consent, of course.

Flint wasn't one of Scarlett's employees. They weren't even business partners. But they helped each other out when needed and Scarlett had an emotional connection to Flint that both were determined to preserve at all costs.

After confirming the deal with Flint, Gaspar had made the leap.

A leap he had, so far, no cause to regret.

Scarlett's assets and Flint's assistance had already served Otto well. Better than Gaspar could have done if he'd remained her partner on the FBI payroll.

Of course, Otto didn't agree with Gaspar's assessments. He'd known she wouldn't. Which is why he never asked or offered. Better to seek forgiveness than permission.

He simply retired and told her afterward.

Since then, he'd sent Flint whenever Gaspar believed Otto needed the help.

She was grateful, even if she didn't gush about it. He respected her all the more for that.

"Sorry I'm late, Carlos," said a husky female voice as a long shadow fell across Gaspar's table. "Do I need to serve myself? Or is there table service?"

He glanced up behind his aviators to see Katie Scarlett, looking as amazing as any woman he'd ever seen. She was sort of a cross between a film star and an army general. Gaspar couldn't say which was dominant.

Oversized sunglasses covered half her face. Her wild hair had been tamed into some sort of updo. She wore a sleeveless sundress with bare legs and high heels.

Gaspar smiled and raised his hand to get the attention of his server. Scarlett settled into the seat across from him.

When the server arrived at the table, Scarlett said, "I'll have what he's having."

Gaspar's grin widened. Otto would never have eaten all that sugar in a million years.

The server hurried off to fill Scarlett's order. "Sorry I'm late. The jet had some weather issues on the way down. And now I'm afraid we don't have much time."

"No problem," Gaspar replied. He preferred to get right down to business, anyway. "What's up that we couldn't discuss through the usual channels?"

"It's not that," Scarlett said, as the server returned with her order.

"What, then?"

She took an exploratory bite of the Danish and then gobbled half as if she hadn't eaten in a week.

"You eat like my wife." He threw back his head and laughed. "I love a woman with a hearty appetite."

Scarlett wolfed down the rest of the pastry and swigged the Cuban coffee. She didn't pretend it was anything other than fabulous.

Gaspar liked her better by the minute. She had a gusto for life, this one.

"We could have covered this on the phone. But I was on my way to Miami, anyway," Scarlett said, pushing the pastry plate aside. "We have a new client with significant potential."

"Who is it?"

"Wants to remain anonymous. At least for now." She shook her head. "Anyway, Flint just came off a tough case. Lots of travel. A couple of close calls. He needs something to do that's not so strenuous. So he's on his way to Pecos, Texas."

"Been there. Not someplace I'd want to vacation," Gaspar replied, wondering where this was going.

"He's planning to meet with the client. And it looks like our interests and Otto's interests may collide on this one," Scarlett said, in her usual straightforward style. "Have you heard from her?"

He shook his head. "A couple of texts. She's in Dallas, or on her way, or something."

"I sent you the file. You can get to work on it, see what you think. Mainly, I wanted you to know that

Flint's already there. So no need to panic." Scarlett glanced at her watch, nodded, and drained her coffee.

"Panic about what?" Gaspar asked, curious.

"Read the file. We can talk later. I thought we'd have more time, but I've really got to run. I'm sorry," Scarlett said just before she left.

Chapter 19

Monday, May 30
Austin, Texas

Pilar's body ached all over from bouncing around in Miguel's van and now Felipe's old pickup truck. Felipe had dropped the workers at a construction site north of Echo, promising to return for them at the end of the day.

Now, they were alone in the truck and Felipe had fallen silent, which suited Pilar just fine.

The road from Echo was flat and dusty and even longer than the interminable ride from Red House

Ranch to Echo had been. The miles passed with nothing to break the monotony.

After a while, Pilar tired of the silence.

“Where are we going?” she asked.

Felipe kept his eyes on the open road. “A private air strip near Pecos. The pilot will take you the rest of the way.”

“To where, exactly?” Pilar arched her eyebrows.

She had never flown anywhere. The prospect was unnerving.

No one had mentioned anything about flying to complete her contract with Baez. She was to be relocated to California afterward. But she hadn't expected to fly to her new home, either.

She preferred to keep her feet firmly on the ground. No one asked or cared about her preferences.

"No idea. Not my concern." Felipe shrugged. "Once I drop you off, my work with you is done."

"Is this what you do all day? Drive workers to jobs? How do they get back?"

"Some I collect at the end of their shifts. Some not," Felipe replied, nodding.

"Who do you work for?"

"Baez Construction," Felipe replied. "The company has several projects underway in this area. Lots of roads need to be built. New homes are coming soon."

"You're Mexicano?" Pilar asked, to confirm what seemed obvious. But she had learned to be careful of strange men. Most were not at all what they seemed.

He nodded. "I live in Ojinaga. Work here during the week. Go home on weekends."

"Your family is okay with you being gone so much?" she asked.

He shrugged. "It's good work. Pays well. Puts food on the table."

Pilar understood. She got the same answer from her mother when she asked about the prostitution business. Puts food on the table, Mamá always said.

“Have you been to this air strip before?” Pilar asked, clearing her throat to disguise her anxiety.

Felipe cast a brief side-eye toward her, scanning for something. Pilar wasn’t sure what he was looking for.

“Not this one, no,” he replied. “Don’t worry. You won’t be late. The place won’t be hard to find.”

Pilar nodded, although punctuality wasn’t the issue. “Why aren’t you coming back to pick me up?”

“I don’t know how long you’ll be gone.” He shrugged again and added, “Boss didn’t tell me to.”

She liked that answer. Felipe wouldn't need to pick her up. She wasn't coming back. Which suited her just fine. After the job, she'd be headed to California. Like she'd planned.

Pilar wanted to live near the ocean. In exchange for the work she'd agreed to do, she'd been promised a job as an assistant to a wealthy family in Los Angeles.

Baez had shown her photos of the mansion, the grounds. Her bedroom on the top floor even had a private bath.

Such luxury. Such a beautiful place. All to herself.

It was a promise too good to be true.

But she wanted to believe Baez would keep his end of their deal.

And so she did.

Not that Baez's promises mattered all that much. She would have agreed to anything to get away from the life she left behind.

Her sisters had spent years engaged in disgusting sex work, always at the mercy of men who used and abused them. They would never earn their way out of Mexico.

Pilar dreamed of leaving from the moment she was old enough to comprehend her horrible future. Even before the disaster that sent her to Baez, she'd been saving and planning and hoping and praying.

Baez was the answer to her problems and her prayers. Pilar was sure of it.

She knew about Baez Construction, of course. Everyone did.

Baez Construction was now one of the biggest road construction companies in Mexico. Based in Durango, with branches in Mexico City and growing areas like Ojinaga.

Ojinaga was where the youngest of the Baez brothers controlled the family's businesses.

Pilar had heard whispers about Cesar Baez's secret illegal activities. No one seemed to know what those activities were, exactly.

But when people wanted to leave everything behind and never return to Mexico, they went to Cesar Baez for assistance.

Now Pilar knew why Baez was the final solution.

Baez had listened to her problems, asking pointed questions, over a two-hour interview. At the end, he offered her one job.

Only one.

In theory, she was free to accept or reject his offer. But they both understood that she was in no position to refuse.

The reward? A new life, a new country. Serving as a house maid for a wealthy family. The work came with free room and board.

The job? Easy peasy.

She could have done it by the age of twelve, if not younger.

Pilar grew up strong, tough, able to take care of herself. She'd perfected those skills by fending off customers who had tired of what her sisters had to offer.

Including the bastard who had tried to choke her. The only regret she had was not killing him when she had the chance.

She'd reviewed that experience in her head many times. Felt his weight crushing her body.

Felt his big hands encircling her neck, squeezing, as he humped like a filthy swine, breathing hard with the effort.

As if she were hovering above the scene, she saw her hand reach under the mattress for the double-edged balisong mamá gifted to every girl on her fourteenth birthday. Mamá taught all the girls how to use the dagger and warned them to keep the weapon close at all times.

That night, Pilar had grabbed the razor-sharp dagger's cold steel handle in her fist. Weakly, before she blacked out, she plunged the blade deep into his belly near where she hoped his vital organs were.

At first, he didn't seem to notice, so intensely was he focused on extinguishing her life at precisely the right moment to coincide with his climax.

With the last of her adrenaline-fueled awareness, Pilar twisted the blade as she pulled it to plunge again.

She got lucky.

At that precise moment, a car backfired twice as it raced down the street outside her open bedroom window.

Or maybe it was gunshots.

Pilar wasn't alert enough to distinguish the sounds.

But the swine heard. He paused to listen.

Which was when he realized blood was flowing from his side.

He howled and released Pilar's throat to grab the dagger and pull it from her hand. The blood poured from the open wound, quickly drenching his body and hers, too.

He dropped the dagger and rolled off her and slapped his flat hands across the gash.

When he moved, Pilar jumped up and away and screamed and screamed and screamed as loudly as her crushed throat would allow.

So much blood.

She'd smiled when she saw the deep red pools.

Surely, no man could lose that much blood and remain alive, she'd thought at the time.

But he survived.

He still lived in the village.

He was, no doubt, regularly forcing her sisters to pay for Pilar's attempt to kill him.

Which was why she'd boldly struck a second bargain with Baez.

In exchange for the work she'd agreed to do, Baez promised to end that bastard forever.

Sure, another bastard would replace him. There seemed to be an endless supply of brutal men.

But this one? Pilar could remove him from the planet.

The knowledge pleased her.

Pilar patted the zipper pocket where the folded eight-inch balisong was resting against her thigh. Its solid weight reassured her once more. Since that night, she'd never been without it.

Now that she was on the last leg of her journey, she was eager to complete her work for Baez.

She was more eager to see justice done to that particular bastard. Then, and only then, could she begin her new life.

She leaned her head back against the headrest in Felipe's decrepit truck.

She could be on her way to California within twenty-four hours.

Pilar closed her eyes and smiled.

Chapter 20

Monday, May 30
Dallas, Texas

It was a miserable day for a funeral.

Traffic and weather combined to slow the drive from the airport to a crawl. The trip consumed more than an hour.

"What's with all the rain?" Miller asked from behind the wheel.

Johnson said, "May's our rainiest month. We usually get at least a couple of real downpours that last all day. This storm is shaping up to be one of them."

Redstone's funeral was scheduled to begin before they had actually arrived. Johnson checked with agents at the church. He confirmed that the service had been delayed in order to give everyone a chance to get there.

The rousing cacophony of the protestors penetrated inside the heavily armored SUV before Miller turned the corner on the final approach to the church. Raised voices, blaring horns, short siren blasts, even a few bad mufflers on large pickup trucks combined to deafening levels.

The crowd size was already overflowing the wide spaces allotted and more protestors continued to arrive. Bus loads pulled up on the side streets and dozens more protestors spilled out.

Bedraggled but determined, they milled about on both sides of the street, spilling into the traveled portion of the roadway, shouting and thrusting their fists into the air. Handmade cardboard signs were as soggy as the people who carried them.

Kim tried to read the slogans, but the rain had smeared the ink or simply washed the words away. The protestors remained undeterred.

Dallas police had been deployed in significant numbers to keep the protestors separated from the mourners and out of the traffic, but the officers seemed to be losing that skirmish.

Protestors were climbing over the barricades or slipping between them to pound on the black SUVs and sedans and shout into the closed windows. The vehicles continued to roll toward their destination and the protestors targeted the next vehicle in line.

Kim noted several SWAT trucks parked along the periphery. Additional personnel filed out of the boxy trucks and vans to join in the crowd control effort.

Cooper shook his head sadly. "Used to be people were respectful at funerals. These days, what should be a solemn occasion is fair game for all manner of offensive behavior."

Just as Cooper finished his sentence, a protester on one side of the road up ahead ran toward the SUV.

He stopped, set his feet, and threw something under the vehicle. Like a softball pitcher lobbing an easy grounder.

Kim's view was obscured, but the object looked like a smoke grenade.

The pitcher's aim was off.

Instead of rolling under the SUV, the grenade hit the vehicle's body near Kim's seat with a solid thud and dropped to the street.

Momentum carried the grenade farther. It stopped when it hit the curb.

Plumes of pink smoke filled the air obscuring the entire SUV.

A loud cheer rose from the protestors.

The smoke was so thick Kim could barely see through the dense pink cloud for a few seconds.

Thanks to the driving wind, the smoke lifted and dissipated faster than it should have.

Kim got a clear view of the guilty protester as he ran back toward the crowd. Just before he reached the opposite curb, he slipped on the wet pavement and fell to the ground.

A couple of his buddies tried to hoist him up. But they weren't fast enough.

Opponents rushed into the fray. They shoved a few more protestors on top of him.

A full-on brawl broke out.

Fists flying, noses bleeding, shouting voices loud enough to wake the dead.

Dallas police officers rushed forward to control the pandemonium.

It felt surreal to watch the riot from inside the SUV and do nothing.

"Should we lend a hand?" Kim asked, reaching to open the door.

"We don't have any riot equipment because we checked on this before we arrived," Johnson answered from the front seat. "They have their protocols in place. They're trained to work together. Police chief asked us to let them do their jobs without interference. Our orders are to stay out of the way."

Cooper straightened his tie. "The locals will have it under control in a couple of minutes. If they change their minds about wanting our help, they'll ask for it."

Kim looked ahead at the long line of cars, vans, and SUVs waiting to enter the church. No one left their vehicles. Perhaps the protocol for violent protests was to stay inside the vehicle's protective shell while the professionals quelled the disturbance.

Before Kim had a chance to argue the point with Cooper, Dallas PD flipped on the lights and sirens atop several squads.

An ear-splitting **Whoop! Whoop! Whoop!** filled the air. The lights strobed across the faces of the protestors, casting their features in strange reds and blues.

When the siren bursts failed to restore order, the officers drew their clubs and shields and waded into the melee, to break up the fights.

“What’s this about?” Johnson asked. “Social issues? Military campaigns? What? Redstone wasn’t that controversial, was he?”

“All politicians are controversial. They make a career out of it. No controversy means no problems for them to exploit," Miller said with a shrug. "Besides, these clowns don't need a reason. Senator Redstone died. Lots of press coverage at his funeral. That's all they need to show up and make trouble."

Kim didn't argue. But according to her quick research, the issue these protestors were energized about was more than a desire to cause a riot and get their faces on the news.

Replacing Senator Redstone in the Senate could upset the balance of power in Texas and perhaps the US Senate as well. Several social and economic issues were on the line. Enough to energize a sizable, dangerous crowd.

Through the usual back room dealing that goes on in government, the senator's job had been temporarily awarded to his son, Teddy Redstone.

He got the job because he was born to the right father. Simple as that.

The challenger was a popular local politician named Luis Trejo. His supporters claimed he should have been appointed to fill the temporary position.

Everyone agreed that the interim appointment was sure to lead to a landslide in the special election for the man sitting in the senator's seat when the voting started.

Reelecting the temporary incumbent was a damned sight easier than climbing up from the masses.

Meaning Teddy Redstone would replace his father indefinitely. At least another twenty years, probably.

Luis Trejo and his supporters would be left without power on the issues that mattered to them most. They saw the situation as now or never.

Both sides of the dispute were outraged and adamant. Big trouble was definitely brewing here.

An ambulance moved slowly through the crowd, shoving protestors aside like the bow of a ship plowing the ocean.

Several loud bursts of thunder broke through the clouds and went ignored by the crowd's angry voices.

After a few minutes, several rain-soaked protestors were cuffed and tucked into the back of the squads. Four were carried on gurneys to the ambulances.

Once their colleagues were safely stashed, the protestors seemed to calm themselves.

Until the next thing, real or orchestrated, happened to set them off.

Through the storm, Miller lifted his foot from the brake and rolled the big black SUV slowly along the line of waiting vehicles outside the church. The waterfall cascade was faster and harder than any rainfall Kim could remember.

Each vehicle was moving slowly toward the entrance. A line of men in black suits waited to usher the occupants under huge umbrellas to keep them dry until they entered the church.

The wind whipped the umbrellas aside or flipped them inside out, permitting the rain to drench mourners long before they reached the entrance.

When Miller reached the line of black-suited ushers, he braked to a stop and slid the transmission into park.

Johnson opened the passenger door and stepped out of the dry, armored cocoon. One of the black-suited men handed him an open umbrella.

Johnson shook his head and shouted into the wind. “You’ll need those. We’ve got ours.”

He strode around to the cargo door, attacked by the storm all the way to his destination. He slapped the back window with his palm to signal Miller.

Miller pushed the button to release the lock on the back hatch. Johnson bent inside and pulled four umbrellas from the interior.

He returned, opened the first umbrella, and held it for Kim. She stepped from the back seat, over the rushing water in the gutter, and up onto the sidewalk.

She took the wooden shaft from Johnson and moved out of the way, soggy but still dry enough.

He offered the second umbrella to Cooper and tossed the third into the SUV for Miller. Johnson kept the fourth umbrella for himself.

Johnson closed the passenger door and Miller pulled the big SUV away slowly, following the other vehicles toward the parking garage on the back side of the church.

“This way,” Johnson said, after getting directions from one of the ushers.

He led them up the sidewalk to the front entrance.

Chapter 21

Monday, May 30
Dallas, Texas

Kim stepped inside the first set of twelve-foot cathedral doors and entered the foyer. She lowered, shook, and folded the umbrella. Water dripped onto the tiled floor in ever growing puddles.

“I’ll hold onto these. We’ll need them again when we leave.” Johnson tucked the three umbrellas under his arm and led the way from the foyer to the already crowded nave of the huge church.

Kim scanned the interior, conducting her own threat assessment.

Given the riot outside, the protesters should be too busy to cause a disruption inside. But things could escalate. If nothing else, some of the protestors would simply want to get away from the storm.

Surely Senator Redstone's people had an adequate plan to secure the church.

Kim noticed security personnel posted strategically around the interior. A quick glance revealed additional security near the entrances and the receiving lines.

She felt the tension in her shoulders ease a little.

The closed casket holding Senator Redstone's body was placed at the opposite end of the aisle from the entrance. Flowers arranged on stands filled the sanctuary, covering every inch of available space. The sweet and cloying fragrance was overwhelming.

The organist played popular Christian hymns Kim recognized softly in the background. The choir had filed onto the risers and began to sing quietly.

Senator Edward Redstone's family stood stoically near the casket, tirelessly accepting condolences from family, colleagues, dignitaries, friends, and enemies alike.

Cooper's gaze fixed on the family for much longer than necessary.

Kim recognized Teddy Redstone standing tall next to his father's widow near the head of the casket. The current Mrs. Edward Redstone was younger than her husband by more than a decade. Even dressed in widow's weeds, Poppy Redstone was stunning.

On Teddy's other side was his wife and their two teenaged daughters.

Mourners filed past the family, offering a quiet word, a silent touch, or a weak nod.

Teddy Redstone looked a lot like his father. According to the press reports Kim had read, the two were also closely aligned on politics. They agreed on every important question of public policy currently under consideration in Washington. It was impossible to detect even a sliver of daylight between them in that respect.

Which meant Redstone's party was anxious to keep his voice in the Senate. Which was why the party's leadership had insisted the governor appoint Teddy to step into his father's shoes shortly after the senator died. There would be a special election. But in the meantime, Teddy Redstone held the seat.

Luis Trejo and his followers had howled loud and long with outrage before and since the temporary appointment. The escalating protests couldn't be avoided.

The fight between the two factions was on the brink of violence, based on what Kim had seen outside. She only hoped that more violence wouldn't break out today. Redstone deserved a decent memorial service. His family's grief should be respected. Politics could wait, surely.

The pews were full, and mourners were standing along the outside walls. If the weather had been better, the crowd might have spilled outside. As it was, they continued to pour into the church through the front doors and wedged themselves into whatever remaining empty spaces they could find.

The air was already uncomfortably warm inside the church, which helped to raise Kim's internal threat meter to the red zone and hold it there. Raw emotions, seething tempers, and hot temperatures had served as a recipe for violent disaster since the dawn of man.

Kim scanned the interior for a place to stand near an exit. Just in case a swift departure was required. She tilted her head in that direction.

Johnson nodded and led the way to a few feet of empty wall space in the walkway behind the last pew.

Cooper, the old soldier, seemed completely at ease here. He stood watching the crowd, waiting for the service for his old friend to begin.

Still on full internal alert, Kim stood quietly next to Cooper, her back to the wall, continually scanning the room for threats.

“Good turnout for Senator Redstone. Particularly in this horrid weather,” she said to break the silence.

“It is.” Cooper’s gaze moved from the Redstone family and swept the pews as if he was looking for someone or something in particular.

“What’s going on with those protestors out front?” she asked, although she thought she already knew.

“Luis Trejo wants Teddy Redstone’s job. Looks like he’s got more support than most of us believed,” Cooper replied, gaze still scanning the church. “That’s why the funeral was delayed a few days. The Senate leadership wanted Teddy appointed to the job first. The governor's appointment is only temporary, but it gives Teddy an advantage over Trejo."

"How much time is left on his father's term?" Kim asked, scanning the mourners individually now, looking for trouble before it landed on top of her.

Who was Cooper looking for?

"Two years. Teddy will need to be elected in the special election and then again at the end of his father's term. He'll need to stand on his own two feet," Cooper said, continuing to watch the crowd. "But he should be okay by then. He'll have the full party machine behind him and no real competition."

"Trejo isn't real competition?"

Cooper snorted in response. "Hardly."

In her periphery, Kim noticed a woman approaching the Redstones standing at the casket.

A small person. Short and slim and dark skinned and fine boned. She weighed maybe a hundred pounds, give or take. Long black wavy hair fell down her back. Dark eyes. Small white teeth.

She looked like royalty.

As if she'd descended from the Aztec Empire.

Perhaps she had.

She turned for a better look at the congregation, allowing Kim to see her face.

Kim nodded toward the casket.

"Carmen Greer," she said quietly, only loud enough for Cooper to hear.

He turned to see for himself. He peered through narrowed eyes. His nostrils flared. "So it is."

Carmen Greer was accompanied by two girls.

One was a teenager. Sixteen or seventeen, probably. Wavy yellow hair. Slender. Taller than her mother.

The only photos Kim had seen of the girl were ten years old. But she hadn't changed much from her six-year-old self.

Ellie Greer.

The other girl was a younger child. Six or seven, maybe. She looked like an even smaller, more delicate, perfect version of Carmen.

"The file I reviewed on the plane didn't mention that Carmen had a second child," Kim said.

"No. It didn't," Cooper replied with an edge in his voice.

After Carmen had paid her respects to the Redstones, she filed away from the casket in her turn. She took her seat next to a handsome Latino near the front of the church.

"Husband?" Kim asked quietly.

"Luis Trejo," Cooper replied. "That's his wife, Selma, seated next to him on the other side."

Kim nodded in response. Selma Trejo was not a particularly attractive woman. No match for Carmen's beauty, but Selma was self-possessed in her own way.

The last of the mourners were finally seated and a hush fell over the crowd as the service began.

The noisy protestors outside had raised their voices loud enough to be heard inside the church, even after the big doors had been closed.

The storm had picked up, too, adding the sounds of nature's fury to the dissonance.

All of which made the pastor's words difficult to hear.

The mourners became restless. Concerned, perhaps, by the ominous soundtrack.

The dignity of the occasion had been spoiled by circumstances beyond Senator Redstone's influence.

Kim felt sorry for Teddy. Losing a parent was always hard. The funeral service should have been a comfort to his family. Instead, the situation outside was out of control and escalating fast toward a full-scale riot.

Quietly, as if he was talking only to himself, Cooper leaned toward her and said, "See anyone else you recognize?"

Kim understood instantly what he meant.

She inhaled sharply and made another quick scan of the mourners.

“Why would Reacher come here?”

A deafening crack of thunder was quickly followed by raised voices out front.

Kim leaned closer to hear Cooper’s quiet reply.

Cooper shrugged. “It’s not like he’s got somewhere else he needs to be.”

Chapter 22

Monday, May 30
Dallas, Texas

Everything happened everywhere and all at once.

Before she had a chance to respond to Cooper, the melee outside burst through the church's front doors and into the foyer.

An ear-splitting crash busted the front door off its hinges and slammed it back against the wall. Protestors fell in and piled on top of each other on the floor.

A moment later, they'd scrambled to their feet and joined the rest of the mob flooding the church.

The mourners jumped from their seats, frightened women screaming, angry men shouting, all unsure what to do, where to go, or how to escape the chaos.

Law enforcement sirens activated.

Rage pelted the church from all sides.

A moment later, Kim heard the unmistakable sound of gunfire.

The first shots were fired out front.

And then more shots inside the church.

Senator Redstone's family swiveled their heads, staring at the scene, bewildered and astonished.

As if they'd never seen such a wild crowd before.

They probably hadn't.

Under cover of the chaos, a lone protester wearing full camo covering his entire body from crown to toe, rushed Teddy Redstone's pew.

He jumped over two pews and stood on the third, arm extended.

From Kim's vantage point, he seemed to be holding his pistol pointed directly at Redstone, but she couldn't be sure.

Cooper lunged forward, as if he intended to defend the Redstone family.

"No!" Johnson and Miller said simultaneously. Johnson restrained Cooper with a solid grip on his bicep. Miller blocked Cooper's momentum with his body. Together, they kept Cooper from the line of fire.

Security personnel pushed Teddy Redstone and his father's wife swiftly aside, knocking him to the ground moments before the gunman fired three shots.

The shooter's marksmanship was subpar. All three shots missed Redstone and his family.

But the bullets hit three others. Each screamed as they fell.

Small mobs surrounded the wounded mourners, sobbing hysterically.

Which suggested the gunman had shot three civilians, although Kim couldn't see the victims.

When the shot was clear, one of Redstone's guards fired back. He hit the protester with four rounds, knocking him to the floor.

Kim's view of the gunman was blocked by the continuing chaos.

Through a momentary gap in the crowd, she witnessed the potential killer's dead eyes staring back at her from the floor where he'd landed. The gun was still clutched in his hand.

The bill of a baseball cap pulled low partially covered his face. Long brown hair protruded from the camo hood he'd pulled over his head.

The milling crowd blocked her view again. An angry woman, drenched to the skin by the storm, rushed toward Kim, arms raised, a rock in one hand, screaming like a vixen in heat.

Kim stepped aside at the last possible moment, as the woman threw the rock. While she was slightly off balance, Kim lunged sideways and knocked her to the floor.

She knelt on the woman's back to hold her in place. She grabbed the arm of a passing patrolman who seemed to understand the situation at once.

"I'll take it from here," he said, grabbing his handcuffs.

While Kim had been fighting off the protester, private security guards rushed in to gather Teddy Redstone, the late senator's wife, and those closest to them, and herd them out the back of the church.

Another team of security officers rushed out Luis Trejo and his wife, who had been in the pew behind Redstone. Trejo seemed unsteady on his feet.

Carmen Greer and her daughters were also swept up and marshalled toward the back exits.

Moments after Trejo and his team disappeared through the door behind the astonished choir, hundreds of protesters flooded though the demolished front door and inside the church.

The protesters brandished baseball bats and clubs. A few carried guns. And there were plenty of them. Like an invading battalion of combat soldiers, they kept coming.

They began destroying the interior of the church. At first, they destroyed the flowers and the hymnals and anything that was easily smashed.

Then they began piling debris into the center aisle, as if preparing for a bonfire.

Reinforcements from all sides were arriving outside. The volume grew louder and louder.

Law enforcement personnel would eventually contain the mob, but Kim's four-man team was vastly outnumbered. They had no tactical gear, no communications, knew nothing about the rules of engagement, and had received no request nor authorization to join the defense.

In short, there was nothing they could do to stop the freight train of the angry mob determined to destroy.

The only option was to protect Cooper and save themselves while they still had the chance.

"Come on. We've got to go." Johnson and Miller grabbed Cooper and led him to the rear exits.

Kim pulled her weapon and followed close behind.

She reached the back exit just in time to see Carmen Greer and her two daughters climb into a black limo and pull away.

Kim swiveled her head to look for the Redstones. They must have been loaded up and were already gone.

Miller pointed. “We’re parked down three blocks.”

He took off at a trot and led the way.

Johnson and Cooper followed.

Kim hurried behind Cooper, bringing up the rear, weapon ready.

They’d covered a couple of blocks in the relentless downpour and were crossing the street when a dark sedan took the corner on two wheels and came speeding toward them.

Kim heard the engine straining under the driver's heavy foot on the accelerator.

He was coming up too fast. They wouldn't get across the street before he ran them down.

"Miller! Johnson! Look out!" Kim yelled as loudly as she could scream into the storm and the noise of the approaching vehicle.

Had they heard her? They didn't change course.

The sedan raced forward, efficiently closing the gap between them with alarming speed.

Adrenaline flooded her body. Her heart pounded and her ears roared and her breathing became rapid and shallow.

She reached forward and grabbed Cooper's arm.

She shoved him to one side.

He tripped over his own feet and fell to the ground.

Kim jumped sideways and tumbled down after him. Just in time to avoid being mowed down by the speeding sedan.

Johnson and Miller turned, aimed, and fired their weapons, attempting to slow the screaming vehicle.

They failed.

The sedan zoomed past and screeched around the next corner.

Kim heard the engine strain to deliver speed as the driver stomped the accelerator and the sedan raced away.

She didn't move for a few moments until her heart thumped a little softer in her chest and her breathing slowed and deepened.

She climbed off the pavement and pushed herself up. Then she offered Cooper a hand.

He brushed her offer aside and stood on his own power.

"What the hell was that?" Cooper said, brushing the dirty sidewalk grime from his expensive clothes.

"We'll find out," she shouted, to be heard over the storm and the riot still happening behind them.

The rain was still falling in heavy sheets. Every inch of pavement was wet and deep pools lined the curbs. Runoff cascaded into the sewers faster than the Merced River.

Kim looked up along the buildings lining the street.

No obvious CCTV cameras, but they had to be there. Downtown Dallas in the middle of the day. There would be video of that sedan, for sure.

"Come on," Miller said, waving them toward the parking garage where he'd left the SUV. "Let's get out of this weather away from the riot and figure things out."

Johnson grabbed Cooper's elbow and Cooper angrily shook him off. "What the hell do you think you're doing? When I want your help, I'll ask for it."

No one needed to worry about Cooper. The realization was somehow comforting.

Kim bent her head and grinned as she hurried to follow Miller's lead. The garage was another half block away. They wouldn't be out of the line of fire until they were inside the armored SUV.

They'd left their umbrellas back in the church. The rain continued to pelt them until they were totally drenched. They kept going.

Miller hoofed along speedily. Cooper and Kim followed. Johnson covered the rear this time.

At the garage, Miller dashed inside. "Third floor," he said as he turned and headed up the ramp.

Cooper was out of breath, panting slightly.

Not for the first time, Kim was glad she spent time running every morning. She was barely winded, although the extra adrenaline added a level of resistance to her movements.

At the third floor, Miller moved to the center of the aisle. The SUV was embassy parked in the middle row.

He pulled the key fob from his pocket and clicked the door locks open. They scrambled into their seats and closed the doors as Miller started the engine.

He pushed the transmission into drive and rolled down the ramp to the exit.

Miller turned away from the church and zigzagged away from the riots, dodging oncoming sirens and staying off the main roads.

Ten minutes later, they'd escaped.

"What the hell was that all about?" Miller asked, as if someone actually had an explanation for the uncontrolled chaos they'd left behind.

Cooper cleared his throat, twice. “Excellent question.”

“Who would want to kill Teddy Redstone?” Miller wondered aloud. “The list of suspects is long, I would bet.”

“What makes you think Redstone was the target?” Cooper snapped.

“You’re thinking it was Luis Trejo?” Miller asked, eyes watching Cooper in the rearview mirror.

Cooper shrugged. “First we need to know who died.”

“Keep our eyes on the prize, folks. We gotta go. While we still can,” Johnson insisted. “Where to, Boss? Back to the airport?”

"Not yet." Cooper shook his head, still staring out the window as if he couldn't quite fathom the rioting protesters they'd barely escaped.

He gave another address, which Miller punched into the GPS.

Kim wondered what the hell he was thinking. Once the dust cleared on the riot, the shooter and the victims would be identified. Until then, speculating wouldn't do any good.

One thing she was fairly sure of, though. Reacher hadn't been inside that church.

She'd had experience now and she knew how to spot Reacher in a crowd. As chaotic as any situation might become, Reacher remained big and obvious in every way.

If he was at that church, before, after, or during the chaos, she'd have known.

Reacher might still be in the vicinity somewhere.

Cooper's intel on Reacher's probable location had never been wrong before.

Chapter 23

Monday, May 30
Austin, Texas

The airstrip, located in the middle of miles of nothing on the outskirts of Pecos, was less than Pilar had expected. It had been abandoned at the end of more prosperous times, perhaps related to the three rusty oil rigs paused nearby.

She wouldn't have realized the long, narrow clearing was an airstrip at all had she merely been driving past. The only indication of the decrepit runway's purpose was the plane, ready and waiting, engines idling.

Pilar's heartbeat quickened. She wiped a thin film of sweat from above her upper lip and stared at the vehicle.

She knew nothing about airplanes. This one seemed impossibly small to her. How could such a craft possibly be safe for flight?

Felipe rolled slowly off the road and brought the pickup to a halt near the plane.

"Here's your stop," he said when she didn't immediately get out of the truck.

"Thanks for the ride," she responded, stalling a bit longer.

Her stomach churned as she climbed out of the truck. Her knees were weak and buckled. A tight grip on the doorframe kept her upright.

“Don’t forget your duffel,” Felipe said.

“Right.” She reached into the back and collected the bag.

“Good luck,” Felipe said.

“Thanks,” she replied over the noise of the engines as she closed the door.

Felipe turned the truck and headed back toward Pecos without further comment.

Pilar watched him leave for a few moments. Knowing she had no alternative, she inhaled deeply and then walked toward the plane as if she were approaching a guillotine.

A man stepped out of the cabin and hustled down the jet stairs. His boot landed on the ground before she reached him.

He watched her approach. When she was within earshot, he said, "Pilar Inez Mendoza?"

"Yes," she said, raising her voice to be heard.

"José Del Campo. This way," he extended his arm, waving her to the stairs. "Let me take your bag."

She handed the duffel to him, grabbed both handrails on the narrow jet stairs, and climbed up. At the top, she took a moment for a more panoramic scan of the dusty brown flat land, wondering why anyone would ever choose to live here.

José was coming up fast behind her.

Pilar ducked her head and stepped inside the cabin.

"Take your seat. We're late," José said as he tossed her duffel into the back.

He secured the stairs and sealed the door while she fastened and tightened her seatbelt. The plane was already rolling before he stepped into the front and settled into the copilot's seat.

A few moments later, the plane's engines accelerated, and the aircraft rolled faster until it lifted into the air like the graceful birds she'd watched for hours as a child.

Just like that, she was flying. She smiled and shook her head. First time for everything.

After an uneventful hour in the air, flying due east, the plane banked sharply and began its descent. Pilar heard the landing gear going down and shortly after, the tires were bumping against the ground.

Another airstrip in another abandoned location. This one less decrepit.

The plane landed, taxied briefly, and came to a stop. José released the four-point harness holding him into his seat and stepped into the plane's passenger cabin again. He unsealed the door and let the jet stairs down.

“Come on. Grab your bag. We’re late. Let’s go,” he said loudly to cover the engine noise, waving toward the open door.

“Late for what?”

José did not respond. Pilar did as she’d been told.

At the bottom of the stairs, she stood aside to wait. José slid down, barely touching the steps, and plopped onto the pavement.

Without comment, he strode toward a black SUV. Pilar followed, hustling to keep up.

He reached into his pocket and pulled out a key fob. He pressed the button to unlock the doors. “Toss your bag in the back. Sit in the front.”

Pilar didn't shout back. No point. He was already in the SUV, starting the engine.

When she was seated with the door closed, he slid the SUV's transmission into drive and accelerated away from the plane.

The quiet calm inside the cabin of the SUV seemed surreal after the constant assault on her senses over the past few weeks. She fastened her seatbelt and settled deeper into the most luxurious upholstery she'd ever experienced, waiting for José's instructions.

He drove another thirty minutes in silence along paved roads in light traffic. Pilar had seen one road sign announcing Austin, Texas, city limits.

"Still in Texas, then," Pilar said.

José glanced toward her. "Yes. Sorry. I've got a lot on my mind."

"No problem. I'm not that chatty," she replied.

He nodded. "Good."

"Where are we going?"

"First, to a hotel."

Pilar's breath caught. Her spine stiffened and she reached to pat the dagger resting comfortably on her right thigh. "Why?"

José replied, "Briefing. Food. Sleep. Tonight's the night."

"Tonight? Can we be ready by then?" Pilar asked, alarmed.

"No choice. The fundraiser is tonight, and the target will be there. We won't have another chance."

José flipped the turn signal on, slowed the big vehicle, and pulled into the driveway of a businessman's motel. He parked the SUV in front of a room in the back on the first floor.

"We've got a lot of work to do. Come on," he said, opening his door and stepping out into the heat.

Pilar followed suit. The heat engulfed her in a stifling embrace of unseasonably hot, humid, air. She collected her duffel.

José was already standing in front of one of the motel rooms, key in hand.

"Food will be here soon." He unlocked the door, stepped inside, and beckoned her to follow.

She paused on the sidewalk. It occurred to her that she could draw the pistol and shoot him. Right here. Right now. Steal the SUV and drive away.

The United States was a big country. She could easily disappear. Baez would never find her. She'd be free to do as she pleased, when she pleased, with whomever she pleased. For the first time in her entire life.

For more than a minute, she actually considered it.

Who would know?

Only one thing held her back.

If she didn't do what she'd promised, Baez wouldn't either. The bastard who'd tried to kill her would live to choke another woman. And another. And another.

One of those women was likely to be someone she knew. Maybe even one of her sisters. Such was the village she'd come from.

So she took a deep breath and squared her shoulders and followed José into the cool dark room and closed the door behind her.

She tossed the duffel on the bed. José had completed his search of the room and exited the bathroom.

"All clear," he said, pulling a cell phone from his pocket. "Get washed up. I'll be right back."

Chapter 24

Monday, May 30
Ojinaga, Mexico

Cesar Baez declined the contract, disconnected, and closed the laptop shaking his head. He poured a second cup of espresso from the pot and contemplated the request he'd received from a returning client.

He stared outside where his children played on the lawn, unseeing.

Cesar spent very little time with his children. They were Gabriella's concern. But he enjoyed displaying them in the same way he displayed other attributes of his wealth. Quietly.

Cesar's father had taught him the essential lessons about human nature.

"Don't brag," Diego had often said. "Let others learn of your success from amigos. Allow them to form opinions on their own. Ignore their fawning words. Watch how they behave toward you. Only then will you know their true nature. When they disrespect you, act accordingly."

The advice had served Cesar well in his personal life and in his business.

"Be selective," the old man had warned. "The more desperate the prospects are the less likely you should accept them."

The old man said, over and over again, "Work only with the coldly calculating. You know them. You know what they will do. And what they won't."

Baez had taken his father's advice to heart, and it had served him well. His clients were men mostly, although he'd found a few women worthy over the years. Very few.

Potential customers occasionally refused to take no for an answer.

"Those are the most dangerous kind," the old man had instructed.

They were also vengeful and vindictive. Such contracts never ended well.

"Avoid demanding men entirely," his father told him. "Never bend to the will of another."

Baez had taken the old man's advice to heart. Partly because he'd found no shortage of amateurs willing to accept his rules or prospective clients willing to pay his prices.

He supposed it was a sad commentary on the human condition in the modern age.

"Patience," his father had cautioned. "Slow and steady will serve you success, time after time."

Baez was patient by nature. Nor was he a greedy man. He was building an empire. Two kills at a time.

Which was why the client had intrigued him for a while before Baez finally accepted him.

The first inquiry, some weeks ago, had been short, succinct, and not even remotely desperate. All good.

The potential client had seemed to lack even a fundamental understanding of the rules. Not so good. But curious.

Anonymity was the fundamental reason users like Baez and his clients operated on the dark web. Clandestine, highly illegal activities such as Baez's operations were commonplace.

Receiving and managing contracts on the dark web had enabled Baez to conduct his empire without limits for quite some time.

Baez's identity and location were completely buried beneath layers of security. Buried so deeply no one could ever find him. Not in real life. And not virtually or electronically, either.

Baez had been successful all these years precisely because he was so careful.

So why had this man skipped the usual encryption protocols? Why had he claimed to use his real name, which was so obviously false?

Baez had initially assumed the initial inquiry was a hoax. He'd ignored the message.

The man who called himself Smith had tried again.

He'd assured Baez that his interest was dead serious.

Which made Baez relax. He took the assurances to confirm that Smith was not his name.

Baez was often contacted by men with false identities. He preferred the careful concealment. He understood it. The activities they were discussing required caution and care and, above all, anonymity.

Beyond that, Baez didn't want to know who his clients were in real life.

All he cared about was whether they paid their bills and left him alone to do the work.

Because Smith insisted that he was using his real name, Baez initially guessed he was probably law enforcement of some sort.

In which case, the contact was a trap.

Again, Smith claimed otherwise.

Could he be trusted?

Perhaps.

If Smith was an undercover operative of any sort, he would most certainly have been more circumspect.

The enigma intrigued Baez. Who was this guy? What did he want?

Baez decided to play the game for a while and see where it led. The first step had been the earnest money. A cool two million dollars, non-refundable, wired to Baez's offshore account established for this specific purpose.

Smith could wire the money. Or not. His action would inform the next steps.

To pay or not to pay? Baez had wondered which Smith would choose.

He hadn't waited long. Smith paid the downstroke on the contract within twenty-four hours.

After that, the first contract proceeded normally. The Greer woman was eliminated. Lopez and his family were also erased. The final fee was received. The matter was closed.

Now, Smith was back with another request.

This time, Smith had four targets on his wish list. Briefly, Baez wondered why Smith wanted to eliminate them. He wasted only a moment on the question.

Baez tapped his espresso cup with his fingers as he contemplated the issues Smith's inquiry presented.

First was timing. When did the jobs need to be done?

Next were means and methods. How could the kills be easily accomplished?

Finally, instruments. Who would do the work?

Baez had much to think about. The happy noises of his children rising from the lawns below barely registered against his ears. His mind was otherwise occupied.

He had named his price. Twice as much per kill as Smith had paid for

Maria Greer. Half paid in advance, non-refundable. Would Smith pay it?

His cell phone vibrated on the desk with a message from José. The messages existed only until he read them, and then they evaporated like ether.

The first was succinct: “Pilar arrived. On track.”

Baez nodded. “Excellent,” he murmured.

The second was disturbingly longer: “Garcia dead. Three more dead. Target survived.”

Baez swore and threw the phone into the burning fire in the fireplace and watched the plastic melt.

Chapter 25

Monday, May 30
Dallas, Texas

Miller drove the SUV expertly through the narrow alleys until they escaped the mass of traffic headed to the riot site. He turned onto a boulevard, following the directions on the GPS.

Cooper relaxed deeply into the plush leather seats as if the chaotic and deadly riot scene hadn't alarmed him at all. He reached up to push a button that raised the privacy glass behind the front seat.

“What the hell was going on back there?” Kim demanded.

A lesser man might have pretended to misunderstand, latching on to one of the more obvious topics such as the riot or the protesters or even the shooter.

None of which was what she meant, and he knew it.

He squared his shoulders and absorbed the assault straight on.

“Win some, lose some. Not everything goes according to plan.” Cooper shrugged. “While you’ve consistently been coming up short hunting Reacher, my track record’s been pretty good on that score.”

"What the hell? Your track record? What track record?" Nostrils flaring, Kim's voice rose and her blunt retort came quickly. "I've been putting my ass on the line out there for seven months, dodging bullets while you've been resting in DC luxury. If you mean you've been one-hundred percent useless, I'll give you that."

"Whatever do you mean?" he replied innocently.

"You know damned well what I mean," was Kim's sharp retort.

"I sent you to the right places at the right times, didn't I? Reacher was there. Every time. You simply failed to apprehend him." Cooper smiled like the reasonable cat who ate the hapless canary. "Whose fault was that? Surely not mine."

“What?”

“Look in the mirror,” he said gruffly.

“You’ve got to be kidding.” Kim’s breath came in quick spurts. She felt the heat rising from her chest to her scalp.

“You think predicting Reacher’s actions is easy? You should try it for yourself and see how easy it is.”

Kim might have punched him squarely in the center of his smug face, but the angle was impossible from her seat next to his in the SUV.

She really hated being captive inside a moving vehicle.

“Okay, okay. Don’t spin out of control.” Cooper grinned and offered a brief nod.

Now that he'd wound her up, he stepped back. Another damned test.

"I confess. I didn't actually **know** he'd be there every time. Let's call it a highly targeted possibility," Cooper said.

Kim was not mollified. "How?"

Cooper shook his head, as if Kim should already know the answer. "I've been monitoring Reacher's prior contacts. Surely you figured that out."

Kim said nothing, still pissed off. She had guessed as much. But it was long past time for him to explain himself. She had no intention of helping him.

“When one of Reacher’s friends is on a collision course with disaster, it makes sense that he might show up, doesn’t it?” Cooper asked.

“Only if he knew. Which, according to you and absolutely everyone else, he wouldn’t. He’s totally unpredictable. No fixed address. Moves randomly. No phone. No way to contact him,” Kim replied, still angry. “So how would he know his friends are in trouble? And don’t hand me your line of blather. You’re not clairvoyant and he’s not a mind reader.”

“Let’s come back to that. For now, we can agree that my, er, informed guesses have been uncannily accurate, yes?” Cooper arched his eyebrows.

Kim nodded sharply. “So?”

“So after Senator Redman died, I **noticed** Carmen Greer’s intention to attend the funeral. She had worked on his last reelection campaign. Maybe she wanted to pay her respects.” He emphasized the word **noticed** to suggest something else.

He didn’t simply come across the intel, that much was clear. Which meant whatever he’d done to find it was illegal, immoral, or both.

She waited.

Cooper continued, “Carmen was in serious trouble when Reacher helped her before, and she seems to be mixed up in something else now.”

"Reacher rescued her once. And you think, if he knew, he might do it again?"

"Not exactly." Cooper frowned and spoke sternly. "Carmen Greer was a piece of work. You saw the files. She lured Reacher into a no-win situation. She was cruising the roads, literally looking for a guy she could bribe to commit murder. She found Reacher, picked him up, tried to pay him to kill her husband."

"Seemed like she had good reasons for wanting the bastard dead. Her husband was no prize." Kim cocked her head. "But of course Reacher refused to kill him."

"It's interesting that you would reach that conclusion," Cooper's scowl deepened. “But you’re right. Money has never been a prime motivator for Reacher.”

Kim considered the point and she had to agree that Reacher wasn’t motivated by promises of wealth.

Although he was one of the best snipers the US Army had ever produced. He had the medals to prove it.

If he’d wanted to work as a highly paid hit man for Carmen Greer or anyone else, he certainly could have done so.

Cooper’s point was spot on, though. Why did Kim instinctively assume that Reacher had refused to kill at Carmen Greer’s request?

She tucked that question away. It was something she'd need to think about privately. Not an issue she intended to discuss with Cooper now, or ever.

"You said you'd recently lost track of Reacher. So you just guessed that he might show up at the funeral because Carmen Greer was there?" she responded skeptically.

Cooper shrugged. "Call it instinct or intuition or informed expertise or whatever you like."

"Not good enough," Kim said, shaking her head. Cooper wouldn't leave his cushy DC location on a whim or even a solid guess. Never happen. "What's the rest of it?"

He paused for a long minute before he finally said, "Reacher knew the Redstones. Edward and Teddy, too. He might have come to the funeral to pay his respects."

"Seriously? Reacher's been out of the army for fifteen years now. Law of averages suggests he's lost several people he knew before. He's never attended any of the other funerals. Not even when his mentor died. You thought he'd show up to a funeral for an old army buddy now?"

Cooper shook his head. "Not exactly."

"What then?"

He looked distinctly uncomfortable for the first time. He straightened his tie and squared his shoulders. Stalling.

"Out with it," she said sharply.

"Like I said, Reacher had history with the Redstones. I didn't say they were buddies. Let's just say he wasn't a fan," Cooper paused and then delivered the blunt truth. "Reacher would have gone out of his way to see the old man dead in his casket. For the satisfaction of it."

"That's pretty cold." Kim shivered as if his words had frosted the air. "You really think Reacher would hold a grudge all these years? Be glad the man died?"

"I don't just think it. I know it. Reacher's like a block of granite.

Nothing much gets him going unless he wants to do it." Cooper smirked and nodded. "The challenge is figuring out how to make him want to."

Kim nodded. She had heard the same story from everyone she'd met on this assignment. Reacher's confidence was as oversized as his body. He moved around in the world like he owned the place and expected everyone else would simply get out of his way.

Most of the time, they did.

And if they didn't, they lived to regret it.

"We agree then," Cooper said, watching her think things through as if he could see the gears turning in her head. "There's one thing that fuels Reacher, pushes him forward when he might not otherwise be motivated in that direction."

"Which is?"

"Revenge."

She shivered involuntarily this time. Cooper's analysis rang true. Too true.

"You haven't talked to him for years," Kim said. "How can you possibly know what motivates him now?"

"Leopards don't change their spots, Otto. Unlike you, I actually know the guy. Known him since he was a kid. I've had many conversations with him," Cooper said. "You don't know him at all."

Kim nodded, simply to encourage him to keep talking.

"Reacher's a hard man. A killer. I've told you that from the start." Cooper flashed her a narrow-eyed stare. "Don't make the fatal mistake of believing otherwise."

Kim said nothing. Her experience of Reacher had been different.

Cooper warned her again. "If Reacher wants you dead, there's no power on earth that will stop him. Don't you ever forget that."

They rode a few miles in silence. There was way more to this situation than Cooper was revealing to her, but he wouldn't share it until he was damned good and ready.

Kim picked up the conversation again from a slightly different angle. "We can agree that Reacher wasn't at the funeral. So where are we going now?"

Miller lowered the glass between the seats before Cooper had a chance to reply.

"Talked to the locals. Redstone is safely tucked in for the night. Trejo and his wife are hospitalized with gunshot wounds. The wife is in critical condition. Still no leads on the gunman's motive or the intended target. Gun was stolen. Owner reported it a month ago," Johnson reported with terse efficiency.

"No ID on the shooter, either.
No wallet, no driver's license,

nothing," Miller said. "They checked preliminary biometrics."

"And?"

"No fingerprints or DNA or matching facial recognition in the system," Miller replied. "They'll keep checking."

Miller paused as if there were more to say, but only if Cooper wanted to hear it.

"What we know so far," Johnson interjected. "Hispanic. A few hundred bucks in cash in his pockets. He's nowhere in our databases. Probably undocumented."

"Why would anyone think they could run into a senator's funeral and kill people and survive the attempt?"

Miller said, shaking his head. "People are crazy."

Kim silently agreed that the idea was preposterous.

Cooper nodded. "Now that the shooter's dead, we can close the case and move on."

Neither Johnson nor Miller agreed nor argued.

"Move on to what?" Kim asked.

Chapter 26

Monday, May 30
Austin, Texas

José left Pilar's motel room and she heard him enter the room next door.

She went into the bathroom, used the toilet, and washed her face and hands. She felt like she was washing off a year's worth of dirt. Maybe twenty years' worth.

When she returned to the room, José was back with a hot pizza and a six-pack of bottled water. Until that moment, Pilar hadn't realized how hungry she was. She fell on the pizza like a starving cannibal. José grinned at her display of ravenous appetite, but she didn't care.

He opened a bottle of water, handed her an electronic tablet, and began the briefing. "That woman is your target. Her name is Emily Brandon. Do you know who she is?"

As she chewed, wiping the grease from her chin, Pilar looked at the image on the screen. A typical American gringo. Pale skin. Symmetrical features. The kind of gringo she'd seen in old movies all her life. They all looked the same to her.

This woman was about fifty, Pilar guessed. She might be older if she had a good plastic surgeon on retainer. Which she probably did.

Shoulder length brown hair brushed straight back from her face. A slight dusting of freckles covered the bridge of her straight nose and her sculptured cheekbones.

She was artificially thin. Bony arms and skinny legs. Dressed simply in casual clothes She wore no jewelry and very little makeup.

Pilar studied her carefully, committing the image to memory. She finished her exercise and the slice of pizza at the same time.

“I’ve never seen her before. Should I know who she is?” Pilar asked as she took another slice of the pizza and a long swig of the water.

“Her husband is Kevin Brandon. He owns a big manufacturing operation.

Global scope. Billions of dollars," José said between bites.

"How nice for them," Pilar replied coldly. She had no frame of reference for a wealthy couple like Kevin and Emily Brandon. They had more money than ten entire villages where she came from. "Why should we care?"

"We don't. I'm just giving you background."

"Okay. She's the target. Is he the one paying the bill?"

José gave her a narrow stare. "Not your business. You have a target. You eliminate her. That's all you need to know."

Pilar shrugged. "Got it. How do I do that?"

José continued to stare at her, as if she'd already failed somehow. She ate the pizza while he made up his mind.

"Baez says you can do the job. I'm not so sure," he said frankly.

"Doesn't matter what you think, does it? You got someone else who can do this job tonight?" she replied between bites and swallows. She hadn't realized how famished she was. "Call Baez. Maybe he's got another option."

He shook his head slowly, displeased by her impertinence no doubt.

"That's what I thought. We don't have unlimited time. So again, how do I kill her?" Pilar asked, reaching for a third slice while he continued to disapprove. She had no idea when she'd be able to eat again.

"She'll be attending a fundraiser at a private home tonight. You'll pose as one of the servers. You've worked as a waitress before, haven't you?"

Pilar nodded. "Yes. Since I was sixteen. In our local café."

"You carried food on a tray? Offered it to patrons?"

"Yes. Thousands of times."

"Good," José nodded. "You'll carry a small tray. You'll offer her an appetizer filled with poison."

"An appetizer?"

He nodded. “A goat cheese-stuffed date. Apparently, it’s a secret recipe that she loves and can’t duplicate. She’ll eat it and death is almost instantaneous. She’ll collapse. That’s it.”

Pilar thought about it, running the logistics through her mind. She imagined a dozen things that could go wrong. The plan was more complicated than he said, but she could do it.

“How do I get away?”

“It’ll be chaos when she goes down. Screaming guests. People crowding in trying to help. Things like that. You slip out the back door during the pandemonium.”

Pilar nodded again. “And go where?”

“You can drive, right?”

“Yes.” Pilar had learned to drive years ago. But she didn’t own a car and she hadn’t driven much. Old trucks and rusty scooters, mostly. The basics weren’t that hard to master.

“You’ll have a car. You’re driving it there and you’ll park it yourself. You’ll simply get back to the vehicle and drive away,” José said.

“Sounds too simple. Why do you think this will work?” Pilar asked after she’d swallowed the last bite.

“Because we have confidence in your ability to do the job,” José replied.

Pilar nodded because she possessed such certainty herself. There were easier, more efficient ways to kill than with a piece of poisoned fruit. But those choices were not hers to make.

"What if this doesn't work? I just walk away?" Pilar asked.

José shook his head. "We need Emily Brandon to die tonight. And she will. If you do the job you're being paid to do."

"And if she doesn't die?" Pilar asked, cocking her head and narrowing her eyes. She wanted to be clear on this point. Would Baez keep his word if the assassination failed?

"She will die. You'll see to it," José said with flat finality.

Pilar nodded. She understood. She was expected to kill Emily Brandon. No excuses. Which was exactly what she would do.

After a few moments of silence, José said, “Let’s get into the details.”

He flipped to another screen on the tablet showing the private mansion where the fundraiser would take place and began to explain exactly how Pilar would accomplish her mission.

The details were extensive.

José explained everything several times, painstakingly answering her questions. Finally, she was satisfied.

“Tell me more about the poison,” Pilar said.

"Carfentinal. It's extremely dangerous. They use it to tranquillize elephants. It's fatal to humans, even in small doses. Stops her breathing. She'll die very quickly."

"She doesn't need to inject it?"

José shook his head. "Just a whiff is enough. Direct contact with her skin will also kill her. Which is why we've put the poison into the food as well as on the outside. Ingesting the carfentinal will work very fast. As soon as she picks up the appetizer and puts it in her mouth, get ready. She'll go down right away. Take your proof of death photo and get the hell out."

"What if she doesn't go down?"

"She will. But you don't leave until she does," José said sternly. "Clear?"

Pilar nodded and summarized quickly. "I'm holding the tray. It's only got one wrapped date on it. I walk up to her. I offer the last piece of fruit to her. She takes it, pops it in her mouth. That's it?"

"Yes. She doesn't even need to chew it. But she will. She loves this particular appetizer. She won't refuse to eat it."

Pilar wasn't so sure. She chewed her lip, thinking. Skinny women like that didn't splurge on high calorie snacks, surely. Pilar needed a backup plan.

"How much time do I have after she touches the carfentinal on the outside of the appetizer?"

"Five minutes, tops. After that, the place will be crawling with first responders. Park close to the house in this space and leave the keys in the car," José swiped to the image of the parking lot near the kitchen again and pointed to the spot where her car would be waiting. "When you get outside, run like hell toward the sedan and speed away."

Pilar continued to think through the steps, nodding slowly as she mentally rehearsed. "Where's my costume?"

"A tuxedo. It's hanging in your bathroom. Dress before you leave here. Take everything with you. Don't come back here under any circumstances," José said sternly.

"Why not?"

José frowned and shook his head, but said nothing.

"Where will I meet up with you after?"

"I've preprogrammed the GPS in your vehicle. Just turn it on and follow the route guidance," José replied. "I'll be waiting for you at the meetup point. We'll ditch the sedan and I'll take you to your plane."

Pilar glanced at the clock. She was tired and wired, all at the same time. "Where do I get the weapon?"

"As I said, the appetizer will be on a tray in the sedan. The tray with the wrapped date is inside a plastic bag. Be very careful not to touch any of it," José said again, for at least the tenth time. "Wear your surgical gloves under your white cotton gloves. When you get there, remove the tray from the plastic and leave the plastic in the car."

"Won't someone notice that I'm walking in with food?"

"No. The event will already be underway by the time you get there. Everyone will be busy. Just walk in the kitchen door and pretend to know what you're doing."

"How do I take the proof of death photo?" Pilar asked.

José handed her a cell phone and demonstrated how to use the camera app. Pilar stood and took several practice photos of the floor, imagining Emily Brandon's body lying there.

When she was satisfied with the photos, she tossed the phone on the bed.

“Show me the layout of the house again,” Pilar said.

They went over the plan three more times before she was sure she thoroughly understood exactly what to do.

José asked her one last time as he was leaving. “You got this?”

“Yes.” Pilar nodded. “See you at the meetup point.”

Chapter 27

Monday, May 30
Dallas, Texas

Miller had driven south of Dallas until they reached the suburbs. He'd turned into the quiet, residential neighborhood populated with modest homes planted on substantial lots.

A mile away from the main road, he pulled up in the driveway of an ordinary looking ranch style house perched in the center of a one-acre parcel.

He stopped at the three-car garage and pushed a button. The door raised and he drove the SUV inside and closed the door again.

Miller lowered the privacy window between the seats and then turned off the engine.

He pushed another button. “Faraday Protocol X activated.”

Johnson said, “Wait here while we sweep.”

Miller and Johnson left the vehicle and entered the house.

“What are they looking for?” Kim asked.

“Surveillance devices,” Cooper replied. “The Faraday Protocol X is extremely secure. It excludes the penetration of electronic signals and surveillance devices from the exterior.”

"All devices?" Kim asked, skeptical that the US government had managed to apply the exclusions completely. Some cell phones worked inside Faraday cages.

Cooper nodded. "Excludes one hundred percent of all known consumer devices."

Kim cocked her head. "Then what are they sweeping for?"

"Tech evolves. New bugs could have been installed since the place was used last. They'll find them and remove them, if there are any."

Kim nodded. "Where are we?"

"Safe house," Cooper said. "We'll regroup. Get food and sleep. Make a plan."

Sleep sounded good to Kim. It had been a while since she'd had any. The break would give her a chance to think, too.

She missed discussing cases with Gaspar. And she'd already thought of half a dozen things she wanted to know that he could help with, if she had the option to contact him. Which, at the moment, she didn't.

If Cooper could be believed, the Faraday Protocol probably made it impossible to connect with Gaspar or anyone else as long as she was inside the house.

While Faraday protection wasn't absolute, the US government had access to the most effective techniques.

The protocol activated here in the safe house could probably be avoided if she had the right equipment, but breaching the protocol was not likely using the devices she had with her at the moment.

When she had the chance, she'd leave the building. Until then, she was stuck here without access to her usual contacts.

Perhaps she could squeeze useful intel out of Cooper in the meantime. He definitely knew more than he'd shared with her so far. No surprise there.

Johnson stuck his head out and waved them forward. Kim followed Cooper into the house. Johnson closed the door and set the interior alarm.

When the alarm's confirmation notice beeped, the place felt more like a prison than a safehouse.

Kim walked through from the garage directly into an open floorplan. The cavernous space was divided by deliberately placed furniture. A sitting room with a wall-mounted flat-screen television and an eat-in kitchen were the two main areas.

The windows were covered with blackout shades, but to preserve the illusion that a family of some sort actually lived here, the shades allowed a sliver of interior light to escape on each side.

Across the open space on the other side of the house, Miller came through an archway jerking a thumb over his shoulder. “Beds and baths back here. Take your pick.”

He began to check the security of doors and windows in the main room.

Johnson walked to the refrigerator and grabbed a bottle of water. “Fully stocked. Get washed up. I’ll pop a frozen pizza into the oven.”

He turned the oven on to preheat and prepared the pizza for baking while Kim and Cooper carried their bags toward the bedrooms.

Through the archway, there were three doors on either side of a wide hallway.

Cooper stuck his head into the first open doorway.

"I'll take this one," he said as he stepped inside the room and closed the door behind him.

Kim continued down the hallway and claimed the room on the end. The equivalent of sitting with her back to the wall and facing the exit.

Kim never entered any place without an exit plan. Knowing she was confined here was already making her twitchy.

The door was steel and heavy, like a hotel room fire door. She slid the deadbolt into place.

She scanned the space quickly.

The floor was carpeted. The walls were painted ivory and totally without adornment.

One closed window was covered with the same type of blackout shade as those in the front room.

The room was little more than a box, sparsely furnished.

Three-drawer dresser with a mirror above it.

Two cots fitted with rough sheets and a rougher blanket.

One bedside table between the cots with a lamp on it.

Single ladder-back chair next to each bed.

Small closet at the far corner.

Bathroom with toilet, sink, and shower directly adjacent.

Kim wasn't particularly fussy about temporary accommodations, but this room was barely more than a cell for two. The place was secure, which was good. It was effectively a prison, which wasn't.

She pulled out one of her phones to confirm that the Faraday Protocol was effectively blocking cell signals. It was.

No reason to spend any more time in here.

She left her bags on the bed and washed up before she returned to the kitchen, following the mouth-watering whiff of baking pizza that pulled her along. Her stomach growled. She spent half a moment trying to remember when she last had a meal before she shrugged and gave up the effort.

Johnson and Miller were seated at a round table talking quietly. They both looked up when she approached.

“What’s your story?” Miller asked. “Cooper didn’t tell us much.”

She shrugged. “He didn’t tell me anything about you, either.”

“Knowing Cooper, the omissions are deliberate,” Johnson said, extending his hand to shake hers as if they were being introduced for the first time. “Clay Johnson. Dallas Field Office.”

“Kim Otto, Detroit Field Office.” She shook his hand and turned to offer her hand to Miller.

“Bert Miller, Houston Field Office” he said with his handshake.

“You guys are not partners?” Kim asked on her way to the fridge. She ducked her head and snagged a water bottle.

“Not usually,” Johnson replied. “Joint task force has us working together on this.”

Kim stood against the counter. The pizza was smelling really good. Her stomach growled loudly and they both laughed.

“Ten more minutes,” Miller said with a grin. “Can’t vouch for the quality, though.”

"We were in DC. Talking to Cooper. He's got access to more intel than we get in the field offices. Seemed easier to discuss the situation in person," Johnson said.

Miller added, "That's how we ended up escorting you two back to Texas. We were coming back anyway, after our briefing. He offered us a ride to Dallas."

"Guess you're on the task force now, too?" Johnson said, eyebrows raised.

Without Cooper to run interference, she had no idea what they were talking about. Or what they knew about Reacher or her covert assignment. It seemed safer to just nod.

"How many cases have you had in Detroit?" Miller asked, taking a swig from the soda can.

"I haven't been briefed. So I'm not sure," she replied. "You?"

"We've been pulling the intel together. It's been a slog. The cases didn't seem connected initially."

"We're not sure they **are** connected," Johnson pointed out. "It's a guess. An educated guess. That's all."

Miller nodded. "Right."

"What suggests they're connected now?" Kim asked, warming to the discussion. Whatever it was, she was intrigued.

"They may not be," Johnson said. "The only real commonalities we've found so far are a murder where the perp dies afterward at the scene. Which is why the project was titled Double Death Task Force."

"Double death?" Kim widened her eyes. "You mean like a gang war or a mass shooter/suicide thing?"

"No," Miller said, shaking his head. "Suicide is a fairly common plan for mass shooters, as you know. They go into the situation expecting to be killed by the officers arriving on the scene. Planning on it, usually. They don't intend to be caught and sent to prison. If we get them alive, it's because they've screwed up their plan somehow."

"And the gangbangers are pretty obvious. Bunch of idiots with guns fighting their turf wars and doing society a favor," Johnson added.

Kim nodded.

“The Double Death Task Force is ruling out gang wars and mass shooters for the moment,” Miller said. “The cases we’re looking at first are individual murders where the killer also dies at or near the murder scene. We haven’t identified any multiple homicides that fit the pattern.”

“Until this one fell in our lap today,” Johnson said.

Miller replied, “Possibly.”

Kim noticed that the pizza smelled better with every passing minute. Surely it would be ready soon.

To distract her growing stomach, Kim asked, “How do the killers die?”

Chapter 28

Monday, May 30
Dallas, Texas

“The pattern we think we’ve identified is pretty specific, at least for now. Like Johnson said, each kill is an individual murder. Afterward, the killer also dies at or near the scene,” Miller explained, warming to his subject.

“That’s odd. They kill and then they just, somehow, die?” Kim asked. “Like it’s an unlucky break or something?”

Johnson nodded. “No obvious homicides have been committed

to eliminate the killers that we've located so far. Although there may be some of that, once we fully sort all of the cases."

Kim nodded slowly, thinking things through. There were a lot of questions that needed answers.

"We have close to twenty-five thousand homicides in this country every year, not including gang related murder, suicides, or drug overdoses," Kim said. "Why are you treating these individual murders as a related group?"

Johnson and Miller looked at each other, as if the intel was too hot to share. The oven timer dinged.

"Pizza's ready," Miller said. "I'll get it. One of you find some paper plates."

Johnson began to open the cabinets, one after another. He grabbed a short stack of paper plates and a roll of paper towels and brought them back to the table.

“The common thread running through all of the homicides we’re considering are certain characteristics of the killer,” Johnson said, giving Miller a look that Kim couldn’t read.

“But you said the killer dies in each case, and always at the crime scene.” And then she realized the connection. She nodded slowly. “Like the shooter in the church today.”

“Yes,” Johnson said. “And the killers are all undocumented. Nothing on them in any of our databases.”

"No fingerprints, no DNA, no papers of any kind. No facial recognition matches. Nothing. We have no idea who these killers are." Miller confirmed as he set the pizza on the table. "Shall I get Cooper?"

"What the hell is he doing in his room, anyway?" Johnson said. "Taking a nap?"

Miller grinned. "Yeah, it's not like he can chat with his lover on the phone while he's inside the Faraday."

"He'll come out when he's ready." Kim shrugged, resisting the urge to say something about how any woman would have to be a masochist to be Cooper's lover.

She placed a piece of pizza on her plate and tore off a square of the paper towel.

While the food was too hot to eat, she said, “So there are two bodies. In each case, you’re able to identify the killer and distinguish which of the two was the victim?”

“Got to have someplace to start unraveling the puzzle. So we’ve made some reasonable assumptions.” Johnson nodded, talking with his mouth full.

“Such as?”

Johnson shrugged. “The victim is the one we can identify. The killer is the one we can’t.”

"Simple but probably accurate." Kim grinned. "Okay, so you have unidentified killers. All are undocumented with no active or inactive records of any kind in any of our databases. The killers are males and females. Ages vary. Killers are mostly Latino, but not always?"

Miller nodded. "Correct on all counts. A few of the killers have not been Latino. We don't know if that means those cases are not connected to the whole. Could be we should exclude them. But for now, we're assuming they're a part of this thing."

"Whatever this thing is," Johnson said.

"Okay." Kim cocked her head. Made sense so far. "What do the victims have in common, then?"

"Aside from being actually identifiable US residents, you mean?" Miller picked the green peppers from his piece of pizza and piled them on the side of his plate.

"Yeah. Besides that." Kim nodded, taking her first bite of the fresh pie, which was actually pretty good.

Detroit had some of the best pizza on the planet and she was normally picky about substandard pies. This one was better than she'd expected. Or maybe she was just hungry.

"The victims don't have much in common, actually," Johnson said between bites. His first piece of the pizza was already swallowed, and he reached for a second. "Most had assets of some kind. They owned personal property like cars and clothes and jewelry, at the very least. A few owned homes and other assets. None were homeless or drug addicted or sex workers."

Miller picked up. "Males, females, all adults, but various ages. Nothing in common there. The killers aren't targeting men or women or children in particular."

Kim cocked her head. "And you said the victims were all US **residents**? So not all were citizens?"

"The ones Miller and I are looking at were all living in Texas when they died. They were all citizens. The task force has confirmed similar cases in other states and the citizenship varies," Johnson said. "Arizona, New

Mexico, Nevada, California, so far. But it might be wider reaching than that."

Kim set her pizza down and stared. "That's crazy. How many cases are we talking about?"

"At least twenty possibles in Texas alone over the past five years. That we know of," Miller replied. "About twenty more possibles in the other four states combined. So far. There may be more. We think it's likely there are more."

Johnson swallowed the last of his second piece of pizza and said, "But we're pretty sure there are more. And the other states are worried they could have more, too, according to those field offices."

Kim sat back in her chair, her appetite gone. "You're saying you've identified forty possible cases, which is eighty deaths, right?"

Miller nodded. "That we know of. That fit what we think is the pattern. So far."

"Yeah, you said that," Kim replied slowly.

"It's worth repeating. We've checked all the homicides in the state of Texas in the past five years. It's been slow going. But we may find more that fit the pattern," Johnson said. "And if we do, we'll need to go back another five years. Because we're not sure when this all started."

"Could be fifteen years or more," Miller said. "We just don't know yet."

He got up from the table and pulled a second pizza from the freezer. He opened the box and slid the pie into the oven before he returned to the table with a second soda.

"I'm still hungry," Johnson said. "And Cooper hasn't eaten yet, either."

Miller gave her a grin. "You look mystified, Otto. How can we help?"

She shook her head slowly, trying to take it all in. "The breadth and scope of the crimes is mind-boggling."

Miller swigged his water. "It gets better. Or worse. Depending on your point of view."

"I'm afraid to ask," Kim said with a weak smile, although the situation was beyond serious.

"The killers died in a variety of ways. A few, like today's shooter, were killed by security teams at the scene of the murder," Johnson said. "But not all of them were."

"What do you mean?" Kim asked.

"Looking just at the Texas cases," Miller replied, "At least four arsonists died in the fires they set. At least three killers died in hit-and-run vehicular incidents. One guy fell off the roof of a building. One died of exposure after killing a victim in the desert. A couple of them died when their getaway vehicles exploded. The list goes on."

They paused to chew the pizza and consider the facts.

Johnson shook his head. “What are the odds that all the killers have such bad luck as to die accidentally and immediately after committing murder?”

“That’s a lot of bad luck,” Miller said.

“Accidental deaths following a murder? I doubt anyone’s calculated that risk,” Kim cocked her head and replied thoughtfully. “But the odds of a regular Joe getting murdered in the US during any given year are nineteen thousand to one. Multiple instances of simultaneous murder followed by accidental death over a five-year period?”

“Infinitesimal. You’re making my head hurt.” Cooper entered the room in time to hear Kim’s last words. “No gambler in the world would bet those odds."

"Which, as you know, is why they've formed the Double Death Task Force. Because these cases are definitely not random," Kim replied as he pulled out a chair and sat at the table. "Someone, or group of some sort, is killing these people."

"That's the working theory." Cooper nodded, filling his plate while Kim wondered exactly why she was sitting here.

The Double Death Task Force wasn't her job. Her assignment was the manhunt for Reacher.

There was no reason for her to be in Texas. No reason at all.

Unless Cooper worried that Reacher might actually be involved in these deaths. Which was preposterous.

Kim's breath caught.

The timing might be right. The murders could have started fifteen years ago. Which was when Reacher left the army and went off the grid.

No serious federal agent believed in a coincidence like that. Certainly, Cooper didn't.

Neither did Kim.

But still…

Why on earth would Reacher get involved in such an operation?

Simple. He wouldn't.

Would he?

Could Cooper actually be entertaining that idea? Was that the real reason he thought Reacher might show up at Redstone's funeral?

The possibility unleashed a flood of issues rushing toward her, fast and furious.

Chapter 29

Monday, May 30
Austin, Texas

After Jose left, Pilar slept a couple of hours. When the alarm clock on the bedside table went off, she awoke somewhat refreshed and headed for the shower.

José had left a duffel filled with toiletries along with the tuxedo and shoes she was to wear this evening.

She showered, applied minimal makeup, and styled her hair into a tight bun at the base of her neck to keep it out of the way.

The tuxedo fit perfectly. It was a bit too large, which enabled her to conceal her balisong in the right pocket and the gun tucked into the waistband at the small of her back.

The surgical gloves rested in her jacket pocket along with the fresh white gloves she would wear over the latex.

She examined herself in the mirror from all angles to be sure she looked presentable and unarmed. Pilar wasn't worried about getting past security at the event. José had assured her he'd already taken care of that.

As instructed, she collected everything they'd brought into the motel room and stuffed it into José's duffel. She picked up both bags, hers and the one José had left, and carried them to the car, allowing the door to lock behind her.

The small silver sedan was parked at the curb in front of her doorway. It was a late model foreign something manufactured somewhere in Asia. Virtually indistinguishable from the thousands of economy vehicles just like it on the roads in and around Austin.

She opened the passenger door and grabbed the keys from under the floor mat, as José instructed. She unlocked the trunk. Inside was a small cooler. She opened the lid to confirm that the serving tray and the weapon were present and secure.

Then she tossed both duffel bags inside before slamming the trunk closed.

So far, so good.

She settled into the driver's seat and adjusted the mirrors and spent a moment scanning the dashboard features.

She was pleased to find icons instead of words on all the knobs and buttons.

Some of the symbols were confusing. Pilar was a native Spanish speaker. She spoke English reasonably well and she could read the language. But anything remotely Asian was beyond her abilities. She'd make her best guess and hope it worked out okay.

Pilar inserted the key into the ignition and started the engine.

The little sedan fired up immediately, its engine purring quietly in the background. Darkness had fallen while she'd been inside. She found the switch to activate the headlights.

A moment later, she located and punched the GPS button.

Two routes had been saved in the memory. The second was the meetup location for later, after the job was completed.

The first was the route to the fancy estate located out in the middle of nowhere. The fundraiser would be held there. Estimated travel time to the Lake Archer home was forty-five minutes.

José told her that everything had been carefully choreographed. He'd warned her to stay within the planned times for things like travel to and from the estate.

She drove the speed limit. The last thing she needed was to get stopped by some cop seeking a date for the night.

Pilar left the outskirts of Austin and drove into dry, hilly land. If there were homes and shops and people out here, they were well hidden from her view. Texas was a big state and there was lots of unoccupied land between the cities and towns.

Briefly she wondered what she'd do if she had car trouble. She could be stuck out here indefinitely waiting for rescue.

Fifty minutes later, Pilar arrived at the long driveway in front of a fenced and gated estate. Before yesterday, she had never entered a gated property in her life. She shook her head in wonder.

“Pilar Inez Mendoza,” she whispered aloud. “You are one lucky woman.”

The Double C Ranch might have been a working ranch at one time, but not anymore. Now, it was a luxury estate, complete with all the attributes of quality and wealth.

The house itself was set back half a mile from the road. Pilar couldn’t see it yet.

Manicured lawns were enclosed by a decorative wrought iron fence running a couple of miles in all directions. The ornate iron work surrounding the iron gate was impressive.

More problematic were the cameras mounted to secure constant CCTV footage of all vehicles passing through the entrance and the exit.

Pilar pulled up to the well-lit gatehouse, which was manned by a single security guard. He stepped out of the guard shack and approached the sedan. Pilar lowered the window.

"Show me your ID please," he said in one of those drawls that could have come right out of an old Western film.

"Sure," Pilar said, handing over the name badge José provided.

He took a quick glance at the badge and ducked to take a look inside the vehicle. “Drive straight up to the house. Park around back.”

“Understood,” she said.

He nodded, handed her badge back, and returned to the guard shack. A moment later, the big iron gates moved slowly. José had warned her about the guard and the gate. She’d need to pass through here after her work was completed.

As the gates swept open, Pilar counted the seconds. At the full ten-second mark, the gates reached a point where she could easily drive the sedan through the gap on the way out. But ten seconds seemed like an eternity.

Any competent guard should be able to stop her in ten seconds or less. Unless she stopped him first.

Pilar patted the pistol resting in her pocket. Nothing she could do about the setup. One way in, one way out. She'd escape, one way or another.

She waited another ten seconds until the gates were open wide and the guard waved her past. She lifted her foot from the brake and accelerated slowly along the drive.

As she rounded the first big curve, the residence came into full view. The videos José had shown her of the twenty-five-acre waterfront estate proved totally inadequate. The sight took her breath away.

For a moment, she panicked. How

would she ever find Emily Brandon inside this overwhelmingly huge mansion? Her breath came in rapid gasps. The edges of her vision blackened.

“Don’t hyperventilate. Breathe. Breathe. Breathe,” she coached herself until she regained control. “It’ll be okay. You’ll find her. She’ll be right where José said she’d be. He hasn’t been wrong yet, has he?”

When her hands stopped shaking, Pilar drove the sedan around to the back of the house where the catering trucks had dropped off supplies. Catering staff had set up the event hours ago.

As planned, Pilar was late. The gala was already in full swing.

She reversed the sedan into her assigned parking space and parked the car. She took a few deep breaths.

“Here we go,” she said quietly.

When she opened the car door, she heard music from a live orchestra traveling from the wide back verandah where guests were mingling in the pleasantly warm evening.

She walked around to the trunk and used the key to open it. She returned to the front seat and replaced the key in the ignition, where it would be ready. The last thing she needed was to waste time searching for the key when she rushed back here after the job was done.

Pilar reached into her pocket and pulled out the surgical gloves. She pulled them onto her slender fingers. Next, she reached into the trunk, opened the cooler, and pulled the tray and the stuffed date from inside.

Both the tray and the appetizer were enclosed in plastic bags. “José wasn’t kidding about not touching this thing,” she murmured.

She closed the trunk. The parking lot was full, but there were no people out here. Still, she didn’t want to drop the damned fruit onto the ground.

“Just carry both to the back door and put the fruit on the tray when you get inside,” she said, impatient with herself.

Pilar made her way to the entrance and slipped inside.

Chapter 30

Monday, May 30
Austin, Texas

The disruption caused by Pilar's entrance became immediately consumed by the chaos. The kitchen was pure bedlam. Catering staff moving here and there and over and under, all rushing to and fro. If anyone noticed her, they said nothing.

Pilar closed her eyes briefly and when she reopened her lids, she found a small flat surface where she could set the tray. She pulled her white gloves on over the latex and opened the plastic bag containing the appetizer. She rolled it carefully onto the white doily resting on the small tray.

José had thought of everything. The doily had several grease smudges, suggesting that it had held half a dozen appetizers earlier, but now, only one was left.

Pilar moved around the bustling staff and reached the swinging door exit from the kitchen that led to the main house. She threaded her way through the guests, shielding the tray from a guest who might try to grasp the fruit before she reached Emily Brandon.

José said Emily would be on the back veranda because she enjoyed the orchestra. Or maybe because he had other people on scene who would maneuver Emily somehow.

Pilar didn't know.

But José had been right about everything so far.

No reason to doubt him now.

At least, not yet.

She stayed away from the guests as much as possible, hugging the walls and avoiding the center of the rooms where most of them seemed to be clustered. She headed toward the music, which was wafting throughout the house now, providing a soft soundtrack for the evening.

Pilar couldn't even imagine the combined wealth of everyone in the building. Emily Brandon herself was one of the wealthiest women in the world. Briefly, Pilar wondered again why José's boss wanted Emily Brandon dead.

Before her thoughts could spin a few billion good reasons from the cool night air, Pilar spied the woman standing with a man straight ahead.

Pilar had watched the other servers passing trays of food among the guests. The approach was simple and straight forward.

First the server offered a cocktail napkin. Next, she held the tray and allowed the guest to select the morsels the guest preferred. Then the server moved on to the next guest and repeated the offer.

That was it. Simple. Straight forward. Anybody could do it.

She squared her shoulders, took a deep breath, and moved toward Emily Brandon to perform the pantomime.

As Pilar approached, Emily and her companion were engaged in lively conversation that suggested they knew each other well.

The song ended and the orchestra's music paused. She waited a few moments until the orchestra began again. She had a clear path to Emily Brandon and her companion. Pilar moved forward, cocktail napkins in her right hand and the serving tray in her left.

"Senora? Would you enjoy a stuffed date?" Pilar said, as she'd been instructed to do.

Emily Brandon turned her head and noticed the tray. "Yes, thank you. These are to die for," she said, raising her hand to the tray. She turned her head toward her companion. "The chef refuses to give me this recipe. Can you believe it?"

"What's so special about them?" he said, reaching faster than Emily to snatch the appetizer off the tray and plop it into his mouth before Pilar had a chance to react.

"Why you scoundrel!" Emily exclaimed, laughing. "You took the last one!"

He wiggled his eyebrows and swallowed the food. “I’m sure there’s more in the kitchen.”

Pilar swallowed her open-mouthed horror. Before she had a chance to move, the companion collapsed, landing in a heap on the floor at Emily Brandon’s feet.

She screamed. “Calvin?! Calvin!!”

Emily knelt down to her friend. The party crowd was distracted and hadn’t seemed to notice Emily’s distress until she yelled, “Call 911! Somebody call 911!”

Pilar’s heart pounded. Her future was falling apart before her very eyes. She couldn’t allow that to happen.

Emily Brandon must die.

Now.

Pilar reached into her pocket and pulled out her balisong. She flicked it open as she knelt down next to Emily.

Under cover of the chaos, Pilar stabbed, plunging the double-edged dagger deep into Emily's body. So intently was she focused on her friend that Emily didn't seem to notice the pain. Her body must have flooded with adrenaline.

Pilar twisted the knife and pulled it out and stabbed again.

Deep red blood blossomed across the middle of Emily's white gown.

She finally registered the pain caused by Pilar's knife.

She slapped her palm across the wound and drew it away covered in the blood that pulsed from her body like a wide-open hose.

The chaos increased with every moment that passed. Women screamed. Men shouted. The catering staff ran forward. Guests rushed for the exits.

Several people were bent over the two victims, attempting to offer aid.

Pilar used the confusion to stand up and walk away.

No one seemed to notice another server headed toward the kitchen. Maybe later, they would recall that Pilar had been with the victims moments before they died. But not now.

Pilar pulled off the white gloves and dropped them in a trash can. She continued to wear the surgical gloves, just in case. She'd left no fingerprints here, nor did she intend to.

She walked out the back door with a knot of escaping guests and picked up the pace as she headed toward her car.

Ten minutes to drive through the gate and she'd be on her way to the meeting point. José knew what to do after that.

As she came around the corner, her parking space came into view. A young man had already jumped into the driver's seat. Had he mistaken her silver car for his own?

Pilar didn't know how he'd made the mistake and she didn't care. She couldn't let him drive away.

She ran toward the vehicle, waving her arms and shouting. "Hey! Hey!"

The distance was too great. She'd never make it in time to thwart the thief.

Pilar stopped running.

She stared, unable to believe her bad luck, as he managed to turn the key in the ignition.

Pilar's promised freedom vanished, just like that.

Half a moment later, the car's engine caught and sprang to life.

Next, the silver sedan exploded.

The noise of the charge blasted through the quiet night.

A ball of fire pushed the sedan's seams apart.

The roof and hood and trunk bucked up.

The doors pushed outward.

The whole car was instantly engulfed in heat and flames and clouds of black smoke.

Chapter 31

Monday, May 30
Austin, Texas

The force of the car bomb's explosion knocked Pilar off her feet. She landed hard on her ass on the gravel drive, mouth and eyes wide, horrified.

Yet, she could not turn her eyes away, as the heat from the fire assaulted her in the already hot night.

The body of the young man who had tried to start her car remained upright behind the wheel even as he was cremated almost instantly amid the flames.

Less than a moment later, comprehension dawned.

The charred body behind the wheel was meant to be her.

Her body began to shake with shock when she absorbed the truth.

The fire in her little sedan spread to vehicles parked on either side. Someone had removed the gas caps, allowing fumes to escape. Puddles of gasoline had been poured on the ground beneath them.

Two more explosions ripped through the night, illuminating the sky and blasting everything nearby to pieces.

A moment later, Pilar realized she was screaming. She clamped her palm across her mouth to stop herself from drawing unwanted attention.

People began pouring outside through the kitchen door. First, the catering staff. Followed by the guests. Soon the area around the gravel parking lot was teeming with terrified spectators.

First responders came speeding along the driveway from the gate, lights flashing atop their vehicles.

They jumped out of the fire trucks and ambulances, attending to their duties all at once in a well choregraphed performance. Moving spectators away from the danger, attending to the injured, and dousing the flaming vehicles kept them fully occupied.

Which wouldn't last forever.

Someone would notice her.

The cacophony was muffled because Pilar's hearing was damaged by the blasts, but she realized the chaos would soon be under control.

She needed to run.

Now.

While she still had the chance.

Pilar had stuffed cash into her pockets along with the gun and her knife. She was still dressed in the tuxedo. Which was better than wearing a skirt and heels, but not as good as the traveling clothes she'd packed in her duffel.

The duffel that had been destroyed along with her car. Her only means of escape.

Pilar backed away from the gathering crowd. She stayed in the shadows and moved along the edges of the chaotic scene until she was running in the dark along the driveway toward the front gate.

The stench of burning petroleum filled the air and gagged her with every deep breath.

Emergency vehicles continued to arrive. She stayed in the darkness.

The gate agent had given up every attempt to monitor the traffic. All focus was on the catastrophe at the big house.

Pilar hid in the shadows and waited for her chance to run through the gate when the security guard wasn't looking.

She didn't need to wait long.

She crouched low and dashed through when yet another ambulance passed between her and the guard shack.

Once on the other side of the gate, Pilar shifted to a jog along the shoulder of the road, heading away from the estate, careful to stay out of the headlight beams. There had been little traffic on the road when she arrived and, aside from the emergency vehicles, there was even less traffic now.

She jogged all the way to the intersection and stood at the crossroads. Which way should she go?

Pilar turned a full three-hundred-sixty degrees, staring into the darkness in all directions. In the aftermath of the murder and the explosions and the chaos and running, she'd become disoriented.

Hills all around blocked her view of the house and the emergency vehicles had stopped for the moment.

She had no idea where she was.

Worse, she no clue what to do next.

Pilar stood in the center of the intersection for a good long time, as if the answer would be revealed somehow. The cloudy sky concealed the stars. The familiar constellations she had relied upon her entire life were unavailable to her now.

She'd had very little sleep and she felt like she'd been running for miles. Her breathing was ragged and her legs quivered with fatigue. She realized how very tired she was.

It would be so easy to give up. To lie down in the dirt and sleep.

She shook her head and forced her eyes wide. She'd come too far to give up now.

Pilar concentrated on slowing her breathing, gathering her wits. After a few minutes, she began to catalogue her limited options.

José had given her a cell phone. He'd told her to use it to take the proof of death photo. Which she'd forgotten to do. He'd be pissed.

She shrugged. Nothing she could do about that now.

After the explosion, she'd become confused. Perhaps that was related to the physical and mental shock. But she hadn't lost the phone, surely.

She patted her back pockets. Yes, the rectangular brick was still there, resting against the flat of her ass. She pulled it out and looked at the screen.

Even in the empty Texas countryside, the phone was able to connect to the cell towers.

José said to use the phone for calls only in case of an emergency.

Her current situation was an emergency. At least, to her.

José had shown her how to call him. She pressed the buttons until she located his number. She hesitated.

The plan had been to connect with José at the meetup point. But that was miles away. Without the silver sedan, she couldn't possibly get there on time.

If she didn't show up within twenty minutes of the designated time, José would leave her. He'd made that perfectly clear.

She looked at the time on the phone. She was very late.

José was already gone.

If she called him, even if she could get there now, would he come back?

Not likely.

And how would he find her if she called him? She couldn't tell him where she was because she didn't know.

Could José track this phone? She'd heard of such things. But it didn't seem likely.

She needed a ride. Going anywhere at all. She would call José when she found a place to meet with him.

She couldn't wait here for a ride to come along. Which meant she had to find traffic.

Where?

Pilar studied the road again. She'd lost all sense of direction. The one thing she definitely couldn't do was go back to the estate. Even if she could find it.

Her legs were pulsing with tension. Soon they would cramp into hard knots, and she wouldn't be able to move at all.

Her breath came in short spurts as perspiration dripped off her face and down her body under the tuxedo. Which was when she realized she was still wearing the tie, which was too tight on her neck.

She ripped the tie off and threw it to the ground.

"Go. Get out. Now."

She felt the breeze brushing across her skin.

"Concentrate, Pilar. Which way was the wind blowing back at the estate?"

She closed her eyes and forced herself to visualize the first explosion and its aftermath.

The wind had pushed the heat away from the house.

Maybe.

She thought so.

But she wasn't sure.

Still, running into the wind was harder than running with the wind at her back.

Had she been running into the wind this whole time?

Pilar shrugged. Maybe so. Maybe not.

But she had to make a decision. She couldn't stay here forever.

She took a deep breath and began to run.

Chapter 32

Monday, May 30
Ojinaga, Mexico

Cesar Baez never put his life on hold for anything. The world he'd created revolved around him. His schedule, his plans, his whims.

He accepted calls when and if it suited him. Usually during a two-hour window in the morning, mid-week.

Otherwise, he decided to whom he would speak and under what circumstances. Which certainly didn't include calls during social events with more than two hundred wealthy, entitled people in attendance.

Baez allowed only one exception.

José could reach him for exigent matters only.

Baez carried an encrypted cell phone in his pocket at all times expressly for this purpose.

The phone had never been used.

Baez was attending a fundraising gala for his wife's favorite charity. When the phone vibrated in his pocket during the last tango of the evening, Baez didn't realize what it was. In truth, he didn't even feel it.

The orchestra's intense tango music filled the ballroom, excluding all else. Enchanted by his wife's extraordinary beauty, the sensual dance held his breathless attention.

He stared into Gabriella's eyes and moved with the music, totally absorbed. They danced as if they were alone in bed.

Dancers paused and spectators stared, embarrassed, perhaps, by the scandalous spectacle. Baez was unaware of everything except his wife and the tango.

When the music stopped, spectators applauded and cheered.

The noise jarred Baez and Gabriella, jerking them back to the present from their trance.

They smiled and bowed to the crowd, as if the incident had been a planned part of the evening's entertainment.

When they left the dance floor, Gabriella still breathless, her face flushed with embarrassment, Baez finally noticed the vibrating phone in his pocket, jerking him fully back to reality.

"I need to take this call," he said to Gabriella.

Her eyes widened and she uttered a breathless, "Oh!"

Simultaneously, they moved apart.

Baez watched as the gossip developed in real time. It amused him to consider how the disapproval would travel through the society of his wealthy peers.

Gabriella walked unsteadily toward the ladies' room, weaving slightly as she crossed the ballroom while spectators tittered behind their hands.

His gaze lingered for a moment longer before he reached into his pocket for a cigar and his lighter. Women smiled and men slapped him on the back as he moved through the crowd and out to the verandah.

Baez had no idea how long the phone had been ringing when he was finally settled away from the partiers and deep into the shadows.

He lit the cigar and reached into his pocket to drop the lighter and picked up the call. “Yes.”

The response was slightly delayed, only a beat, as if the caller was shocked speechless because Baez answered.

José said, “We have a problem.”

“Which is?” Baez replied, aware that his side of the conversation could be easily overheard.

“The target was eliminated.”

“Fine.”

“Something went wrong. The site is a disaster. The story is breaking news on every channel here.”

“I see,” Baez said angrily while clenching the cigar in his teeth. Sensing there was more bad news coming, he said, “What else?”

“Our asset is lost.”

"Lost? That was the goal, wasn't it?"

"No. She's missing," José said nervously. "If they find her..."

"That's your problem, not mine," Baez growled, chewing on the stogie as he walked farther from the house seeking privacy.

"I'll need resources."

"We have none to offer." Baez walked down the back stairs from the verandah to the gardens and kept walking. "She's your problem. Fix it."

"I'm searching for her now. But if we don't find her and someone else does," José said, breathing heavily into the microphone, "she will identify us to remain inside the US."

"Then I'd suggest you find her before that happens," Baez said curtly.

And then he crushed the phone with a vise-like grip. The phone's cheap plastic cracked. José's call was immediately disconnected.

Thus the conversation with José ended abruptly without solutions.

Baez swore and slammed the broken plastic to the ground, stomping it with the heel of his boot into a million tiny pieces.

He paced the garden, finishing his cigar. In all the years he'd been running this operation, the amateur assassins had never failed to eliminate their targets. Nor had one, not one, escaped immediate death.

Where did this operation go wrong?

He had vetted the girl himself. She was perfect for the job. Pretty, but not beautiful enough to attract undue attention. Capable with weapons. Highly motivated.

She definitely possessed the capacity and the desire to do the job. The target was dead. She had completed her mission.

Which meant that Baez would get paid tonight, as promised.

But the danger to his operation was unacceptable.

How could she have escaped her fate?

He should have held his temper until he'd acquired more facts.

Had the bomb failed to detonate properly?

José had installed dozens of car bombs.

What did José do wrong?

Baez shook his head savagely.

There would be time enough for failure analysis later.

At the moment, his focus must be damage control. José had to find Pilar as soon as possible.

Which meant reconnecting with José using the encrypted communications devices in his office.

After he contacted the client and collected his fee.

He would also dust off the plan B he'd created years ago, before the business became a success. Using undocumented migrants as assassins presented its own challenges. Eliminating them afterward was the insurance required to sustain the business.

His enterprise had accumulated enough profit to assemble a stable of professional killers. Much easier.

After the current series of deployed assets completed their contracts, he would make adjustments going forward.

He'd start by eliminating excess personnel.

José would go first.

After José's recent insolence, tardiness, and now complete failure, the man simply had to go. There was no room for incompetence in plan B.

The idea cheered him somewhat. José was his brother's wife's brother. Not really family to Baez, but he liked his brother's wife and eliminating José would cause her pain. Unfortunately.

Killing José would also infuriate his brother. A significant bonus. Baez smiled.

Baez hurried to the house, up the stairs, and across the verandah, seeking his wife. Time to leave. He had much to do before he could join her in bed to finish the dance.

Chapter 33

Tuesday, May 31
Dallas, Texas

The pizza was long gone, and they were all fatigued, but it was too early to go to bed.

"Let's move to more comfortable chairs," Miller said, standing and heading toward the TV room. "My ass is complaining about these seats."

"I'll grab a couple of beers," Johnson replied as the others relocated. He pulled four long-necked bottles from the fridge and handed them around before he plopped into one of the recliners.

Cooper had removed his sport coat and unbuttoned his collar. He accepted the beer, twisted the cap off, and swigged.

Kim took the only chair in the room that didn't make her feel like a child visiting a giant. Even so, her feet barely touched the floor. Why did men go for such oversized furniture, anyway? She shrugged. One of the mysteries of life.

Miller emerged from the hallway after a trip to his room. He slid into the last recliner and twisted his beer open.

The chair shifting had given Kim a few more minutes to think about Redstone's funeral and the Double Death Task Force. After Miller came back, she hit the subject again, this time at a tangent.

“Let’s say the man who, we think, attempted to kill Teddy Redstone today did fit the double death pattern,” Kim said.

Johnson nodded. “Raises a whole lot of other problems, doesn’t it.”

“Such as whether the task force had early warning that the shooting was planned,” Cooper said. “Is that what you mean?”

“It’s a legitimate question and someone’s going to ask it,” Kim replied evenly, casting a pointed look in return.

“They will,” Miller said, swigging the beer. “The situation has come up before, believe it or not. We’ve got a few cases where there were agents on scene when the murder happened."

"As far as we've learned so far, it's not that the agents had advance notice. We think it's the other way around," Johnson explained. "The murders were committed in situations likely to result in law enforcement or private security killing the shooter."

"Meaning the shooters meant to die after they completed the murder. Similar to a mass shooter," Miller added.

"Or he was set up in a situation where he was likely to die, whether he wanted to or not," Kim said slowly, working through the facts.

A hard triple rap on the front door sucked all the oxygen from the room.

Cooper raised his eyebrows. “Are we expecting company?”

Johnson and Miller said, “No,” at the same time.

“I’ll take the front door,” Miller said, gesturing. “Two more. Back entrance. Garage entrance where we came in.”

Johnson said, “I’ll take the garage.”

Cooper said, “I’ll handle the back entrance. Call out if you need assistance.”

“There must be exterior surveillance cameras, surely,” Kim said, glancing around the room. The only screen immediately visible was the wall-mounted television.

The four agents drew their weapons and fanned out.

Miller had reached the front door by the time Kim located the remote for the television and punched up the exterior cameras.

The screen came on, visually divided into multiple squares like a game show. Each square displayed a different exterior location feed from a CCTV security system.

Kim's quick visual scan showed the image of only one person captured in any of the frames.

"No breaches of the perimeters," she reported. "One man at the front door. An SUV parked in the driveway."

“Anybody inside the SUV?” Cooper called out.

Kim replied, “Can’t confirm. We don’t have eyes on the interior.”

“Thermal images?” Johnson called out. “Check the remote. Infrared options should be there.”

Kim examined the various buttons until she found the infrared. She made adjustments to the remote. A moment later, another square on the screen showed the dark SUV in the moonlight. Only one splash of red in the front of the vehicle under the hood.

“The engine is still warm. Not showing any live bodies inside, humans or dogs or otherwise,” Kim said.

Cooper said loudly, "So a lone uninvited visitor drives up the driveway in an SUV, gets out, knocks on the front door."

"Sounds about right," Miller confirmed. "Happens in every neighborhood in America several times a day."

"Nobody knows who he is?" Cooper asked, seeking confirmation.

"Hang on," Kim said. "Surely there's a lens to capture images of potential visitors at the front door."

She continued pushing various buttons on the remote to adjust the images reflected on the television screen.

One of the buttons popped up a new camera angle from a lens mounted in the center of the front door. Probably a part of the peep hole.

The visitor’s full face was now displayed on the screen.

Kim grinned.

“Stand down. I know this guy,” she said to the others. “He’s okay. We can let him in.”

Nobody left their stations or holstered their weapons.

“Who is he?” Johnson demanded.

“Michael Flint. His security clearance is higher than mine. Probably higher than yours or Miller’s, too,” Kim replied. “I’ve worked with him. He’s more than competent. I’m guessing my former partner, FBI Special Agent Carlos Gaspar, sent him."

Johnson and Miller remained vigilant.

"I know Gaspar," Johnson said. "Liaised with him a few times before he retired. Never met Flint."

"I've heard of Flint. Never met him." Miller nodded. "But yeah, Gaspar was a good agent. Works in Houston now. Ran across him a couple of times since he joined Scarlett Investigations. A reliable outfit."

"The Faraday Protocol is fully engaged," Cooper scowled. "How the hell did Gaspar find you here?"

"Guess we should ask Flint," Kim said, although the answer was obvious.

Gaspar must have tracked her here. When he lost the signal, he sent Flint to check things out.

When nobody moved, she said, “But we’ll need to let him inside first. We can’t question him through the door.”

“What makes you think he’s not coming in hot? He could have a bomb or a grenade,” Miller said.

“There’s four of us and one of him. You think the guy has a death wish?” Kim shrugged. “You’re wasting time and creating a spectacle for the neighbors.”

Miller turned his gaze toward Cooper, the boss. “Let him in?”

Cooper didn’t look happy about it, but he nodded approval. Johnson walked in from the laundry that led to the garage.

When the four were reassembled, Miller deactivated the alarm and opened the front door.

“Michael Flint,” he said calmly from his spot on the porch. He held both empty hands open in front of his body. “May I come in? Or do you want to come out here and search me first?”

Miller stood aside, allowing Flint to enter the room.

Miller closed the door and reset the alarm. “You’re fairly bold, just walking up to the door like that. How’d you know I wouldn’t shoot you and be done with it?”

Flint shrugged. “Just a hunch. Friends of yours in Houston said you’re a little slow on the draw.”

“Wise ass,” Miller said with a grin.

Flint looked around the open space, nodding to each of them in turn. When he spied Kim, he grinned. “Agent Otto. Long time, no see.”

“Flint,” she said, nodding. “Didn’t hear your helo outside.”

Truth was, she’d seen Flint not so long ago and she was glad to see him again now. She didn’t know much about Miller and Johnson. And she didn’t trust Cooper.

But she knew Flint was as loyal as a Doberman and twice as fierce.

All of which meant that Flint's appearance was welcome, indeed. **Gotta love Gaspar**.

After introductions all around, Flint said, "I know who you are, Mr. Cooper, sir. And you guys, Johnson and Miller, are members of the Double Death Task Force, aren't you?"

"How'd you hear about that?" Johnson said.

"It's not a secret, is it? Buddies in Houston mentioned it to me a couple of weeks ago," Flint replied.

"Why'd they tell you?" Miller wanted to know.

Flint said, "I've been hired to investigate a case that might be related. I'd heard some rumors, so I followed up."

"Why are you here, Flint?" Cooper demanded, serving him a strong glare.

Flint responded with a steady look.

The little staring contest lasted about three full seconds, until Flint tired of the drama.

"How about a soda?" Flint turned to ask Johnson.

"We've got beer, if you'd rather."

"Can't. I'm flying tonight," Flint replied.

Johnson nodded toward the fridge.

The television screen continued to display live CCTV from the cameras placed around the exterior of the safe house.

Flint scanned the room and the surveillance video in a wide sweep. Then he helped himself to the soda and joined the others in the sitting area.

“Nice setup you’ve got.” Flint’s tone was friendly.

“Again,” Cooper said coldly. “Why are you here?”

Flint shrugged and offered a friendly grin. “Heard Otto was here. I’ve done her a couple of favors. Thought she might be able to help me out. She’s good with stuff like this.”

“Stuff like what?” Cooper didn’t like it. Not even remotely.

But he'd be forced to admit he'd isolated Kim for some specific reason if he wanted to pursue the matter further.

For the moment, he let it go.

"Since you're all here," Flint nodded, signaling that he accepted the temporary cease fire, "Maybe you guys can help me out, too."

"How so?" Miller asked, now that Flint had been admitted to the conversation.

"I'd like to share intel. As I said, I think my case might also be one of yours," Flint replied, sipping from the water bottle. "I've got a double death I'm dealing with. Rural location south of San Antonio. Arson and murder."

"No question about the arson or the murder?" Johnson asked.

"Clear evidence of accelerant. The house burned to the ground. When the locals sorted through the rubble, investigators found two bodies," Flint replied. "The woman who lived there died in her upstairs bed. The other was a man's body found in the kitchen."

"Two people died in a house fire. Not that uncommon." Johnson said, draining his beer bottle. "Why do you think it's a Double Death Task Force situation?"

"The locals figure the man first killed the homeowner and then set the fire? Could have killed himself by accident, maybe," Miller said. "Fell down. Knocked himself out. Died of the blunt force trauma or fire killed him while he was unconscious."

"Possibly. Not much left to work with on the house or the bodies. Everything was burned to a crisp," Flint replied. "They sent the human remains to the crime lab."

"And?" Miller asked.

"Neither the man nor the woman died of smoke inhalation, according to the autopsies. She died in her bed. It's possible the body wasn't the woman who owned the place, but no reason to believe she wasn't the homeowner," Flint said. "And we did a quick DNA on the body along with DNA on dirty dishes at the scene. Inconclusive, but close enough.

Unless we find a reason to conclude otherwise."

The others nodded, paying attention, digesting the information and comparing it with facts they already knew.

"What about the man?" Johnson asked.

"The lab got some usable DNA. Dentition. That's about it." Flint shrugged. "Locals figure he killed her first. Otherwise, she'd have awakened and tried to get up, at least."

"Yeah, but what about ID on the arsonist?" Johnson asked.

"No luck there," Flint shook his head. "He was probably undocumented. No other way to explain him so far. They want to notify his next of kin. So they'll keep trying."

As he talked, the hairs stood up on the back of Kim's neck. The facts identical to one of the files on Cooper's flash drive.

Which meant Cooper knew the case, too. Frowning, he silenced Kim with a meaningful look. He didn't want to discuss the files on the flash drive. Briefly, she wondered why.

"Who's your client, Flint?" Cooper demanded.

Flint replied, "Can't reveal that without the client's permission."

"What's the victim's name?" Johnson asked.

Kim held her breath, waited for the confirmation.

Flint set down his empty bottle. "Maria Greer."

Just as she thought.

"Motive?" Miller wanted to know.

"Good question," Flint replied.

"Care to guess? Since you have a client you're investigating for, you've got some ideas, don't you?" Cooper demanded.

"Ideas, sure. Firm intel, not yet. But it's Murder 101, right?" Flint shrugged again. "Who benefits?"

Cooper replied, "Excellent question. What's the answer?"

"Dunno yet. Several possibilities I'm running down. Too many problems with all of them, so far. Which is why

I thought Otto might be able to help me out." Flint stood up to leave. "I left my helo a few miles from here. I can make it before sunrise if I go now."

"Where are you going?" Miller asked. "Back to Abilene?"

"Witness interviews. Place called Red House Ranch. South of Pecos," Flint replied. "You know it?"

Miller and Johnson shook their heads.

Kim looked hard at Cooper. After a bit, he nodded.

"You're right. I might be able to help. I'll come with you," Kim said to Flint, on her way to collect her bags from her room.

Chapter 34

Tuesday, May 31
Austin, Texas

Pilar had been pounding the pavement for what seemed like hours, running away from the estate.

The gun was heavy in her pocket. Much heavier than the knife and phone she'd stuffed into the opposite pocket for balance. Now and then, she needed to stop and pull the pants up over her slim hips.

She realized she'd left the main road, somehow, and turned onto a nearly deserted two-lane.

The road was in good shape, which made running easier. But she was tired and thirsty, and losing hope.

How much farther could she run before she collapsed?

She pushed through the exhaustion and ran two more miles before she reached another intersection. She stopped and plopped down on the pavement to rest. Her breathing finally slowed, but she was parched and exhausted.

“There’s no reason to keep running. Just stay here and wait. Eventually, someone will come along. There wouldn’t be roads here if no one ever used them,” she said.

Pilar had no idea how long she'd be required to wait, but she didn't have the energy to run any further.

After a good long time, she saw a dim set of headlights in the distance coming toward her. Finally. She might have cried if she hadn't been so dehydrated. As it was, tears were impossible.

She stood up and dusted herself off, trying to make herself look as non-threatening as possible.

Pilar walked into the middle of the intersection and stood there, waiting. The approaching headlights were higher off the ground than a car. Which probably meant this was a pickup truck or an SUV.

She didn't care. She'd take anything at this point. She hoped she looked harmless as well as dirty and exhausted.

The lights came closer. She moved into the traveled portion of the road and stood directly in front of the oncoming vehicle.

Pilar had heard stories about Texas cowboys hunting illegals at night. Maybe that's what this was. Maybe a couple of good ole boys looking for brown people to kill, just for the sport of it.

The truck's headlights nearly blinded her as it drew closer. But Pilar didn't move. The driver slowed and stopped ten feet from where she stood.

He opened his door and stepped out.

He was a cowboy, all right, complete with boots and jeans. But he wasn't holding a gun. So far, so good.

She approached, walking past the headlight beams, and stopping a few feet away near the front tire.

"What are you doing out here in the middle of nowhere?" he said, friendly enough.

She'd had some time to think about an appropriate answer to this question. She'd rejected several responses before she came up with one that didn't make her sound like a moron, or worse.

"I had a fight with my boyfriend. He was drunk. He kicked me out of the car and left me stranded. Any chance you could give me a ride?" She had no trouble looking desperate.

He didn't answer right away. Instead he looked around as if he expected the boyfriend to jump out and attack him or something.

After a couple of minutes of thinking things over, he shrugged. "Sure. Hop in. If you're not afraid of me, I guess I'm not afraid of you, either."

Pilar's knees buckled with relief, but she managed to trudge around to the passenger side of the pickup and climb inside.

"Thanks for picking me up. I might have died out there before somebody came along."

She didn't bother with the seatbelt. Too restrictive. She might need to move out of the seat quickly.

He simply nodded. "Where are you headed?"

Pilar wasn't that familiar with Texas geography. She said the first thing that popped into her head. "Pecos."

"You've got a long trek, then. It's probably six hours to Pecos from here. Maybe seven." He glanced toward her. "Wish I could help you out, but I'm going north. To Abilene."

"That's okay." She gave him a grateful smile. "I'll get out at the first place we come to. I'll call a friend to come pick me up."

“Sounds reasonable,” he replied with a nod, obviously uneasy with the situation. “You don’t mind me saying so, your boyfriend doesn’t sound like a keeper. You could do better.”

“He’s okay. He’s got a wicked temper is all. Crazy jealous, though,” she said, to head off the advance she sensed was coming.

The last thing she needed was to hook up with a lonely cowboy in the middle of nowhere. She’d done more for worse reasons, but not now.

Pilar waited for him to make the first move, hoping he wouldn’t do it, but knowing, in the pit of her stomach, that he would. They all did, sooner or later.

The gun was still resting in her pocket. Shooting him while the truck was moving at seventy miles an hour wasn't a solid plan, for sure. But she was too tired to struggle anymore.

The less she had to talk to him, the better.

The cowboy drove another few miles before he said anything more.

"It's not too far, by Texas standards, to a gas station convenience store. Maybe fifty miles. Maybe an hour or so. That be okay?" he asked as if she actually had options.

Maybe he'd decided not to press her. Maybe something about her vibe had warned him off.

"Yeah. That's great. You can be on your way. I'll call my friend from there."

"Sounds like a plan," he said with another nod to punctuate the decision.

But now she thought maybe she should eliminate him anyway. She'd managed to get away from the fundraiser. If investigators did come looking for her, this guy might feel like it was his civic duty to report the disheveled hitchhiker he'd picked up.

He reached across to turn on the radio. He pressed the scan button to search for a station until it landed on country music. The song was heavy on twang and steel guitars, about a guy whose woman done him wrong.

Pilar cast a furtive look at his left hand gripping the steering wheel.

He wasn't wearing a wedding ring. He hadn't mentioned a job or a wife or kids. Maybe he was a loner, like her. Maybe he wasn't as harmless as he seemed.

How long would it take for someone to miss him and come looking for his truck?

Chapter 35

Tuesday, May 31
Dallas, Texas

Kim had not unpacked, so gathering her stuff didn't take long. She joined Flint in the main room.

"Let's hit the road," Flynn said as he headed toward the front door. "Miller, can you let us out?"

Cooper gave Miller a nod of permission. Miller walked to the control panel and turned off the alarm.

"It's open," Miller said, handing Kim a small, padded manila envelope. "Keep in touch."

Kim accepted the envelope and stuffed it into her laptop bag. No reason to open it here. The envelope was from Cooper, and she could easily guess what was inside.

Had to be a cell phone with a special frequency that would allow her calls to penetrate the sophisticated Faraday protocol at the safe house.

Which also explained why he'd spent so much time in his room before dinner. Cooper had had access to the outside world all along.

"Will do," she replied, loud enough for Cooper to hear. The envelope proved two things. First, Cooper was as big a snake as she'd expected.

For a moment, she'd thought maybe her instincts had been wrong about him all this time.

She wasn't wrong.

Good to know.

And the second thing? The advanced surveillance tech she'd believed Cooper had access to was, once again, confirmed.

The futuristic stuff science fiction stories imagined was completely within his grasp now.

Cooper could see her and hear her and follow her in ways that the average citizen, friend or foe, would never believe or even guess.

Also good to know.

Kim followed Flint through the doorway and into the warm night air. Miller closed the door firmly behind her and probably reset the alarm. Ironically, she felt safer outside the house than inside it.

Flint unlocked the SUV and stepped into the front seat as Kim stowed her bags in the back. She reached into her pocket for a low-tech alligator clamp as she returned to the front.

Kim climbed into the passenger seat, closed the door, and buckled up.

"You know carrying Cooper's phone around with you is like sending him a constant update on your activities," Flint said, shaking his head.

"I'm aware."

"You could leave it here. Solve the problem. Just sayin'." Flint flashed a big grin her way as she loosened the shoulder harness and put the clamp on the webbing below the retractor.

The shoulder harnesses on these big vehicles cut high across her petite body and locked to imprison her. A fast brake or a slight collision activated the SUV's safety restraint, and the strap practically beheaded her.

"What if that thing fails when we have a crash? The shoulder harness wouldn't lock. You could fly right through the windshield," Flint teased.

"With luck, the clamp will fall off on impact and the strap will keep me in the seat. I'll be battered and bruised but with my head still intact. That's the plan, anyway," Kim replied. "Problem is, most people in this country are so damned huge. When you're my size, life is deploying a series of equalizers. I've got to figure out how to survive in the giant's world."

Flint shook his head as he put the transmission in gear and reversed down the long driveway like a pro. Because he was a pro. Gaspar wouldn't have sent him otherwise.

"And you're keeping Cooper's phone because?"

"Because we might need it." She didn't say that the connection to Cooper wasn't always a negative. He wasn't the best backup she'd ever had, but he was better than nothing. Sometimes.

Flint arched both eyebrows and flashed her an **oh, please** look.

"Where are we going?" Kim asked instead of arguing the point. She peered into the darkness as he turned onto the main highway.

"Private helipad nearby. I'd have been here sooner, but it took Gaspar a while to find me a place to park."

"Yeah, run that down for me quickly, will you? How did Gaspar know where I was? Why did he send you in?"

"He got your texts. He knew you were with Cooper. He started following your signal. When you went into the safe house your signal disappeared," Flint paused to fiddle with the dashboard. "He knew right away what had happened. He tried all of our usual methods for getting past Faraday shields, but we weren't able to get through to you. That's when Gaspar asked me to check on you because—"

"Let me guess," she interrupted dryly, offering his usual excuse. "You were in the neighborhood."

He gave her a quick side-eye and laughed.

They traveled a few more minutes before he turned into an industrial park. Kim counted eight buildings on either side of the street. All were quiet for the night.

As the SUV rolled past, she saw the helipads.

Kim said, "I guess helo travel is better for miles in the great state of Texas, eh?"

"Definitely," Flint replied as he pulled up to the driveway of the last building in the cul-de-sac at the end of the road. "Big state. Lots of ground to cover."

He pushed a button on the dashboard of the SUV, which activated the chain link gate blocking the driveway.

The gate engaged and slid slowly open until the SUV could slip inside. Flint rolled forward through the opening.

The big vehicle must have activated a sensor on the opposite side of the gate, because it closed again behind them.

Flint drove around to the side of the building, approaching a helicopter secured at the fixed tie down points holding it to the pavement. He parked the SUV and turned off the engine.

"I'll get the helo ready. Can you bring your bags?" he said, halfway out the door.

"Yeah. Let me take a minute to send some stuff to Gaspar. He can get to work on it while we're flying to Red House Ranch," Kim replied.

Flint stopped a second. "We're going to Pecos first."

"Why?"

"Interview a lawyer who has helpful intel," Flint said before he headed to the helo.

"I'll bet," Kim replied to his retreating back.

She climbed out of the SUV and walked around to the cargo door. The earlier storm had chilled the oppressive heat and humidity out of the air. It felt like seventy-five degrees, maybe. No wind. With any luck, they'd have weather like this all the way to Pecos.

Kim opened the cargo door and pulled her laptop out of her bag. She sent all of Cooper's files from the flash drive to her secure server for safe storage.

Then she sent them again. To Gaspar's secure portal this time. She didn't include a note. He'd know what to do.

She closed the laptop and stored it again. Then she pulled her travel bag and her laptop bag from the SUV, closed the cargo door, and walked toward the helo like a woman headed to the guillotine.

Man, she hated helo travel. If she drove the SUV, she'd get there almost as fast as the helo. In theory. If she knew where she was going. If there were no tie-ups of any kind.

But Flint wouldn't travel with her in the SUV, and he had intel she needed.

Flint had removed the tie down straps and completed his preflight check. The helo had started to spool up. She picked up her pace.

The big rotors were already spinning, pushing air and building noise in the otherwise quiet darkness. Kim stowed her bags and climbed up into the copilot's seat.

She fastened her four-point harness and gave Flint a big thumbs-up as she positioned her headset.

Slowly, the helo began to rise straight up off the ground.

"How long will we be in the air?" she asked, ignoring her churning stomach.

"Don't worry. We have plenty of fuel," Flint's voice came through her headset. "Beautiful out here tonight, isn't it?"

Before she had a chance to respond, the headset signaled an incoming transmission. Flint accepted with the press of a button. "Yeah, Gaspar, what's up?"

Chapter 36

Tuesday, May 31
Austin, Texas

Gaspar's voice came through Kim's headset. "No trouble collecting the package, then?"

Kim grinned. "Appreciate your help, Chico."

"Good to hear your voice, Suzy Wong," Gaspar replied with the kind of warmth that suggested he'd been concerned for her safety.

"No need to worry about me. I can take care of myself," she said, a bit more harshly than she'd intended.

"It's the company you keep that worries me," Gaspar replied.

She couldn't argue. Cooper worried her, too. And he wasn't the only one. "You've checked out those files I sent you?"

"Ten-four," he replied. "You want the rundown now?"

Flint would hear the conversation, which would give Cooper apoplexy when he found out. But it couldn't be helped. Not if she wanted the information now instead of hours from now when they landed in Pecos.

"Start with the file on Maria Greer," Kim said. "Flint already knows more about that one than I do, I'm sure. He thinks it's a Double Death Task Force case."

"Why do you have a file on Maria Greer?" Flint asked, frowning.

"Cooper gave it to me," she replied. "Usually he offers intel because the subject is a lead of some kind. I'm supposed to follow up and figure out the rest."

"Which means the file's got something to do with Jack Reacher," Flint replied, digesting the situation quickly. "How is Maria Greer related to your search?"

"First," Kim said, as a kind of test, "confirm that your client is Carmen Greer."

"I told you, my client's identity is confidential. I need permission to disclose it to you," Flint replied. "I'll ask. And if the client approves, you'll be the first to know."

"Right," Kim said with a sharp nod. "But since Gaspar's on this transmission and he already knows more than either of us, let's just skip the formalities. We all need to get on the same page, Flint."

Gaspar and Kim waited while Flint paused a couple of beats to consider.

Which was the moment the helo hit an air pocket and dropped straight down in the air.

Kim grabbed the hand hold and clamped her lips together to keep the pizza where it belonged.

The drop was fast and hard. She had little time to compensate.

Not that there was anything she could do.

Flint managed the controls expertly.

After a very long few moments, the bird climbed to altitude and leveled out.

An eternity later, Flint had stabilized the helo and she was flying levelly again.

But Kim's already weak confidence in the helo had taken a direct hit. Her stomach churned like a rock polisher. She felt the pizza threatening to escape her clamped lips.

She couldn't reach the antacids she kept in her pocket without releasing her hold.

She took a deep breath and let one hand go while maintaining her death grip on the hand hold with the other. She found the antacid and popped it into her mouth.

Then she pulled her harness tighter. "Do you have any parachutes handy?"

Flint laughed. "You want to go skydiving?"

"I was a Girl Scout. Be prepared and all that."

Why did pilots think bouncing around in the air was fun? Kim would never understand it.

"You worry too much, Otto. We're not in a vortex ring or losing lift or anything like that. Just a little bumpy air is all," Flint said as if soothing a wild bird. "We're past it now."

"Are you two done fooling around up there?" Gaspar's voice interrupted. "I've got a lot to cover with you and more to do before I can grab some sleep."

"Yeah, sure. Like she said, we need to be on the same page. So tell us what you've got," Flint replied into his headset microphone.

He removed one hand from the controls and pointed to the parachutes packed and stowed in the cabin behind Kim's seat. She nodded, glad to know they were within easy reach. Should she need to use one. Which she sincerely hoped she wouldn't ever need.

Kim wiped the nervous perspiration from her upper lip and pulled her attention back to the briefing.

Gaspar was talking about the files she'd sent him thirty minutes ago. "You already know that Maria Greer is the niece of Rusty Greer. Before Maria died, Rusty had three living blood relatives. Now she has two. Her son, Bobby Greer. And her granddaughter Ellie."

Flint said, "And how is that related to Otto's hunt for Reacher?"

"Ten years ago," Kim explained, "Reacher spent some time at the Red House Ranch. We're not sure why he was there or what, exactly, went on. At the time, Maria Greer was the maid. We suspect Reacher liked her."

“Ah,” Flint replied as if he were connecting the dots. “Which means Reacher met Rusty and Bobby Greer back then as well.”

“That’s right. Also Carmen and Ellie Greer. And Reacher dealt with Carmen’s lawyer, back then, too,” Kim said, giving Flint a moment to catch up.

“So you’re thinking Reacher, what?” Flint asked. “I’m not seeing any connections here.”

“You know what my assignment is,” Kim said, cocking her head.

Flint replied, “Find Reacher. Cooper wants him for a classified assignment, he says. Which may or may not be true.”

"Right. So if Cooper is sending me down this trail, he probably believes Reacher is back here now, or he was here recently, or he's on his way here," Kim explained. "Predicting Reacher's behavior is not an exact science, as Cooper recently reminded me."

"I see," Flint said, thoughtfully. "How does Maria Greer's death come into play?"

"I don't know."

"Does Cooper know?"

Kim shrugged. "Your guess is as good as mine. You arrived at the safe house before I had a chance to ask him."

"I might be able to help shed some light on this." Gaspar's voice came through the headset. “Maria Greer lived alone. She was an artist. Painter. Not a very good one. But she’d been supporting herself with her painting since she left her job at the Red House Ranch when it burned down, and Rusty Greer went to prison ten years ago.”

“It’s odd that Maria Greer survived the fire at the Red House Ranch back then, only to be consumed by another fire a decade later,” Kim said thoughtfully.

“So when she died,” Flint picked up, “at first, the locals thought the fire was an accident. Maria used oil-based paints and she had gallons of paint thinner laying around, too. Both oil paint and paint thinner are highly flammable.”

"And she liked to paint by candlelight," Gaspar added. "Not a smart combination."

"So accidental fire wasn't an unreasonable assumption when the first responders arrived at her home," Kim said, finishing the thought. "Until the second body was found."

"And they figured out the accelerant the arsonist used wasn't paint thinner. It was gasoline," Gaspar said. "Pretty quickly, they concluded Maria Greer was murdered and the arsonist screwed up, causing his own death afterward."

"We looked at her bank records. Maria wasn't wealthy, by any stretch," Flint said. "Nobody would have killed her for her piddly fortune."

"Was Maria well insured?" Kim asked. "A lot of arsons are done to collect insurance money on the building."

"The house and the land it sat on was only worth about a hundred thousand dollars. Maria had no will. And Maria's heirs are the same as Rusty's," Flint said. "That's why I'm heading to Red House Ranch. To tell Rusty and Bobby Greer about Maria's estate, such as it was."

"The estate will be tied up until they settle the questions surrounding Maria's death, though," Kim said. "Is that why you have an appointment with the lawyer first? Maria Greer's lawyer?"

"She was Maria's lawyer, yes," Flint hedged.

Which was when the truth occurred to Kim. She nodded slowly. "So your client **is** Carmen Greer, as I suspected. The lawyer you're planning to talk to was Carmen's lawyer when Carmen was accused of killing her husband. And she still is."

"That's confidential," Flint said.

"Which means Carmen Greer hired you to find out what happened to Maria Greer," Kim said.

Flint shrugged. "I can't confirm your hunch."

"So the question is, why does Carmen care so much about Maria Greer?" Kim mused aloud.

Gaspar chimed in. “Do you two want to keep playing twenty questions or would you like to hear what I called to tell you?”

“We’ve got nothing but time, Chico. Dying to hear all about it,” Kim said.

Chapter 37

Tuesday, May 31
En route to Pecos, Texas

Kim heard Gaspar's voice come through the headset, but the words made no sense. She blinked and shook her head to clear what felt like brain fog.

"Sorry. Can you clarify?" she asked. "What did you say?"

"Reacher contacted me. That's one reason I sent Flint in to pick you up," Gaspar replied. "I know you'll have a thousand questions, but just let all of that go for now and take my word for it. The caller was definitely Reacher. Let's move on from there."

While the world around her looked the same, the situation instantly became bizarre and surreal.

Kim blinked a few times to clear her head.

After all these months, Reacher simply called Gaspar? How could that be? How did he get Gaspar's contact number? Where had he called from? Where was he now? Why did he call, anyway?

"Okay. We can circle back to most of my questions. But what did he want?" Kim asked, getting a grip on her galloping astonishment.

"I have no idea what he wants. I'm not a shrink, Suzie Wong," Gaspar replied. "He asked me to deliver a message to you. He said, and I'll quote here, 'Tell her to go ask Alice.'"

Flint laughed like a man watching a hilarious comedy.

"Yeah, that's what I did, too," Gaspar said. "He told me to keep my head. I thought he was being a smart ass and got the lyrics wrong. I said **feed** your head. He acted like I'd lost my grip."

Flint chuckled again. "Well, that last line is odd, you gotta admit. "White Rabbit" **is** a good song. Grace Slick certainly had a set of pipes on her back in the day."

"Reacher's not a classic rock 'n roll guy. He wouldn't know Grace Slick from Grace Jones. There's a book with the same title, **Go Ask Alice**.

Reacher's not much of a reader, either. What he meant was to go interview Alice Aaron, I gather," Kim said in an effort to keep the conversation on track. "And ask her what?"

"It was a short conversation. Sounded like he was calling from a roadside pay phone. I located the phone, but Reacher was long gone," Gaspar said. Kim heard the clacking sound of his keyboard while he pulled something up. "I record all calls from unrecognized numbers. Here's the entire message."

The playback was barely audible through the helo's headset. Kim asked Gaspar to repeat it. On the third round, all the words finally came through.

"Gaspar, it's Reacher," the voice said, straight forward, no small talk.

Kim recognized him instantly.

Reacher had left voicemails for her in the past. And she'd heard an old recording of a witness interview he'd done once. The voice was exactly the same.

"Copy that." Gaspar had replied as if a call from Reacher was as common as the sunrise.

"Can you pass along a message to Otto for me? Tell her to go ask Alice."

Gaspar's hearty laugh sounded tinny on the recording.

"Keep your head, man," Reacher said without humor.

“**Feed** your head,” Gaspar said.

“What the hell are you talking about? This is no joke.”

“Right.” Gaspar cleared his throat. “Where will Otto find Alice?”

“Alice Amanda Aaron, J.D.,” Reacher said. “Lives in Pecos. You can find her address in the phone book. She’ll be expecting to hear from Otto. Sooner is better.”

Kim smiled. Only Reacher would think people still used phone books.

“Will you be there when Otto arrives?” Gaspar asked.

“I’ve got something else I’ve gotta do. Otto can handle this. Sooner is better,” Reacher said again.

"Yeah, copy that," Gaspar replied. "Anything else she'll need to know?"

"Tell her this thing is bigger than she thinks. Watch her six," Reacher said. "My ride's waiting. I'll call again when I can."

"That was the end of the recording?" Kim asked.

"That's it. He hung up. I filtered out the extraneous noises on the audio you just heard. But on the original, there are big diesel engines idling nearby. And the pay phone is located at a rest stop on the highway," Gaspar said. "He's hitchhiking. He found a ride. Stopped to call me before he caught a lift that would take him farther south."

"Can you get eyes on the phone? Find out whether Reacher hitched a ride on one of those big rigs? And which one?" Kim asked.

"Already done, Sunshine. The satellite views are not as crisp as we'd like. The phone was blocked from view by the trucks. When the trucks moved out, Reacher wasn't near the phone," Gaspar replied.

"But you can match the timing of the call to the departure of the trucks, right?" Flint asked. "Could be the one he hitched with since he said he had to catch his ride."

"Possibly," Gaspar said. "Or he was in the men's room or went inside to get coffee. Or maybe he hitched in a different vehicle. There were SUVs and pickups and a couple of sedans there, too."

"That's just great," Kim said dryly.

"We're working on it. It's a busy rest stop. There were six private vehicles and eight semis that departed within a ten-minute window of Reacher's call," Gaspar said. "We're tracking them all. Nothing promising yet."

"Which direction was he headed?" Kim asked, visualizing the map of Texas.

"Three of the big rigs are headed south. Toward Mexico," Gaspar said. "Which makes sense. If Reacher called because he was planning to leave the country and couldn't rely on finding a phone to place the call from the other side of the border."

“That’s a solid theory.” Flint shook his head, exasperated. “Why can’t he just get a cell phone like everybody else in the world?”

“Because then he’d have to carry it around,” Gaspar replied. “Everything Reacher owns amounts to a few pages of paper and fits in his pockets and weighs close to nothing and cell phones are heavier. Because he doesn’t want to add more stuff to keep track of. Because he’d have to make a regular cell phone payment. Which would mean a credit card or a checking account and a fixed address. None of which Reacher has.”

“And who’s he gonna call, anyway?” Flint said. “It’s not like the guy has a posse or even a single best friend that he talks to regularly.”

"All true. But the real reason he doesn't carry a cell phone is the same reason Reacher doesn't do a lot of things," Kim replied. "He simply doesn't want to. So he doesn't."

For a few minutes, the noisy helicopter drowned everything out.

Gaspar picked up the conversation. "I located Alice Aaron. She's been out of town visiting her family in New York. But she got back a few hours ago."

"Thanks, Chico. Can you send the address to my server? I'll download everything when we land," Kim said.

"Ten-four, Suzy Wong," Gaspar said with his usual easy humor. "Flint, you're cleared to land at Pecos Executive Airport. There's an SUV parked there for you. Fully stocked."

"Got it," Flint replied. "Get some sleep. We'll call if we need anything."

"Thanks, Pepe. I still can't do this job without you," Kim said with absolute sincerity.

Gaspar chuckled. "So you've been reading Pepe Carvahlo now?"

"Spain's best loved detective, according to his hype," Kim teased.

"Next to me, of course," Gaspar joked in response. "If Pepe were Cuban, that is."

"Spain's close enough to Cuba for our purposes. Pepe's a great detective, almost as good as Suzie Wong. Which is all that matters here," Kim replied.

"Speaking of detecting, one last thing," Gaspar said, "I've got eyes and ears on Cooper. Also checked out Johnson and Miller. I'll send that intel to your secure server, too."

"Give me the short version now," Kim said.

"Both Johnson and Miller look okay, based on what I've found so far," Gaspar said. "And you already know Cooper's a lying snake. No news there."

Kim smiled. "But why is Cooper here? That's what I need to know. He says he's here to draw Reacher out. Which is probably a load of crap."

"Working on it, Sunshine. Like Pepe, I've only got two hands," Gaspar said before he rang off.

Kim gave the conversation a rest for a while. She couldn't quite wrap her head around Reacher contacting Gaspar.

She'd been hunting Reacher at Cooper's direction for seven months. Looking for a cunning man who couldn't be found.

Or so she'd believed.

Perhaps Reacher had been the one in control all along.

Kim activated her headset and paused to let Flint do the same. "Now we know why I'm headed to interview Alice Aaron. But why were you already on your way there when you stopped to pick me up?"

Chapter 38

Tuesday, May 31
En route to Pecos, Texas

Alice Amanda Aaron, J.D. lived in a small stucco house a couple of miles east of downtown Pecos. The bare lot was dotted with a few succulents and the rest was covered by landscaping rocks of various sizes and shapes.

Xeriscaping, they called it. The point was to eliminate the need for irrigation.

Kim was sure her mother would be horrified by the xeriscaping style.

Kim felt more comfortable around the lush green gardens of her childhood.

She imagined Alice had found the dry brown land unfamiliar. Alice was born and raised in New York. She went to law school at Harvard in Boston. Lawns and flowering annuals planted in the spring must have been baked into her DNA, too.

But Alice had been in Pecos more than ten years now. Whatever she thought about the land, she'd chosen to make her life here. Like everything else that felt strange at first, Alice probably got used to it after a while.

The house was a rectangular box, maybe twenty feet by forty feet. One end was a two-car garage.

The house was painted the color of sand and blended into the xeriscaping seamlessly.

The front door was closed, but there were lights on inside, which suggested Alice was home and awake.

Flint parked the SUV in the circular gravel drive near the front door and turned off the engine. Kim removed the alligator clamp, unlatched her seatbelt, and allowed it to retract. She slipped the clamp into her pocket and opened the door.

She slid out of the cool interior of the SUV's cabin into the sunbaked heat. Instantly, Kim began to perspire. Almost as quickly, the perspiration evaporated.

They walked abreast to the recessed front door, which had been painted a dull turquois sometime in the distant past. The paint was faded now, unable to withstand the constant sun and heat.

No need for an overhang across the door.

Kim had read that Pecos was blessed with an average of thirteen inches of annual precipitation. From the looks of things, there hadn't been rain or snow around here in a very long time.

But a shield over the door from the unrelenting sun would have been welcome.

Kim pressed the bell. She heard the tinny sound peal from a small box mounted on the inside wall. Which was probably all the notice of visitors or deliveries Alice ever needed. The house wasn't large enough to require a more elaborate system.

After much too long, Kim heard the deadbolt slide back. Cool air rushed out to meet them when Alice Aaron opened the door.

She was tall and thin and dressed in white pleated trousers paired with a white tank top tucked into the waistband. No makeup. No jewelry. Her dark hair was cut short.

Her skin was brown and weathered, as if she'd spent way too many hours in the hot Texas sun. She looked forty-five, but she was ten years younger according to Cooper's file.

The total effect was casually elegant and mature without Alice having given her appearance an ounce of thought, probably. She didn't seem like the type to obsess over superficial things.

"I'm Michael Flint. This is Kim Otto. May we come in?"

"You're late. I expected you earlier." Alice stood aside to allow them to walk into the gloriously air-conditioned house. She closed the door and threw the deadbolt behind them.

"Yeah, sorry," Flint said.

The layout of Alice's home was similar to the safe house in Dallas. Maybe they called it a Texas ranch style. The garage was on Kim's right and the bedrooms were on the left. The center of the house was an open floor plan decorated in a minimalist Southwestern style.

The interior palette was the same as the exterior. Sand and turquoise with a few yellow and red accents. The wood was stained dark, but there was precious little of it.

The walls and cabinets in the kitchen were painted the same sand color as the exterior of the house. The countertops were turquoise laminate. Even the appliances were turquoise. The floors were terra cotta tile.

If Alice meant to leave her east coast sensibilities behind, she'd made a good start with the decor.

Kim heard the faint noise of a television playing in one of the bedrooms. Otherwise, the house seemed quiet.

Alice noticed Kim's visual scan of the room. "Yeah, it's a little much, isn't it? This was the builder's model. His decorator went a little crazy with the Southwestern charm. I bought it completely furnished. I keep thinking I'll change it someday, but I've been here seven years, so…"

Her voice trailed off and she shrugged, leading them into the kitchen.

"Coffee?" she asked, nodding toward a carafe that was almost empty. "I can make a fresh pot, if you like."

"Just a bottle of water, if you have it," Kim said through her parched throat, pointing toward the water bottle in Alice's hand.

"In the fridge there," Alice nodded toward the appliance.

"Grab one for me, would you?" Flint asked.

Kim opened the fridge, which was full of bottled water and condiments. Whatever else she was, Alice Aaron was no gourmand, for sure. Kim collected two cold plastic bottles and handed one to Flint.

"Thanks for coming to the house instead of the office," Alice said to Flint. "I just got back in town, and it's been one crisis after another. I thought we'd have a bit of privacy here, but no luck."

"What do you mean?" Kim asked, craning her head around to look.

"Somebody else here?" Flint asked.

"Yeah. A client. It's an evolving situation, so we may have to cut this short," Alice said. "She was arrested last night. I managed to get her a hardship release from jail, but then she didn't have anywhere else to go."

"Arrested for what?" Kim asked.

"Existing on the wrong side of the line. I'm an immigration lawyer. I do pro bono work for migrants who have entered the country illegally," Alice replied, offering a steady stare. She would brook no disparagement of her work or her clients.

“Sounds like tough duty,” Flint said. “The individual situations can be tragic, but Texas has a tough policy on illegal immigration for a lot of good reasons.”

“The work is definitely not easy.” Alice nodded. “I don’t handle the criminal cases or the drug runners or any of that. We have plenty of those in the country already. We don’t need any more. If we manage to catch them and kick them back, so much the better.”

“Can’t argue with you there,” Flint replied.

“The migrants I represent are just normal people looking for a better life. They believe they can find it here," Alice continued. "But most of the time, that's just a lie someone used to steal everything they own."

"So what can you actually do for the ones who qualify for your help?" Kim asked.

"Not much. Sometimes, I can get them asylum. In some circumstances, they can get temporary visas while we work toward something more permanent." Alice shrugged, swiping a weary palm across her forehead. "But usually, it's a matter of making sure they get back across and returned safely to their homes south of the border. Many don't even have homes to go back to, so they'll have to start over once they return to their own countries."

"Are they Mexicans?" Flint asked.

"About half," Alice nodded wearily. "Some come from farther south. There's a sizable group from other continents, too."

"How'd you get started in this work, anyway?" Kim asked. "You have a law degree from Harvard. You could have any number of great jobs."

"Yeah, and they'd pay better and be way less heartbreaking," Alice replied with a smile. "Are you sure my parents didn't send you here?"

Kim smiled, too, and shook her head. "No, but I have similar parents myself. My law degree's from Georgetown. Divorced. No kids. Mom tells me every day that I could settle down and have a great life."

"I hear ya, sister," Alice raised her water bottle and they touched plastic. When she'd swallowed a healthy swig, she said, "Actually, I came here on a five-year plan. Young, starry-eyed, you know? Trying to give back and all that. I had a girlfriend at the time. We were supposed to get married in year six, move to New York, represent hedge fund managers and make millions."

"So what happened to the plan?" Flint asked.

"We broke up before year five and I just never left Pecos."

Flint laughed and Kim chuckled.

Alice said, "How about you, Flint? Should we start a support group?

Are you a colossal disappointment to your parents as well?"

He shrugged and drained his water bottle. "Dunno. I grew up in an orphanage. Never met my parents. I'm sure they'd be just as embarrassed by my choices as yours are. How much time do we have before you need to leave?"

Chapter 39

Tuesday, May 31
Pecos, Texas

“Hard to say how much time we have. Not long enough, probably,” Alice replied, tilting her head toward the back of the house. “My client, Elana’s, pregnant. Due any day now. And she’s developed a medical problem with the pregnancy, which is how I got her out of jail last night. A friend called me and asked me to help her. So I did.”

“Why didn’t she go directly to the hospital?” Flint asked. “Too afraid?”

"And they didn't have a bed, anyway. Hospitals here are seriously overcrowded with migrants, many of whom have serious health problems," Alice nodded. "I've made some calls. We're expecting to get a bed for her at the hospital any minute now. We'll need to leave right away so they don't give her bed away."

Kim cocked her head. "She's more than eight months pregnant? Why is a woman in her condition crossing a dangerous border alone in the first place?"

Alice's shoulders slumped. "That's really the problem. But in her defense, she wasn't quite eight months pregnant when she got here. Unexpectedly, she got the chance to cross, so she wanted to do it. And she wasn't alone. Her boyfriend was with her."

"Where is he now?" Flint asked.

She shook her head. "He had to leave for work four days ago and now she can't reach him."

Kim and Flint exchanged glances.

Flint asked, "Since he's undocumented, what kind of work did he get?"

"Probably some sort of manual labor. I don't know. Never met the man," Alice said tiredly. "Elana says he plans to return before the baby's born. Tomorrow or the next day at the latest, she said. But he might not make it in time if they have to do a C-section today."

"If she has any idea where her boyfriend is, we might be able to find him for her," Kim said, with a nod toward Flint.

"Thanks. I appreciate the sentiment. But you practically exude law enforcement from every pore of your body," Alice grinned. "No way will any of these people trust you."

Kim nodded. "So what will you do?"

"I've been in this game awhile now, so I've got contacts. If Elana knew where her boyfriend was, I could probably find him," Alice sighed. "But she doesn't know. I've already asked."

"Let me know if you change your mind or if there's any way we can help. Meanwhile, let's move on for now. That okay with you?" Kim asked.

"Sure," Alice nodded. "This will be my last chance to talk with you for a while, so we need to make the most of it."

Kim paused a moment to choose her words. This was always a pivotal moment in every interview. Reactions from witnesses to questions about Reacher were always a crap shoot. They ran the gamut from hostile to tearful, and everything in between. Kim needed to be ready for whatever came her way.

"Alice," Kim took a breath before plunging straight into the fire. "We weren't properly introduced before. I'm an FBI special agent. I'm looking for Jack Reacher."

"Yeah, he told me you'd be coming," Alice replied, nodding. "He said I should answer your questions."

Well. That's a first. After seven months of dodging her, Reacher had decided to cooperate. Why? Kim was already considering the angles.

"Have you seen Reacher recently?" Kim asked.

Alice shook her head. "Haven't seen him in years. He was in Pecos when I was out of town, apparently."

"What makes you say that?" Flint asked.

Alice gave Flint a long solid look. "Carmen Greer told me he was here."

"When did you talk with Carmen Greer?" Kim asked.

"While I was in New York. She called me. Said Reacher was here and wanted to ask a favor. I said she could give him my number."

"Why?"

"Why not?" Alice replied with a shrug. "Call me curious. We worked together on a tough situation ten years ago and I haven't seen or heard from Reacher since. I was surprised, frankly."

"What kind of case did you work on together?" Kim asked. Cooper's files had been vague on this point.

"Carmen Greer's wrongful arrest for the murder of her husband."

"You were a pro bono lawyer back then," Kim said. "The Greers have money and lots of it. Why did Carmen need to hire you?"

"That's a complicated question. Basically, Carmen was accused of killing her husband. Understandably, the Greers weren't too happy to pay for her defense," Alice explained, draining the water bottle, one ear cocked toward Elana's room. "And Carmen didn't have any money of her own back then."

"I guess that makes some sort of sense. Except Carmen didn't kill her husband. I guess by the time you figured that out, she didn't need money from the Greers," Kim nodded slowly. "How wealthy are the Greers, anyway?"

“By Texas standards, back then, not very. A few million or so,” Alice said. “But a few years after that, new drilling techniques came on board and the Greers’ oil properties have pushed their net worth into the stratosphere.”

“Yeah, I see the Greer name regularly in the Texas business press,” Flint added. “Nobody’s collecting food stamps if their last name is Greer these days.”

Alice cocked her head. “Look, we’ve already established that I don’t have a lot of time here. Why don’t you ask me the things you don’t already know?”

Flint nodded. “Sounds reasonable. Where did Reacher go? Where is he now? Is he coming back? When?”

Alice smiled. "You really don't know much, do you?"

"No. And I'm the kind of guy who likes to know things."

"Right," she replied with amusement. "I don't know where he went. I don't know where he is now. And I don't know when, or if, he's coming back."

"Look, Alice," Kim cleared her throat. "Reacher called a mutual friend because he couldn't get in touch with me. He had something he wanted me to know. He told me to come here and ask you."

"Ask me what?"

"That's the question," Kim nodded. "What's the answer?"

"I would tell you if I knew. I swear," Alice replied. "He called me. He said Maria Greer was murdered. He said he knew who killed her. But he didn't tell me who the killer was."

Kim let the intel sink in for a moment. She had so many questions it was hard to know where to start. "Why did Reacher think you'd be interested in Maria Greer's murder?"

Alice paused a long beat. "Because she was my client. And I liked her. And so did he. And she didn't deserve to be murdered."

"How did Reacher know that Maria Greer was your client?" Kim asked.

Alice shrugged. "Maybe he's got a source. Maybe he's dating a fortune teller. How should I know?"

"No one deserves to be murdered," Flint said. "Reacher said he knew who the killer was. Did you have the impression he was planning to go after the killer?"

"Interesting question, since what Reacher said makes no sense. Maria's killer also died in the fire," Alice replied. "What we don't know is who he was or why he killed Maria."

Or whether Reacher knew him and how Reacher could go after him now since he was already dead.

"Are you worried that the killer might have been one of your clients, too?" Flint asked.

Alice's mouth opened into an "O" and her eyes widened. She coughed uncontrollably and reached for her water bottle to soothe her throat.

When she'd calmed herself, she said, "Sorry. Honestly, the idea had never occurred to me. And I was about to say absolutely not. I told you, I don't work with killers, gangbangers, or drug dealers."

"But then—" Kim prompted.

"But then I realized that there's no way I can say for sure that Maria's killer was or wasn't a client. I represent a lot of undocumented migrants and the killer hasn't been identified. He's a John Doe. So I guess he could have been a client and I wouldn't have known about it. Which would well and truly suck," Alice finished weakly, her voice trailing off into uncomfortable silence.

Before Kim could ask anything else, a woman emerged from the hallway that led from the bedrooms. She was young, Hispanic, pretty. Very very pregnant. And pale as milk.

She was also crying uncontrollably.

“Elana?” Kim asked, to alert Alice.

Alice jumped out of the chair and rushed toward Elana. “What’s wrong? Is it the baby?”

“No, no, no. Javier.” Elana’s ragged voice was barely audible over her sobs.

“What about him?” Alice said, wrapping her arms around the sobbing woman.

She pointed a shaky finger toward the television.

Flint found the remote and turned it on.

The story came up as breaking news. Coverage of the riot at Senator Redstone's funeral yesterday in Dallas.

Images of the chaos filled the screen as police tried to quell the rioters.

The reporter showed a photo on the screen. She said authorities were asking for help identifying this man who was killed inside the church.

Elana's keening grew louder and more heartbreaking. "Javier, Javier," she sobbed, pointing at the photo.

"This is Javier, Elana? What's his last name?" Amanda asked, while comforting the woman as best she could.

"Garcia. Javier Garcia," Elana sobbed.

"Is he your baby's father?" Kim asked kindly.

"Sí, sí," Elana's sobs became wails and screams as she crumpled to the floor.

Flint bent down and picked Elana up. "Where can I put her?"

"This way," Alice said, leading him down the hallway to the bedroom.

Flint left Elana in bed and returned to the kitchen a few moments later without Alice. "Elana's vomiting now, she's so upset. Alice needs to get her to the hospital as soon as possible. She's calling about the availability of the bed now."

He handed Kim a cell phone. “This belongs to her. Look at the photo on the lock screen.”

Kim took the phone and pushed the button to turn on the screen. When the screen came up it displayed a photo of a young couple, smiling, obviously in love.

The woman was Elana. And the man was unquestionably the dead shooter from the photo on the news.

“Javier Garcia is a fairly common name. Not likely we’ll be able to find anything else about him until Elana is capable of coherent speech,” Kim said, pulling out her phone and snapping a few shots of the picture.

She sent the photo to Gaspar along with the name. He texted back. **I’m on it.**

"What about Miller and Johnson. Cooper, too, for that matter," Flint said. "They'll want the intel as quickly as possible."

"Yeah. I'll have to use Cooper's phone to get a message into the safe house. I left it in my bag," Kim replied, dropping her own cell phone into her pocket.

She examined Elana's phone. Javier Garcia was not listed in Elana's contacts.

The call log showed no outgoing calls in the past two weeks. The last incoming call was four days ago. The number had a Dallas area code.

Kim sent the number to Gaspar. He'd know what to do.

Chapter 40

Tuesday, May 31
Pecos, Texas

Alice emerged from the hallway looking worn down and defeated. She rummaged in the cabinets until she found a jar of peanut butter and a sleeve of saltines. “You guys want to stay for dinner? Or breakfast? Or whatever the hell time it is?”

“What’s going on with Elana? Is the ambulance coming?” Kim asked, accepting the knife and slathering a cracker with peanut butter. She passed the jar to Flint.

"Not unless she's unconscious or dead or worse," Alice said, shaking her head. "I called my friend. They're still working on getting Elana a bed. But I've also called a doctor. He's willing to make a house call, but he can't get here for another hour."

"I've delivered babies before," Flint said, around a mouthful of peanut butter.

"Me, too," Alice smiled. "Let's hope it doesn't come to that."

A few moments of silence passed as Kim washed the sticky meal down with the water. When she could speak again, she said, "Where did Elana cross the border? Do you know?"

“Finally, a question I can actually answer,” Alice said, preparing another cracker. “There’s an official entry point south of Pecos at Presidio. Elana and Javier came through there.”

“Why did they cross the border at all?”

“Javier was promised construction work, she said. But when they finally came across, she was not feeling well. Javier left her and continued without her,” Alice replied. “She got picked up two days ago by border agents in a sweep. The plan was to bus her back to Mexico, but she’s not able to travel at all now.”

“Which means the baby is likely to be born here and will automatically become a US citizen,” Flint said.

Alice nodded. “But that doesn’t mean the baby’s parents can stay in this country. The parents definitely don’t become citizens. If Javier is dead and with no other way for her to support herself and the baby, I’m not sure what Elana will do.”

“Does she have family in Mexico?” Kim asked.

“I don’t know. That’s something we’ll need to figure out. But the first thing is to get her admitted to the hospital,” Alice said as her phone began to dance around on the table. “Everything else will need to wait. This is my call. Excuse me.”

Alice picked up the phone and headed down the hallway toward Elana’s room.

Flint turned to Kim. “Now what?”

She slid off the chair and headed toward the door. “First call is to Cooper. I’ll give him the intel we have on Javier Garcia. And see what he’s willing to share that could help us.”

“Us?” Flint said with a grin. “I already have a job, Otto. I don’t need another one.”

Kim kept walking, ignoring the smack talk. “You coming or not?”

“Depends on where you’re going.”

She reached the front door and went outside. The SUV was unlocked. She opened the cargo door and located the envelope containing Cooper’s phone. She fired it up and waited for it to connect to the secure satellite.

The call rang four times before he picked up. When he did, she heard background noises she couldn't immediately identify.

"What did you learn?" Cooper said, as if he were genuinely curious.

"The most important thing is the identity of the shooter at the Redstone funeral yesterday. He might be an undocumented migrant named Javier Garcia."

A long silence.

"And you know this how?"

"I'm at Alice Aaron's home in Pecos. She is on her way to the hospital with a woman who claims Garcia is the father of her unborn child."

"And you believe her?"

"Definitely. Her devastated reaction when she saw the photo of the dead shooter on the news was genuine."

More silence.

"OK. I'll pass that along to Johnson and Miller. Did she tell you anything else that might help us?"

"Potentially. She came across from Mexico with Garcia at the border crossing in Presidio from Ojinaga. He was promised construction work somewhere north of Pecos. She says she hasn't heard from him since he left here, but he was scheduled to be back in a couple of days."

"Who promised him the work?"

"She claims she doesn't know."

"Is that true?" His terse responses suggested there were others within hearing distance of the call.

"Possibly. She had received a call on her cell phone from a Dallas phone number. Could've been Garcia. It's tenuous, but a possible connection to the Redstone shooting."

"Okay. What's the woman's name?"

"That's all I have at the moment," Kim replied, ignoring his question. Cooper had been more trustworthy lately, but she wanted to know more about Elana Fernandez before turning her over to ICE. "What about you? Anything to report?"

"We've put the Redstone shooting into the Double Death Task Force database for now. Until we decide it doesn't belong there," Cooper said.

"Who was Garcia's target? And did he succeed in his attempt to kill?" Kim asked. This was one piece of information that wasn't contained in the news reports. Probably because of a desire to first notify next of kin.

"Officially, we have no idea who the targets were, or if there were targets, for that matter. The shooter might have been one of the rioters. Several of them had guns and there were more gunshots inside and outside the church," Cooper reported as if he was reading from a prepared statement. "Off the record, they think the target could have been Teddy

Redstone. But he and his family were spared. Luis Trejo was shot but survived. His wife was killed. A man unconnected to either the Trejo or the Redstone families but sitting near them in the church was wounded. The doctors say he will make it."

"Seems like Garcia wasn't a very good shot, thankfully," Kim said. "Who is conducting the Redstone investigation now?"

"Dallas P.D. at the moment. We'll probably leave it that way," Cooper said.

"Unless Johnson and Miller can tie Garcia to the task force's other cases."

"Exactly."

The background noise was unrelenting. Kim had tried to filter it out with little success. Nor could she identify it.

Finally, she asked, “Where are you, anyway?”

“Did you find Reacher or any evidence that he’s been near Alice Aaron?” Cooper asked, ignoring her question.

She could have asked him the same thing, but she didn’t. No point. She already knew the answer. If he’d found Reacher, he wouldn’t have taken her call.

“You already know that he called her. Alice says that’s the extent of it. She claims she hasn’t seen him for ten years.”

"Do you believe her?" he asked, repeating his earlier question about Elana.

Kim gave it a moment's thought. "Possibly."

"Why are you hedging?"

She couldn't answer that question without telling him Reacher had called Gaspar. She changed the subject. "The task force has had two murders in the past two weeks. Is that time interval between murders unusual?"

"Probably. Why?"

"I'm wondering why these murders would be speeding up. The more murders there are that fit the fact pattern, the more this begins to look like a coordinated plan. If the murders are weeks or months or years apart, it's more difficult for law enforcement to connect them."

Cooper replied, "Yes. That's why it took so long to recognize the pattern and identify possible cases."

"Which means there's a puppet master behind these murders," Kim said slowly, thinking aloud. "Someone orchestrating them. Hiring the killers, eliminating them when they've done the job."

Reacher had said he was going somewhere to find Maria Greer's killer. Did he mean the man who had set the killer's mission?

"Why would this hypothetical puppet master engage in such behavior? To what end?" Cooper asked bluntly.

She shrugged, although he couldn't see her. To what end, indeed.

"The usual answer is money. But you have access to more data than I do. Maybe you can figure that out. I'm heading to Presidio, Texas," Kim said.

"Why?"

"It's a small town. The border crossing is not as busy there as other towns. It's more likely someone might have usable intel," she said, thinking aloud.

“And what if they do? How is that helping you to find Reacher?” Cooper asked.

“I don’t know. But it’s an odd coincidence that seems relevant,” Kim replied.

“Okay. But don’t waste too much time in Presidio before you head to Red House Ranch. The Greers are more likely to know something useful,” Cooper said before he disconnected the call.

Chapter 41

Tuesday, May 31
Pecos, Texas

Kim returned Cooper's phone to her bag and glanced around. She'd been caged too long. She felt like a prisoner in her own body. Her daily five-mile run had been put on hold and her muscles were complaining about the forced inactivity. She needed to move.

Alice didn't live in an upscale area, but there were worse neighborhoods in every city in the world.

Kim walked away from the SUV and the house and strolled along the street. Every ounce of moisture was continuously being sucked from her body by the arid heat. She'd soon look like a dried peach.

After half a mile to limber up, she pulled out the burner that connected her to Gaspar and pressed the redial button. He picked up right away, as he always did.

"What's up, Suzy Wong?" he asked with his usual good humor.

"Ah, Pepe, you are always amusing," she replied with a grin.

"Yiyiyi," Gaspar laughed. "Flattery will get your everywhere."

"I'm counting on it," Kim put a smile into her voice and then turned to more serious matters. "Reacher told Alice Aaron that he was going somewhere to find Maria Greer's killer."

Gaspar paused briefly. "So he's at the morgue? Or the cemetery?"

"Very funny. A point Cooper mentioned suggests Reacher's onto something."

"Which is what, exactly?"

"You know about the Double Death Task Force. They've had two murders in less than two weeks," Kim said, stopping to perform a few squats.

"That they know about." Gaspar sounded distracted by something else going on in his office.

"What?"

"Sorry. Working on a fresh coffee con leche." Gaspar slurped his favorite espresso with milk and loads of sugar. "The task force has identified two murders in two weeks. There could be more they haven't discovered yet."

Kim nodded slowly. "Yes, I suppose that's possible. Anybody else in Texas been murdered lately by a killer who died at the scene?"

"Funny you should ask," Gaspar replied, after a moment.

Kim stopped walking and stood very still. "You're serious?"

"Completely."

"When did this happen?"

"Last night. It's all over the news. I'm surprised you didn't see it," Gaspar said. "Victim was Emily Brandon."

Kim widened her eyes. "Emily Brandon, wife of Kevin Brandon, one of the richest men in America?"

"Ten four. One and the same," Gaspar replied

"Wow."

"Yep. Seems she was at a big fundraiser in Austin. Stabbed to death," Gaspar said.

"And her killer?"

"Burned beyond all recognition when his sedan parked at the scene exploded shortly thereafter," Gaspar said.

“Vehicle-Born Improvised Explosive Device attached to the ignition?”

“Most likely.”

“Very reliable weapon. Use it when you want to be absolutely positively sure,” Kim replied.

“You bet. Saw a few of those VBIEDs deployed during my army days, myself,” Gaspar said.

Kim resumed her slow pacing along the street in front of Alice’s house, thinking things through. She’d walked up and back the length of the lot three times before Gaspar interrupted.

“You want to call me back? Or should I just keep sitting here while your gears are turning?” he said.

"I guess the Emily Brandon killer's body is not identifiable," Kim said slowly.

"They'll try DNA, see if they can get a match as soon as they can. But it's not likely to lead anywhere, given the condition of the body. I saw the photos. It's bad," Gaspar reported. "That's all I know at the moment. I'll keep you updated. Meanwhile, why don't you tell me what you've found out and maybe I can contribute some of Pepe's brilliance."

She cleared her throat, which was as dry and scratchy as the gravel under her feet. She gave him all the same intel she'd shared with Cooper in a raspy whisper. After she'd finished, she had barely a drop of her own saliva to swallow.

“Got any good news?” she said.

“Possibly. The fundraiser was held in a mansion owned by some tech billionaire. The place was loaded with surveillance cameras. There’s tons of footage,” Gaspar replied.

Abruptly, Kim stopped walking. “Way to bury the lede, Pepe. So you’ve got images of the murder as it happened?”

“The killer was wearing a tuxedo and his face somehow escaped all the cameras.” Gaspar explained slowly, as if he were running through the video feed as he spoke. “But it looks like Emily Brandon’s companion was served an appetizer by one of the staff. He collapsed almost immediately. She knelt down to help him. At that point, the server kneels down, seems to be offering assistance, and then stands up and hurries out through the kitchen. Shortly afterward, it's apparent that the server stabbed Brandon."

"She must have bled out quickly."

"Very. She was already dead when first responders got to her. Emily and her companion were standing apart in a quiet corner of a large open ballroom. She cried out when he fell," Gaspar said.

Kim thought about the logistics. Stabbing was personal. The killer needed to be very close to the victim. A woman like Emily Brandon would also have been closely guarded, presumably.

"Seems extremely risky. The killer has to get in close enough to touch her, deliver the vicious attack, and then escape. Not a crime of opportunity, surely. Something like that would have been meticulously planned."

"Dunno enough to say that for sure yet. But that's a reasonable theory. I'll follow up. You should let Cooper know. The task force can do more with the intel than I can."

"Yeah. I'll call him back as soon as we hang up."

"Can you get anything more out of Elana Fernandez?" Gaspar asked after a few moments to digest everything and finish slurping his coffee.

"Probably. But not until later. Could be a couple of days, even." Kim could drink a gallon of his coffee right about now. If she had access to it. Which she didn't. "Elana will be headed to the hospital very shortly."

"Send me a photo of her. I can run it through facial recognition. I'll run the boyfriend, too. I might get a hit if either of them is listed in Mexican databases," Gaspar said, clacking the keys on his keyboard, probably looking for the names.

"Yeah. I'll send you a snap of the one she's using on her screensaver as soon as we hang up. You'll have to upgrade it, probably."

"You have her phone still? She may have more photos on there.

Try to send them directly to me. And anything else on the phone that might be useful. Such as fingerprints."

"Copy that," she said, mimicking one of his standard responses.

"So you're on your way to Presidio, then?" Gaspar said, distracted now by his new direction. "Flint can fly you down there. The place is small enough to cover quickly, but not on foot. I'll arrange a vehicle. It'll be there when you land."

"We'll need to ask some delicate questions of the locals. Do we know anyone working that border crossing?" Kim asked. "Because if we don't, check out a member of the Michigan National Guard. Martin

Weber. He might be deployed there. He should be friendly enough to tell us the truth."

"And who is he, exactly?" Gaspar said, preoccupied with whatever was going on in his office.

"He's apparently dating my sister. But that's not why I want to question him," Kim replied.

"Sure, Suzy Wong. If you say so. Your plan to interrogate Weber has nothing to do with the lovely and adorable Sunny. Absolutely nothing at all," Gaspar teased before he hung up.

Chapter 42

Tuesday, May 31
Ojinaga, Mexico

Cesar Baez had confirmed the murder of Emily Brandon and received payment in full that had been transferred to his offshore account. Collecting his full compensation improved his mood slightly.

José had managed to close one project, albeit a significant loose end remained, which was not ideal. Baez frowned, staring across his land from the verandah with unseeing eyes.

The whore, Pilar Inez Mendoza, was missing. Which wasn't the least bit okay. Pilar had always been trouble. He should never have given her the Brandon assignment, he knew now.

Baez had been Pilar's first lover almost ten years ago now. She was barely fifteen at the time. She had caught his attention with her flashing dark eyes and impertinent behavior.

He'd expected her to be wild in bed, and he wanted her.

Her mother said she wasn't ready. Baez argued Pilar was two years older than her sisters had been.

They'd negotiated for a few weeks until he'd finally agreed to pay significantly more than the usual rate for Pilar's virginity and Señora Mendoza had seemed satisfied.

He'd soon tired of her temper and inexperience, which was fine. He hadn't been looking for a wife, after all. Baez promptly moved on and gave Pilar less than a moment's thought afterward.

Eight years later, Pilar was in trouble. She'd stabbed a prominent man during sex. He was gravely wounded. He'd spent days in the hospital and barely recovered. He insisted Pilar be prosecuted.

Pilar's mother had been frantic. Not only would Pilar go to prison, but the man would make sure that no customers came to her brothel again. Señora Mendoza and her family had owned and operated the brothel, under Baez Cartel protection, for generations. The women had nowhere else to go. They would starve.

At her wits end, Señora Mendoza dressed in her finest outfit and, for the first time in her life, took the bus from her village. She came to Baez's office and begged for Pilar's life as well as the brothel's business.

Like his father before him, Baez had a soft heart where mothers were concerned. The hardworking whores with no man to protect them were especially vulnerable.

Baez also remembered the girl fondly. She'd been beautiful and innocent and a wild and exciting hellcat. Yes, he'd enjoyed his time with Pilar.

And, as luck would have it, he'd been searching for an assassin with similar physical characteristics for the Emily Brandon job.

Dios proveerá, his father always said. **God will provide**.

Baez told Señora Mendoza to send Pilar to him. "I will send her away. You will never see your daughter again. You understand?"

"Sí, sí." The mother had nodded furiously, bowing and backing her way out the door before he could change his mind.

That was weeks ago. Baez had accepted the Emily Brandon

contract. José had implemented the plan. Everything had unfolded as it should.

Pilar eliminated the target.

Kevin Brandon was a husband now free of his wife's claims to his money.

And Baez was considerably richer.

The loose end had become a significant problem. José failed to eliminate Pilar. Now he'd lost her. Baez paced to control his fury.

Not only had José failed with Pilar, the ambitious politician contract, Luis Trejo, also remained open. That situation required new personnel now that Javier Garcia no longer lived.

On top of his recent inadequacies, José's failures had become too costly. Baez could no longer trust him.

Baez stomped back and forth along the length of the verandah, becoming more angry instead of less.

After a while, an idea began to form itself in his mind.

"Perhaps the politician contract could still be satisfied," Baez murmured as he reached for José's phone vibrating in his pocket.

"Pilar has resurfaced. I'm on my way to collect her. She'll be dead before nightfall," José promised, perhaps anticipating his boss's fury.

"Change of plans," Baez said.

"Oh?" José replied.

"Take her to Red House Ranch," Baez instructed. "I will meet you there."

"Sí," José replied. "Anything else?"

Baez disconnected. He hadn't traveled into the US for several months. Border crossings were becoming more and more difficult, even with a false passport and a willing border guard.

Locating the corrupt guards and paying them off was simpler when his father ran the cartel. These days, illegal crossings kept the guards overwhelmed and overtired. Temporary reinforcements were deployed and recalled too frequently.

There was little time to find the weak guards and exploit them. His brothers complained about the problem often. They were losing personnel and product with alarming frequency, cutting into their profits.

Even so, the Pilar and Trejo situations must be dealt with immediately.

José was no longer up to the task. That much was clear. Until Baez found a replacement, he would handle José's duties himself. No one else on his payroll could be trusted.

Which meant a trip to the Red House Ranch to meet with Pilar Mendoza personally. She could be redirected to handle the politician, with a bit of guidance.

He knew exactly how to handle her. Pilar had no friends or family in the US, and nowhere to go.

Baez had been her first lover.

He could persuade her to do anything for him. He was sure of it.

"Cesar, my love," Gabriella came onto the verandah looking as beautiful as always. She was dressed in riding clothes. The form fitting garments accentuated her figure in arousing ways.

"Yes?" he cast a lustful gaze upon his wife, making her blush.

She smiled and lowered her gaze. She cleared the huskiness from her throat. "Will you be home for dinner?

I'm on my way out, but I will stop in the kitchen to speak with the cook."

Cesar enfolded her in his arms and nuzzled her neck. She smelled as good as she looked. He was the envy of every man in Mexico, and for good reason.

"Sadly, no," He stared into her eyes before he gave her a long passionate kiss. "I'm leaving for a few days on business. I'll make it up to you when I return."

She pouted prettily and gave him another kiss. He walked into the house with his arm around her waist. They parted and she headed toward the kitchen.

Cesar watched her go for a few moments longer. He took a deep breath, pivoted, and strode toward his den with renewed purpose.

There was much to prepare before he could leave for Texas.

Cesar had barely reached his desk when doorbell chimes rang deep in the house. He glanced left when recorded video activity from the surveillance camera at his front door caught his attention.

The screen reserved for the surveillance cameras around the villa came to life, as it only did when movement was detected.

The front door was equipped with a wide-angle camera that captured activity along the private driveway inside the wrought iron gate.

Cesar rewound the video and punched play at the point where a diesel pickup truck pulled up. The truck stopped on the raked gravel at the bottom of the broad steps leading to the double door at the front entrance.

A huge blond gringo stepped out from behind the steering wheel and closed the driver's door.

His shirt was tucked tight into the waistband of his pants, giving his torso a triangular shape. Cesar zoomed the view to confirm the unmistakable outline of a handgun shoved into his right hip pocket.

His shirt sleeves were rolled up all the way to his shoulders, the veins in his biceps showing big and obvious. Steroids, probably. No human looked like that naturally.

He walked up the steps to the doorbell and pressed it. Cesar heard the chimes deep inside the house. The man waited patiently for a good long while until the maid opened the front door.

“I’m here to see Cesar Baez,” the man said.

“Do you have an appointment?” the maid asked. “He always tells me when he’s expecting visitors.”

“Tell him I work for a bank in Boston, and we’ve just discovered a private box owned by his father. It contains stock worth more than a million dollars," the man said. "We've had trouble finding him and now we're short of time. If he doesn't claim the money today, it will be turned over to the state of Massachusetts."

"Very well. One moment, sir," she said, turning to walk deeper into the house.

Because of the time delay in the recording, while the maid had climbed the stairs, the man had plenty of time to follow.

When she knocked timidly on Cesar's office door, the man towered right behind her.

Chapter 43

Tuesday, May 31
Austin, Texas

When the cowboy had pulled into a rest area for a short break, Pilar left him and hitched a ride with an older couple headed west. All she'd wanted was to get as far away from Austin as possible.

But as they covered the miles, a new plan began and grew in her mind.

Pilar Inez Mendoza was done with running away from men who sought to use her. If she didn't take that stand now, she'd be running for the rest of her life. José and Baez would never rest until they found her and silenced her forever.

She left the old couple behind and hitched another ride back toward Austin. A long-haul trucker headed east picked her up.

When he stopped to refuel close enough to Austin, Pilar thanked him for the ride and headed toward the toilet. She waited long enough to let him get back on the road before she came outside again.

Away from the convenience store, where her conversation wouldn't be overheard, she found an available picnic table. She slid the cellphone from her pocket and turned it on.

She thumbed through to the screen with José's preprogramed number and pressed the call button.

He'd seemed shocked to hear from her. Which he definitely was. The panic in his voice made her smile.

She gave him her location and he told her to wait for him there.

Afterward, Pilar wandered into the air-conditioned convenience store. Her mouth gaped open, and she clamped it shut to avoid making a fool of herself.

So much food in one place available for anyone who had the money to pay for it was mind-boggling. Americans complained about poverty in their country, but Pilar had never lived amid such riches.

She approached the big coolers with glass doors where soft drinks, beer, and milk were displayed. For a while, she simply stared.

Finally she spied cold bottles of water lined up like little soldiers. She opened the door, feeling the cool air on her face and neck, and pulled the water off the shelf.

On her way to the register, she collected a bag of tortilla chips and a jar of cheese dip. She hadn't eaten in several hours and suddenly realized she was famished.

She placed her items on the counter and reached into her pocket for the cash José had given her back at the motel two lifetimes ago.

The clerk was talking on the phone

and messing with the buttons on a board that somehow both released and restricted the gas at the pumps.

He rang up her purchases and pointed to the total displayed on a small screen. Pilar paid for the food, and he gave her change. He offered a plastic bag for her purchases and returned to his other duties.

As she was filling the bag, Pilar glanced at the small television playing behind the clerk. He had the sound turned off. But the images were startlingly clear. The ticker running across the bottom of the screen reported the headlines.

The images jumped off the screen like a tiny reproduction of the events she'd witnessed.

A stand-up reporter was talking while fire trucks and ambulances and police vehicles filled the background. Bedraggled men and women huddled together behind the crime scene tape, their expensive clothes, hairstyles, and fancy party destroyed.

The camera panned to the burned-out cars in the gravel parking lot behind the kitchen.

Next, the screen showed publicity photos of a smiling Emily Brandon and the man who had been standing beside her. The reporter said both were dead. No further details at this time.

Pilar learned nothing new from the story, which, she supposed, was okay. At least there were no images of her serving the last of the dates or wielding her knife before they both died. Not yet.

But those images would leak out soon enough. Cameras had been placed everywhere around the estate. It was only a matter of time.

Pilar turned and left the store.

She sat on the picnic table with her feet on the bench and tore into her food. She finished the chips and half the cheese dip before José's SUV pulled up.

He lowered the tinted window and waved her over. She hurriedly collected her trash, stuffed it back into the bag, and dropped it into the bin on her way to the SUV.

“I waited for you at the meetup point,” José said aggressively the moment she was seated, and he rolled the big vehicle onto the road.

As if Pilar was the one who had failed.

She clenched her jaw in the dark cabin, feeling the gun in her pocket where it rested against her leg, resisting the urge to scream **Liar!**

“Sorry.”

She’d had a lot of time to think since the little sedan blew up right in front of her.

Only José knew her car, knew where she’d parked, knew how long she’d be gone, knew she would return in a rush to get away.

José planted that car bomb or paid someone else to do it. No other conclusion was possible.

Once her head cleared and she'd figured things out, she realized she hadn't left José stranded at the meetup point, either. Because he was never there.

He'd never intended to go there.

He certainly didn't hang around waiting for her to show up.

José had expected her to be cremated on the spot, just like that young man who tried to move her car.

Until she called him, José must have believed his plan was successful.

Pilar’s heart pounded hard in her chest. She felt her face flush, barely able to control her fiery temper. She glanced at the built-in compass on the dashboard.

“Where are we going?”

“The Red House Ranch. Baez said we can wait there to see what comes out in the news about the Brandon murder. When things cool down, he can place you in California, as planned,” José replied, still defensive, still angry.

“Okay.”

The mention of Baez and her plans to live in California enraged her like a hot poker in her belly.

José was scum.

José didn't take a piss without Baez approving it first.

José would never have tried to kill her without approval from Baez.

"Will Baez be at the ranch? I need to talk to him," she said through gritted teeth as calmly as she could manage.

"About what?"

She flared her nostrils and itched to shoot the bastard right where he sat.

Breathing hard, she forced her rage under control.

For now.

"It's personal," she said coldly. Which, indeed, it was.

José gave her a hard side-eye. "Yes. He'll be there."

They continued traveling in silence for more than an hour. Speeding along the country roads, he put the miles behind them quickly.

"Shouldn't we leave the state of Texas while we still can?" Pilar asked.

The question was a sort of test.

How loyal was José to Baez?

She needed to be certain.

"And go where, exactly? You killed Emily Brandon. Her powerful husband will use all of his resources to find her killer. Public opinion will demand no less," José responded harshly. “Just where do you think you’ll be safe?”

Pilar said nothing. In truth, she had no idea where to go. She didn’t want to spend the rest of her life hiding from hunters who would never, ever give up until they found her and killed her, too.

“Unless you want to return to Mexico, your only alternative is Baez,” José said with slightly more compassion. “He’ll know what to do. Surely you see that.”

She nodded. What José said made sense. Baez was a powerful man. He had placed her in this position, and he **could** get her out of it.

But would he?

Baez had wanted her dead.

She'd survived, proving she had more guts than he'd believed.

Would Baez see her merit now? She could be a valuable member of his cartel.

Or would he kill her anyway?

She thought about the question along the next thirty miles of darkness until she reached the only answer.

Not if she killed him first.

The longer they traveled, the calmer José seemed to get.

Pilar stared through the tinted windows, barely noticing the miles and miles of unoccupied land.

Occasionally, another vehicle would approach and then zoom past.

Pilar checked the clock on the dashboard. They'd been traveling west for a good long while now. She'd seen a couple of signs pointing toward a place called Fort Stockton, which was south of Pecos.

Echo and the Red House Ranch were south of Fort Stockton.

She waited until José made the turn southward. Another hour passed.

She inhaled deeply and cleared her throat, which captured José's attention.

"Pull over," she said. "I need to pee. And stretch my legs. I'm cramping up. It's so damned dry here."

José flashed a deep scowl in her direction, but he slowed the SUV and pulled onto the shoulder. He slid the transmission into park, which allowed the front doors to be unlocked and opened.

“Come on. You’ve got to need a break, too,” she coaxed as she opened her door and slipped onto the gravel shoulder.

Truth was, she wanted him out of the vehicle.

He didn’t shift his weight at all.

She shrugged and said, “Suit yourself.”

She closed her door and strolled twenty yards from the vehicle where she squatted and waited. After a bit, he opened his door and strode a short distance in front of the SUV.

He unzipped and stood with his feet apart and his hands occupied and his gaze into the distance ahead.

Pilar stood up, slipped the gun from her pocket, and ran as silently as possible toward José.

She would only have one chance. She intended to make it count.

The idling engine covered the sound of her quiet footsteps.

José never saw her coming.

When she had a clear sight line to his broad back, she stopped, raised the gun, took aim, and fired.

The first shot hit him squarely between the shoulders.

He turned slightly, an astonished expression on his face, his penis still in his hand.

She fired again.

The second shot caused his knees to buckle. Momentum dragged him to kneel on the ground.

She fired the third shot directly at his head as he fell forward, smashing what was left of his face into the dirt.

Pilar stood watching José's body, breathing hard, heart pounding.

Curiously, José's death didn't make her feel better at all. Her rage was still burning hot in her body, threatening to consume her.

If she'd had the extra gasoline, she'd have set him on fire and joyfully cremated the bastard on the spot.

She approached his body and gave him a good, solid kick. Another. And another. She could have stood there kicking him forever.

Then she bent and searched his pockets.

She found his cell phone and a few hundred dollars in cash. He had a wallet, which probably contained fake ID and phony credit cards. She took that, too.

Pilar stood over him, breathing as normally as she could manage, struggling to calm herself.

She gave José's body two more vicious kicks before she hurried back to the idling SUV.

Pilar climbed into the driver's seat, adjusted the seat and the mirrors and slid the transmission into drive.

She tossed the gun and José's few treasures onto the passenger seat and rolled westward toward Fort Stockton.

The Red House Ranch was still hours away. Which was fine.

Chapter 44

Tuesday, May 31
Pecos, Texas

Flint flew the helicopter expertly, battling exceptionally strong winds from Austin to Marfa and then along US 67 south to Presidio, Texas. Kim kept her jaws clamped shut and controlled her breathing to make sure her stomach contents stayed where they should be.

There was no direct road to travel. The flight path cut at least an hour off the ground travel time. Maybe more.

The last sixty miles of US 67 was mostly flat, open sunbaked land with more cattle than people.

“If your car broke down on this road, you’d wait a long time for someone to find you,” Kim said into the headset.

Flint craned his neck to take a wider look. “Yeah. There’s a bit of traffic. But not enough to depend on, that’s for sure.”

“Have you seen any homes since we left Marfa?”

“Not many. A handful. No gas stations, either. They’d better fill up before they make the trek, for sure,” Flint replied.

When they came closer to Presidio, she began to see a few trees and scrub dotting the tan ground here and there. She counted ten surveillance towers with high-tech cameras used for digital security placed around the perimeter of the town.

"How far do you think they can see with those things?" Flint asked.

"Probably read a license plate from a mile away. Cuts down on border personnel and it's more effective," Kim said. "The cameras record what they see, which can eliminate mistakes, too. The records are stored and can be reviewed later."

"So Cooper could find Elana and Javier on those recordings?"

"In theory, I guess. I mean, first he'd need to narrow the time frame. We don't know when they entered the country. Then he'd have to spend a few hours watching video." Kim shrugged. "None of that's likely to happen. But the task force guys might do it, if we can give them a firm lead."

After a few minutes of silence, Flint asked, "How about a short observation tour of the place before we land?"

"Please."

At this point, Kim noticed, the Rio Grande was narrow enough to cross from one side to the other with little difficulty.

The U.S. Customs and Border Protection Point of Entry was obvious from a significant distance.

Never-ending ultraviolet radiation on border agents and personnel was a serious problem along the border, particularly in places like Presidio where there was no natural shade at the entry point. Various forms of tactical infrastructures had been developed by the US government to manage the various impacts of the ultraviolet border.

A security canopy had been constructed to cover the Presidio station and protect people from the unrelenting sun. A long line of vehicles waited to pass through the checkpoint and cross over the river at the two-lane bridge.

Inside the canopy, an array of surveillance cameras hosting facial recognition software for biometric processing were constantly gathering data on people passing through the checkpoint.

"Seen enough?" Flint asked.

"Yeah, thanks. We need to get on the ground," Kim replied, adding the data from the checkpoint cameras to a long mental list she'd pass along to Gaspar and to Cooper.

Flint circled again and headed north along US 67. As they approached the tiny Presidio Lely International Airport, which was not much more than a nicely paved runway surrounded by dirt, Kim tightened her grip on the armrests.

Flint grinned. "Don't worry. You've held onto your stomach this far. You won't lose it now."

Kim didn't bother to argue. She wasn't afraid of flying. She was properly cautious about all of the possible pitfalls, that's all. No point in explaining that to him again.

He landed the helo as gently as possible, which she appreciated.

Flint began shutting the helo down while Kim reconnected the burner cell phone that connected her with Gaspar via a secure satellite.

He'd sent three texts. The first had been copied to Flint and he probably picked it up earlier.

The first text gave coordinates for the Presidio airport and helipad. They were sitting in the exact spot now.

The second text confirmed the SUV's position in the parking area nearby.

"Gaspar came through. Our SUV is in the lot. I'll meet you there," she said as she removed her headset.

Flint flashed her a thumbs-up.

She settled her sunglasses on her nose, climbed out of the cabin, and set her feet on solid earth. Finally. She exhaled a pent-up breath.

The oppressive Texas heat was supplied by the unrelenting sun blazing almost directly overhead. The forecast high temperature for the day was one hundred ten degrees.

"Dry heat," she reminded herself, as if it mattered. A hundred and ten degrees was hot regardless of the humidity levels.

Kim grabbed her laptop case and left her travel bag in the helo. The extreme heat would probably melt her toiletries, but there was nothing she could do about it.

She headed around the building to the parking lot.

There were a few vehicles parked together. The black SUV waited exactly where Gaspar had said it would be.

There was a security keypad placed under the door handle. Kim punched in the code Gaspar provided and heard the door locks pop open.

She stashed her laptop case in the back and moved to open the driver's door.

The temperature inside had to be hot enough to fry an egg. She touched the leather seat with the palm of her hand and pulled it back fast, as if she'd been burned.

Kim wondered how long a human body would last when confined inside a space so hot. She certainly felt like she was melting.

She leaned inside and started the engine and cranked the air conditioning to full blast, circulating cooler air. She left the front door open for a couple of minutes, allowing some of the heat to escape. She hoped.

Kim climbed into the driver's seat, which felt hot on her ass even through her pants.

Whoever delivered the SUV had been a much larger person. She adjusted the seat and the mirrors.

She closed the door and pointed the cool air vent directly at her face.

She retrieved the phone and read the third text from Gaspar again.

Martin Weber's residential address. He'd also included Weber's duty schedule. She punched Weber's address into the GPS system. A ten-minute drive, according to the maps.

"Weber is working the early shift today. Gets off at three. We have time for lunch before we connect with him," Kim said when Flint opened the passenger door and joined her.

“Fine by me.” He settled into his seat.

When he touched the hot metal of his seatbelt buckle, he yelped and dropped it back into the retractor.

“How do people live out here? It’s impossible to breathe the air. It burns your windpipe all the way down to your lungs,” Flint said, sucking on his burned thumb.

“Can’t argue with you there.” Kim hadn’t buckled up either and for the same reasons. “Let’s find a burger somewhere that has air conditioning. We’ll leave the SUV running while we eat. Maybe it’ll cool off in less than an hour.”

"Sounds like a solid plan," Flint said, still examining his sore digit.

She rolled the SUV out of the parking lot and onto the pavement on US 67 headed south to the center of town.

Heat radiated from the pavement, shimmering above the blacktop. Even wearing polarized sunglasses, the shimmer distorted her view.

The first eatery they found was a fast-food joint.

"How about this?" Flint said, sticking his thumb toward the giant neon burger advertising a drive through option. "We can't get a beer, but we can eat without leaving the cool air again."

“I don’t drink at lunch when I’m working, but I would like to find a couple of locals to question. That parking lot looks deserted, though,” Kim said as she drove past.

“What are you going to ask the locals? ‘Seen any killers lately?’” Flint teased.

Kim nodded. “Yep. That’s my opener. We should have this case wrapped up before lunch.”

Chapter 45

Tuesday, May 31
Pecos, Texas

“This town is pretty small. I’ll bet everyone knows everyone else’s business around here,” Flint said.

“I’m counting on that, actually. With luck, anybody new who shows up will stick out, too,” Kim replied.

Flint cast a side-eye her way. “Anybody like Reacher, you mean?”

“Possibly.” She shook her head. “Gaspar said he was traveling south. He could be here. But I’m thinking he’s not here now.”

"Why?"

She shrugged. "Just a hunch, really. But Cooper didn't send me to Presidio. He would have, if he'd thought Reacher was around, or likely to be around. And Cooper has a lot of resources at his disposal. He's rarely wrong where Reacher is concerned."

"Where is Cooper anyway?"

"Good question," Kim replied. "On our last call, he seemed more secretive than usual, if that's even possible."

"You think he's got a lead on Reacher?" Flint asked.

Kim considered the question. Cooper told her that Reacher had fallen off his radar. Maybe he had located Reacher again. It was certainly possible.

Cooper also said he was using himself as bait. He thought Reacher would come to him, under the right circumstances. He'd refused to tell Kim what those circumstances were.

The border crossing was straight ahead, but there was a long line of traffic waiting to pass through the checkpoint. Border guards would be too busy to talk while processing vehicles passing through on both sides. Perhaps traffic would slow down a bit later.

She glanced at the clock on the dashboard. Martin Weber's shift wouldn't end for a while yet, either.

"I saw a cantina as we drove through town. Looked like it was still open. That okay with you?"

"Yeah, sure."

She turned into a parking lot, drove around the back and out again, headed north. The cantina was on the north side of the main street. There were three old pickup trucks and a couple of ancient cars parked in the side lot.

The pickups were probably customers. The cars likely belonged to the cantina staff. She pulled the SUV into an open spot near the front entrance.

"Wish we could leave the AC running while we're inside the cantina, but there's probably an experienced car thief within running distance," she said, glancing at the empty sidewalks. "We don't need a broken window and a stolen SUV to deal with."

"And I didn't see a single car rental or taxi in the whole town," Flint said, nodding.

She shut the engine down, opened the door, and stepped out. The heat hit her like a steelyard furnace. It was so intense she could barely catch her breath.

Flint climbed out and joined her. Kim pressed the lock button on the key fob and slipped it into her pocket.

She pulled her sunglasses off and dropped them into another pocket. She opened the cantina door and smacked into a solid wall of dimly lit cold air.

The temperature change was a physical jolt that raised gooseflesh on her arms.

She stood inside the door for a couple of minutes to let her eyes adjust. There was a register next to the door and a tired waitress sitting sideways on a counter stool.

Three tables were occupied. Two men seated across from each other at two of the tables glanced up briefly when Kim and Flint walked in and then returned to their meals, as if she wasn't particularly interesting.

The third table was occupied by a single man eating alone who didn't seem to notice Kim and Flint at all.

There were no women in the place except the waitress and now Kim. Maybe the cook. Kim couldn't see into the kitchen.

She walked toward the occupied tables and sat close enough to overhear conversations. Flint pulled out a chair and sat across from her.

The waitress brought a pitcher of water, no ice, two sticky plastic menus, and a pad with a fountain pen. She poured the water into cloudy plastic glasses and pulled a couple of straws from the pocket of her apron. Then she stood poised to write down their orders.

"What's good here?" Flint asked.

She shrugged. "Locals like chicken with rice and beans mostly. But we're out. Served the last order ten minutes ago."

After a quick glance at the menu, they ordered chips and salsa and guacamole and taco salads. It was too hot outside to think about warm food.

A white man about sixty wearing jeans and boots and a white short sleeved shirt was finishing his meal. His face was weathered leathery and as brown as cowhide.

He clicked his tongue and said, "Too bad about the chicken. Best thing on the menu."

Flint nodded. "Yeah, I thought that might be the case."

"You live here in Presidio?" Kim asked with a smile.

“All my life. Just like my daddy before me and his daddy before him,” he replied. “Born here. Probably die here, too.”

“What kind of work do you do?” Flint asked.

“Ranching. Place just up the road a ways. You drove past it if you came in on 67.” He reached his big paw toward Flint. “Alan Macomber the third. People around here call me Mac.”

“Flint,” he replied, shaking the man’s hand. He nodded toward Kim. “That’s Otto.”

Mac grinned and dipped his head. “Otto’s a funny name for a woman.”

"It is," she replied pleasantly but without elaboration. "Everybody in here local residents?"

Mac nodded. "Yeah. We don't get a lot of visitors. Family, mostly, of folks who live here. You two don't look like you're related to anybody lives here."

"Houston," Flint volunteered.

"The only visitors we get who aren't family are border agents of one kind or another. Or politicians and reporters," Mac said pleasantly enough while chewing on a wooden toothpick protruding from his lips. "The illegals don't hang around long enough to visit. They're just passing through."

"Do you get a lot of illegal migrants crossing here?" Flint asked.

"Not as many as some places, and more than some others, I guess," Mac nodded. "This is a border town. People been crossing back and forth for more than a hundred years, I reckon."

"What about Ojinaga? People come to visit from over there?" Kim asked.

"All the time. Nice people. We'd have a harder time around here than we already do if we couldn't rely on those folks," Mac said.

"How do they help you out?" Flint asked.

"Lots of ways, really. There's nothing between us but the river. If we have a power outage, we can get power from Ojinaga," Mac warmed to his subject. “Many Presidio folks have family in Ojinaga. They visit back and forth. It’s a nice place. Been there plenty of times myself.”

Kim said, “Ojinaga is a larger city than Presidio, so I imagine it’s got more to offer in the way of nightlife and jobs.”

Mac nodded. “It does. And good restaurants, too. Some of the best Mexican seafood you’ll ever find. You want recommendations?”

Kim smiled and shook her head. “Not today, I’m afraid. We won’t be in town long enough to enjoy whatever Ojinaga has to offer.”

Mac cocked his head. “You know, I had a similar conversation a couple of days ago with another guy who came in here asking about Ojinaga. Big dude. Looked like some kind of giant compared to most of us."

"Yeah?" Kim's heart rate picked up. "Did he give you his name?"

"He did. Can't recall it right off the top of my head. Kind of an odd name. Jack something, I think?" Mac said thoughtfully, working the toothpick around with his lips. "He the one you're looking for?"

Flint smiled.

Kim said nothing.

Mac gave Kim a half wink. "It's obvious you're looking for someone. Otherwise, why would you be here? It's not like Presidio's got a Disneyland or anything."

"Right," Kim replied. "He could have been one of the ones we're looking for. Jack Reacher. Was that his name?"

Mac cackled a loud laugh. "Yep. That's it. Damned unusual name, I said when he told me. No wonder I couldn't remember it."

"Is he still in Presidio now?"

"Doubtful," Mac chewed the toothpick and pushed it around with his lips from one side of his mouth to the other like an ex-smoker. "He said he was headed to Ojinaga. Doesn't take too long to get there from here. Likely he went through there the same day I talked to him, far as I know."

"Did he say why he was going to Ojinaga?"

"Said he was looking for a guy. Just like you are. Didn't say the guy's name," Mac said, chewing the toothpick slowly. "Reacher in some kind of trouble?"

"Not that we know of," Kim replied. She found her cell phone and pulled up the photo of Elana and Javier. "Have you seen this couple around at all?"

Mac accepted the phone, pulled out a pair of readers and slipped them onto his nose. He studied the photo a while. Then he shook his head and handed it back.

"Sorry. They look like a nice couple, though. Who are they?"

"Elana Fernandez and Javier Garcia," Kim said. "They crossed over from Ojinaga through the border checkpoint here."

"When was that?" he asked.

"Within the past month. We can't pin it down more than that," Kim replied.

Mac shook his head again and worked the toothpick. "You can see there's a line at the border crossing all the time. If they simply drove through, nobody around here would have seen them except the border guards."

The waitress walked up with their food and placed it on the table.

"How about you, Frieda? You ever seen these two kids?" Mac said, handing her the phone.

Chapter 46

Tuesday, May 31
Pecos, Texas

Freda took Kim's phone and squinted at the faces. "Was she pregnant? The woman? There was a couple who came in about a week or so ago. She looked like she was about to deliver on the spot. She wasn't feeling well. He seemed jumpy, like he was worried about something. Could've been these two."

"Did they say anything about where they'd come from or where they were going?" Kim asked.

Freda shook her head and handed the phone to Kim. “They stayed about half an hour. He ate the chicken and rice and beans. She didn’t eat anything. Then they left.”

“Were they driving? Alone?”

“Probably. But I didn’t see where they went after they stepped outside. We don’t have any windows in here,” Freda said.

“How’d they pay the bill?” Flint asked.

“Most folks pay with cash,” Freda said. “US money only. We don’t take pesos anymore.”

Kim cocked her head. “You said he was jumpy. What made you think so?”

"That's why I remember the couple. She went straight to the restroom, as if she was sick. He sat facing the door. His leg bounced the whole time he was at the table. Sat over there," Freda tilted her head toward a table in the darkest corner. "That table's a little unsteady. I had to warn him that it might collapse if he kept bouncing it around like that."

"Did they speak English?" Flint wanted to know.

"Not to me. Not between themselves. But sure. Most folks do," Freda said with a shrug as she turned to deal with the other tables.

Mac pushed his chair back. "I need to get going, too. Can I help you folks with anything else?"

"If you don't mind," Kim nodded, as she swiped through the photos on her phone until she found what she was looking for. "Is this the man you were talking about earlier? The big guy?"

She handed him the phone again. He put his glasses back on to look at the photo of Reacher. It was an old photo. His army headshot taken more than fifteen years ago. She'd cropped out the uniform so the photo showed only his face.

Mac worked the toothpick and frowned at the photo for a bit. "Hard to say. I guess it could be him. The guy was older. More worn out, kinda. Possibly could have been him."

"Thanks," Kim said, retrieving the phone and swiping through the photos until she found the one she wanted. "One more, if you would be so kind. Do you know this fellow?"

"Yeah," Mac said, nodding, and then returning the phone. "I've seen him around recently. Border patrol, isn't he? Weber, I think he said his name was."

"National Guard. But yeah. Helping out at the border," Kim replied, accepting the phone and clicking the screen off. "Where'd you see him?"

"Right here. He's been in the cantina a few times. This is about the only decent place to eat in town, to be honest," Mac replied, removing the readers and folding them again. He slipped the glasses into his shirt pocket. “I think he works days. Which means he’ll be getting off soon. Might even come in for an early supper. This place has the best air conditioning of all the eating places, too. Most folks come in just for that.”

Kim and Flint thanked him for the help as he got up to leave.

“Glad to do it,” he said, waving on his way out.

Flint fell onto his food like a hungry wolf. Kim watched Mac’s broad back as he walked into the blazing sunshine on the other side of the heavy front door. She picked up her phone, found Martin Weber’s cell number and texted him to meet them at the cantina after work.

"Copy that," he texted back. Kim smiled.

"How'd you get his personal cell number?" Flint asked. "From your sister?"

"Not a chance," Kim replied swiftly.

Asking Sunny for Weber's details would imply way more than Kim wanted her to know. Plenty of time to tell Sunny about the meeting afterward. Assuming it went well.

"You can eat and think at the same time, you know," Flint said after he'd swallowed a big forkful of the taco salad.

Kim nodded. Mac had been right about the food. It was uniformly great. The guacamole was some of the best she had ever eaten, and the salsa was hot enough to set her mouth on fire. Exactly the way she liked it.

Between mouthfuls, Flint said, "So what does the National Guard do here, anyway? I mean, Weber's not a trained border agent, right?"

"I'm not sure exactly what his job is. The Guard fills in at the border crossing if needed," Kim replied. "But it's mostly providing infrastructure, operational and aerial support, information and detection support for the trained law enforcement officers."

"Makes sense. The law on these border crossings is complicated and it seems to change frequently. It's gotta be hard to keep up, even for the full timers," Flint said. "How long has Weber been deployed down here?"

"Almost six months, according to my sister." Kim licked the cheese from her fingers and wiped them with the napkin. A big gulp of water helped with the fire in her mouth. "They're shorthanded. So he's been out in the field more than originally planned."

"Where does he live? I mean, there's no military base close by, is there?" Flint asked.

"Government contracted housing. He'd be in a hotel except there aren't any beds available at the local places. So he's sharing a rental house with three other guardsmen," Kim said. She glanced at the big clock on the wall above the door. "It's after three o'clock. He'll be here shortly."

Flint had finished his food. He wiped his hands and tossed the crumpled napkin into his plate. "Elana said she and Javier came through the Presidio border crossing. Freda says they were here in the cantina, so we've confirmed that they came across somehow. Mac says Reacher was here, too. How do you think all this fits together?"

Kim shook her head slowly. "I'm not sure it does. But I suspect Elana Fernandez might be the thread we can pull to unravel the situation. She knows a lot more than she's told us."

"For sure."

The front door of the cantina opened allowing a bright rectangle of blinding sunlight to enter the cool, comfortable darkness inside. A group of six men, backlit shadows, strolled inside and closed the door behind them.

After the light was extinguished, Kim saw nothing but spots for a moment. She blinked a few times to clear her vision.

The men had moved deeper into the cantina and pulled a couple of tables together in the back. They settled down and Freda took their orders, which was when Weber left the group to join Kim and Flint.

“Kim Otto?” he said, extending his hand to shake. When she nodded, he said, “I’d have known you anywhere. You look exactly like Sunny. I’m Martin Weber.”

Given her conflicted feelings for her sister, Kim simply nodded toward her companion.

“This is Michael Flint.”

“Martin Weber,” he said to Flint as he pulled out a chair and sat between them. “Sorry. I must smell like an old goat. It’s been another long, hot day patrolling out in the field. No chance to shower before we came over here.”

“Why were you out in the field?” Flint asked. “Thought you guys were mostly here for support functions?”

Freda came by with a tall glass of water and handed it to Weber on her way to his buddies. He thanked her for it and downed it in one long gulp.

“I don’t think I’ve ever been as thirsty in my life before I came to Presidio,” Weber said. “Freda will be bringing my food soon. Why was I out in the field? Just luck of the draw. They’re shorthanded here. We all go where we’re sent, you know?”

Flint nodded, as if the answer satisfied his curiosity. Maybe it did.

“How can I help?”

Chapter 47

Monday, May 30
Presidio, Texas

“We’re not exactly sure,” Kim replied, pulling the photos of Elana and Javier up on her phone. “We’re looking for information on three people. These two,” she swiped to the next photo, “and this guy. Have you ever seen them before?”

“I see a lot of people every day and I’ve been here for a while now. But I’ll try.” Weber took the phone and studied the two photos.

He tapped Reacher’s picture with his index finger. “Maybe this guy. Was he here in the cantina recently? He sorta looks familiar. But I don't think I talked to him. Don't remember the conversation, if I did."

Kim nodded. "What about the young couple?"

Weber shook his head slowly. "Don't take this the wrong way, but they look like hundreds of attractive Latinos I've seen around here. From just this headshot, they don't jump out at me. Anything special about them that would help me recall?"

"She's pregnant," Kim said.

Weber shook his head. "A lot of the ones I see are pregnant. What are their names? If I checked them through, I'd have read their passports. I've got a better memory for names than faces. Especially if they're traveling together."

"Elana Fernandez and Javier Garcia," Kim replied.

"Pretty common names," Weber said without looking up from the photo. "You understand that I don't work the point of entry station that much? Just fill in when they're shorthanded. Usually at night, mid-week. I don't have a regular post or anything."

"Are there specific officers assigned to the checkpoint stations? Or do they rotate?" Kim asked.

"There's a duty roster. The permanent staffing rotates. Guardsmen fill in where needed,"

Weber explained. “Why are you asking me about all of this? You could just pull the intel off the computer systems, couldn’t you?”

“Fair question. If we pull the records, we’ll put a big flag on the issue. Whoever’s involved is likely to go underground for a while. We want to avoid all that.” Kim paused a moment, wondering how much she could trust Martin Weber, and then made her decision. “Have you heard about the FBI’s Double Death Task Force?”

“We’ve been briefed.” Weber sat back in his chair. “And of course, I’ve heard the gossip. There’s not a lot of entertainment around here. Gossip is about all we have to fill the downtime. That, and poker.”

Flint said, “Tell us the gossip.”

Weber tilted his head. “That’s what the other guy was asking when he was in here.”

“What other guy? You mean Reacher?” Kim asked, showing him the photo again.

“Is that his name? Yeah. He was sitting here with Mac Macomber. Shooting the breeze, you know? He asked if anybody had heard about the situation,” Weber said. “Mac said no. But we were over there, at our usual table, playing poker. Mac told him we might know.”

“How did that go?” Kim asked. “Any specific details you can remember would help.”

Weber closed his eyes to think back.

When he opened them, he said, “He wanted to know whether the Mexican gangs around here were torching homes.”

“Gangs?” Flint asked.

Weber nodded. “He said a friend of his had died in an arson fire and he thought one of the gangs was responsible.”

“Did he say which gang?” Kim asked.

Weber shrugged and filled his water glass and gulped it down again.

“I don’t think he knew. Or if he did, he didn’t say. There are quite a few gangs, anyway. Some are pretty hard-core. We think they’re responsible for thousands of fentanyl deaths. We told him what we knew, but I had the impression he was looking for something or someone specific," Weber said. "He didn't say who or what. He just asked about the arson."

"Nobody had any intel to offer?" Flint asked.

Weber shook his head. Freda walked past with a big flat tray filled with food. His nose lifted to follow the aroma trail behind her.

"The biggest cartel around here is run by the Baez brothers since their old man died. The youngest, Cesar Baez, owns about half of Ojinaga. But he's out of the family business, they say. Legit contractor now, he claims. Lots of business here in the states. Sends workers over frequently. Do you mind?" Weber said, jerking a thumb in the direction of his food and then getting up to follow his meal. "See you back in Michigan in a few weeks, Kim. Call me if I can be of further service. Sorry I couldn't help more."

"Thanks." Kim took a hard look at his companions. Five men dressed in jeans and t-shirts, wearing work boots.

Three of the five were merely tan from recent hours in the sun.

Two others sported the leathery skin she'd seen on the locals. The kind that was produced by years in the hot, arid weather.

“Now what?” Flint had been eating during the conversation. He’d made short work of more than half the food.

Kim shrugged and hurried to finish her share. “If Elana and Javier came through the port of entry, how did they do it?”

“Fake passports? Fake visas?” Flint said, crunching the last of the ice left in his glass.

“Not likely.” She cocked her head, thinking things through. “Two people with no money and no connections would have a hard time getting counterfeits good enough to pass through the sophisticated equipment we have now for detecting them.”

"We only have Elana's word for it that they went through the entry point. Maybe there's a place where the Rio Grande is shallow enough to walk across. With Javier helping her, she could have managed it," Flint said, finishing the last of the chips crumbled in the bottom of the basket.

"And then what? Walk for miles, avoiding detection of the border guards on quad bikes or horses? Hide her pregnant self behind the mesquite, running from one bush to another for miles in this heat?" Kim shook her head. "There's a simpler answer. You know Occam's Razor."

"Entities should not be multiplied beyond necessity," Flint recited. "Or the simplest answer is usually correct."

“So the simple answer is to believe Elana when she said they came through the checkpoint. If they did, they had excellent counterfeit documents and we should be able to find the records almost instantly. Or…”

Flint nodded like a good student paying attention. “Or there’s a corrupt border patrol officer facilitating illegal entry by letting them cross without proper documents. Why would he do that?”

“Money, usually,” Kim shrugged. “Probably wouldn’t take as much as we think, either. People around here don’t have vast fortunes. A few thousand dollars would go a long way toward improving a local family’s quality of life.”

"You think Javier Garcia's thwarted murder at the Redstone funeral is related to the Maria Greer arson and by extension, to the Double Death Task Force cases," Flint said, nodding slowly, trying the idea on, looking for holes in her theory.

"More importantly for my purposes is that Reacher seems to believe there's a connection."

"We could follow him to Ojinaga," Flint offered a bit half-heartedly.

She shook her head. "I'm not sure he ever went there. Or if he did, whether he's still there. Trailing around after him won't work. I've been doing that for seven months now. I need a better plan of attack."

Kim looked toward Weber, who had rejoined his colleagues with gusto. He'd be finished eating soon. She didn't want to cut him from that herd, alerting the gossip mongers to her suspicions.

One of Weber's companions put some money in the jukebox and chose a half dozen ear-splitting tunes to accompany their meal. The music made it impossible to think, let alone talk.

"Can you pay the bill? I need to make a couple of phone calls. I'll meet you outside," she said, finishing off her food. "Watch Weber and his crew. If any of them try to leave by the back door, call me."

"I'm not chasing anybody down on foot in that heat," Flint nodded toward Weber's table. "Not likely one of these guys is passing illegals through the checkpoint anyway, is it? USBP is probably the best paying job in Presidio. Any halfway decent agent would know the penalties. Weber's group doesn't look like men who would take those risks. They're too relaxed, for one thing."

"The pressure must be overwhelming, too. Whoever hired him to look the other way will kill him if he stops passing illegals through. On the other hand, if Uncle Sam catches him, he's going to prison for the rest of his life. Or worse," She pushed back from the table preparing to stand. "With any luck, he's ready to make a deal. But first, we need to identify him."

Chapter 48

Monday, May 30
Presidio, Texas

On her way to the SUV, Kim scanned the immediate vicinity for threats, as she routinely did everywhere. No one wandered the streets. Perhaps there were lurkers in the shadows, seeking respite from the blazing sun. If so, they were blocked from view.

She noticed dark clouds to the west. Maybe Presidio would get a break in the weather. The place could use some rain.

Kim climbed into the SUV and flipped the air conditioning up to full blast.

She was well positioned to see anyone who came through the front door of the cantina.

She used her cell phone to text Weber. **I need to talk to you alone. Black SUV parked out front.**

After a bit, he replied. **Copy that**.

The cantina door opened, and Weber emerged from the dark interior. He cleared the door and reached into his shirt pocket for sunglasses.

As he slipped them onto his face, a deafening noise that could only be two gunshots rang out nearby.

The shots went wide of Weber and hit a few feet from the cantina's heavy door.

Stucco splinters flew off slashing Weber's bare left arm. Blood trailed down to his hand, even as he dropped low. He ran to the driver's side of the SUV and crouched behind the engine block.

The shooter moved from the concealing shadows to fire off two more rounds, missing the moving target completely.

Kim drew her weapon, got off a couple of defensive shots, and slid to the ground next to Weber. "Are you armed?"

"Usually, but not at the moment," he said, shaking his head. "This SUV armored?"

"Didn't think we'd need it. Stay behind the engine block and you should be okay," Kim replied, peering in the direction of the gunshots.

Observations rushed through her head, in no particular order.

For some reason, the shooter didn't fire again. Maybe he needed to reload.

No one came outside from the cantina. Why?

The gunshots were loud enough to be heard. That damned jukebox.

"He's tucked away between the cantina and the building next door. What's behind there?"

"A gravel parking lot. Trash dumpsters. No residential housing," Weber replied.

"So he's probably got a vehicle ready for a quick escape. He'll try again," Kim said as she inched forward, preparing to rush the shooter.

Assuming he was still there.

Weber grabbed her arm. "Get yourself hurt on my account and your sister will never forgive me."

She grinned. "Are you kidding? Sunny would give you a medal. We're not exactly close."

"Let's not test your opinion, okay?" he said seriously.

"He knows you're unarmed because you didn't shoot back or try to come after him. He'll try again," she explained rapidly. "Stay down until I signal. Flint will show up in a moment. We've got it under control."

"Copy that," he said.

Kim said nothing more as she dashed from her position behind the SUV. Flint emerged from the cantina at the same time.

The shooter tried to hit her and missed.

She didn't shoot back. If he knew Weber wasn't armed, maybe he thought she was unarmed, too.

Kim flattened her back against the cantina wall and, weapon ready, inched toward the shooter's position at the corner of the building.

She was almost there when Weber stood up and yelled, "Look out!"

The shooter had inched closer to the opening and extended his weapon.

He shot directly at Weber. This time, he got lucky. Weber went down.

Flint shot twice to draw the man's fire.

The shooter stepped out to put Flint down.

Kim fired three rounds in response. All three hit the target. The shooter fell to the ground.

The gunfire brought two of Weber's companions running through the cantina's front door, weapons drawn.

Three more of Weber's group must have run out the back door. They came around between the buildings, running full out, weapons ready.

A moment ago, Kim had been defending alone. Now the shooter was encircled by men with guns.

But they were too late. The shooter was already dead.

“What’s your name?” Kim said to one of Weber’s guys, willing the adrenaline surging through her system to slow.

“Ralph. Oscar Ralph,” he replied.

“You know this guy?” Kim asked him when Flint rolled the body over onto its back.

“Pablo Gomez. CBP Officer. Meaning he’s one of the full-time border guards here.”

Kim snapped a few photos of his face and quickly collected fingerprints on her phone app. She sent them to her secure server and returned her phone to her pocket.

"Any idea why he's shooting at Weber?" Kim asked.

"They'd had a few exchanges lately. Weber reported him a couple of weeks ago. Gomez didn't appreciate it. They had words," Ralph said.

"Pretty extreme to shoot the guy for something as minor as a workplace dispute."

"Maybe he just wanted Weber out of the way. If he'd been wounded, he'd be sent home."

"I see," Kim nodded. "When was Gomez suspended?"

"Yesterday."

"He lives here in Presidio, right? Any family?" she asked.

"He rents a room from one of the widows in town." Ralph shrugged. "As far as I know, his wife and kids and the rest of his family lives in Ojinaga."

Kim took a deep breath, reached into her pocket, and pulled out a business card. She handed it to Ralph. "Okay. Follow whatever your protocols are now related to death of an officer. Call me if you need statements or anything like that."

Ralph examined the card. "FBI? Guess we're on the same team here. We can find you if we need to."

He didn't ask for her weapon and she didn't offer it.

Kim holstered her pistol and returned to the SUV with Flint.

Weber was seated on the dirt holding his left arm. One of Weber's men was kneeling near him when Kim approached.

"The bullet just grazed my arm," he said to Kim.

Flint added, "He's okay. He'll need some first aid. Maybe a few stitches. Might miss a couple of days work."

"Okay."

"What about the other guy?"

"Ralph says his name is Pablo Gomez," Kim replied.

Weber's eyebrows arched and his nostrils flared. "Are you kidding me? That crazy bastard. What the hell is he doing shooting at me?"

"Unfortunately, we can't ask him. He's dead." Kim replied.

"Help me up, will you? I want to see him," Weber said, struggling to his feet while holding his left arm with his right hand. He did it more gracefully than Kim would have.

"We can't get stuck here. You can file the reports and answer questions about what happened," Kim said to Weber while handing the key fob to Flint. She gave Weber her card. "Call me if you need anything from me. I'll report to my boss."

"We need to get going." Flint glanced at the dark clouds, climbed into the SUV, and started the air conditioning again.

Weber's colleagues had moved over to deal with Gomez. Weber stood kicking the dirt, looking down. "I'm sorry I got you into this. Gomez was mad as the devil when I reported his conduct. He got a two-day suspension. I thought that was the end of it."

"What did he do, exactly?"

Weber shook his head. "What I saw was a few times when he didn't check the paperwork as closely as he should have. He was territorial about it and cussed me out when I objected. It wasn't all the time. Just now and then."

"Why didn't he do the job properly?"

Weber shrugged. “I don’t know. He’s been on the border for years. He knows what to do. I mean, if we can keep one undocumented person out, that’s one less we need to rescue. Gomez didn’t see it my way.”

“How’d the matter come to a head, then?” Kim said.

“A van full of Mexican citizens were coming through the other night. Construction workers, headed north. I asked for the paperwork and the one in the passenger seat handed it to me. While I was going through the documents, Gomez came over with a flat out lie and took the job away from me.”

“What did he say?”

Chapter 49

Monday, May 30
Presidio, Texas

"Gomez said the boss wanted to see me. He demanded the paperwork and sent me over to the supervisor," Weber explained. "Only when I got there, the boss didn't have any idea what Gomez was talking about. I was tired and ticked off and I reported what Gomez had done because he'd wasted my time and made me look like a fool."

Kim nodded. "And then what?"

"The supervisor took my complaint. He investigated. Gomez got suspended for wasting resources. That was it," Weber said. "I'd cooled off by then. Thought he had, too."

"Guess not," Kim replied thoughtfully.

Gomez was dead because he'd tried to shoot a member of the National Guard deployed to assist border personnel. The situation made no sense. Something else was going on here.

"You're not going to get in any hot water over this, are you?" Weber asked with real concern. "This is my problem, not yours."

Kim shrugged. "It's my problem now, too. I'm the one who shot the guy."

Weber's frown deepened, but he didn't argue.

“Flying into Presidio, we noticed the high-tech surveillance towers installed around the town. Ten of them. Seems like a lot of expense for such a small place,” she said. “What’s the illegal crossing situation like here?”

“We have our share of coyotes, criminals, drug mules, and all the trouble that comes along with them,” Weber replied. “But mostly, we get normal people who just want to live peacefully in the US.”

“And do you see a significant number of migrants like that?”

“Thousands. The numbers are overwhelming. Presidio is no better or worse than any of the other places where people can cross over unseen in the dark," Weber said, nodding wearily.

"How do you deal with it?"

"If they're lucky, we catch them, send them back on a bus before they die of exposure trying to make it further inland. But many of them return again," Weber said, wiping a palm across his tired face. "It's like a deadly game of wack-a-mole. Tempers are short. We're exhausted and often heartbroken. How many dead families can we accept before we fix this?"

Kim nodded in sympathy. "Once they come across, are there any stash houses in Presidio where they can rest and get supplies before they move on?"

"No. If we find them in a stash house, we clear them out, and shut the house down," Weber replied, shaking his head. "I've heard about a place east of here, but it's just gossip, really."

"Where is this place?"

"Echo County. An old Texas family has a ranch. Rumor is that coyotes pay to stash illegals for a day or two. But every time the place is raided, there's no illegals there," Weber said, shaking his head. "Wack-a-mole. Like I said."

A shot of electricity ran through her spine like she'd been tapped with a cattle prod when he mentioned Echo County. "You know the name of the place?"

"They call it Red House Ranch. Because the ranch house is painted red," Weber said. "But that might not be the name. Could be just the way they describe it among themselves."

"Okay. We'll follow up." Kim nodded. "Get your arm checked. Last thing you need is an infection."

"Yeah," he said, not like he meant it.

A siren sounded in the distance, rapidly approaching.

"Look, don't worry. Take care of yourself. Make a full report. Tell them everything. Don't feel like you have to hide anything to protect anyone, including me. I'll do the same. Let the bosses sort things out." Kim gave him a solid clap on his good arm. "See you back in Michigan."

Weber nodded, still troubled, and headed toward the others waiting for law enforcement to arrive.

Kim climbed into the SUV with Flint.

She placed a call to Cooper on his dedicated phone.

She would give him a full report. The sooner he took care of erasing her involvement in the Gomez situation, the better.

Kim said, “Next time, Gaspar should get us an armored vehicle.”

“I’ll be sure to make a note of it,” Flint replied, backing the SUV away from the cantina and heading toward the helicopter.

Cooper didn’t answer. Briefly, she wondered why. He was up to something and not knowing what it was made her nervous.

When an FBI agent who was unauthorized but hanging around asking questions, killed a border patrol officer, and left the scene before checking in with the locals, there would be plenty of tricky details Cooper would need to handle to avoid the blowback.

Kim left a detailed message about the Gomez shooting.

Too bad she couldn't see his face when he got **that** message.

Cooper wouldn't be happy about her report, but she was absolutely confident he'd be apoplectic if she hung around to give official statements of any kind to anybody for any reason whatsoever.

Kim had barely finished her voicemail message when Gaspar returned her call. She located his cell phone. "What's up, Chico?"

"Reacher called me again," Gaspar replied in a disgruntled tone. "It's like we're becoming BFFs or something."

Kim frowned. "He could save himself some time and call me."

"Yeah, but given your lack of privacy, that would be like calling a straight line to Cooper. Reacher's not gonna do that. When he's ready to talk to Cooper, he'll do it directly," Gaspar said, moving on. "Flint there with you? I'd like to say all of this just once."

She put the call on speaker.

Flint said, “I’m here. What’s going on?”

“Reacher gave me a name. Told me to gather whatever intel I can find. He thinks this guy is behind the Maria Greer murder.”

“What’s the name?” Kim asked.

“Cesar Baez. Either one of you heard of him?”

“Weber said he had been tied to the Baez cartel, but he now runs a legitimate construction business. Has projects going inside the US and sends his workers across the border at Presidio,” Kim replied. “Wouldn’t think he’d want to compromise all of that.”

"Yeah, well, Weber's got half the story correct. The legal half," Gaspar said absently as if he were scanning materials onscreen. Which he probably was.

Flint grimaced. "What's the rest of the story?"

"According to Homeland Security, the Baez Cartel business goes way back. Drug trafficking, human trafficking, and prostitution, mostly. The Capo, Diego Baez, was an old-fashioned gangster. He ruled with an iron hand," Gaspar explained while clicking the keys on his keyboard and scanning and mumbling the salient points. "He died a few years ago and the cartel business seems to have fragmented since then."

"Fragmented how?" Flint asked, slowing behind a farm truck traveling ahead.

"Speculation in the reports I'm reading says the old man wanted his sons to take the business legit after he died. There were three sons. The two older ones didn't agree with their father. They're still running drugs and human trafficking across the border and prostitution inside Mexico and protection rackets and who knows what else," Gaspar said, still clacking those keys. "Whatever they can get away with."

"And Cesar? What about him?" Kim asked.

"He's the youngest son. Went to Harvard. Married an American from

Boston. Gabriella Adams. Got a few kids. Lives in a palatial villa in Ojinaga," Gaspar replied. "Looks like there's more money in the construction business than his tax returns probably reflect."

Flint increased his speed now that they'd traveled past the city limits. "We need to get going. There's some dark clouds moving this way. Flying a helicopter through a storm is not a lot of fun."

"Where is Reacher now?" Kim asked, thinking things through. "Possible he's on his way to Ojinaga to deal with Baez?"

"I asked," Gaspar replied before he disconnected. "Reacher said nothing."

Chapter 50

Tuesday, May 31
Near Echo, Texas

As he regained consciousness, Cesar Baez opened one swollen eye. His right eye was pressed closed by the pressure of the side of his head resting against the gravel. He had no idea what time it was or how long he'd been lying in the dirt.

Cesar tried to remember exactly what had happened after the big man entered his office back in Ojinaga, but he could not.

Cesar closed his eye again and tried to concentrate. His mind felt like his son's kaleidoscope, fractured shapes and colors constantly reforming themselves. A picture of the big man refused to complete itself in his mind's eye.

Cesar saw only fragments out of order, moving from one to the next.

The man was huge.

And unnaturally calm.

And angry.

And violent.

He'd said his name was Rutherford B. Hayes. Which was a lie, of course.

Hayes said he would come after Cesar's family. Lots of accidents, one after another, he'd said. "You'll never know when the next one is coming. It'll drive you crazy."

He'd thrown a priceless heirloom, an antique crystal pitcher filled with iced tea, over the balcony. It shattered into a million pieces on the patio stones below.

Hayes threatened to throw Cesar's children over the balcony, too. He was certainly big enough and strong enough to complete the threat, but Cesar hadn't totally believed him.

Somehow, he didn't seem like the kind of man who would kill children for any reason. Not that Cesar would take that bet. Not in a million years.

Hayes was definitely unhinged. Crazy men did crazy things. Nothing was impossible.

Cesar tried to move, testing one limb at a time.

His body felt the bruises caused by a thousand bounces in the back of a pickup truck driving along the desert floor.

The big man had hit Cesar several times, too, leaving bigger, bolder bruises everywhere he'd punched. Cesar had a sharp headache where Hayes had head-butted him like a randy ram during rutting season.

At some point during the beating, Cesar had lost consciousness.

He'd awakened for brief moments here and there, realizing he was lying in the open bed of a pickup truck, bouncing with every bump in the road. He suspected Hayes was driving through ruts and potholes intentionally, simply to torture Cesar into oblivion again.

Cesar closed his eyes and went back to sleep.

The next time he awakened, Cesar pushed himself into a sitting position on the gravel. His throat was parched. His lips dry and swollen.

His eyelids were crusty. He rubbed the crust away with his fingers and pried both eyes open. His eyeballs felt like tennis balls covered in fuzz.

Cesar's vision was blurry. He tried to focus. After several attempts, he realized Hayes had dumped him along the shoulder of a paved road.

The big man was gone. His pickup truck was gone, too.

Cesar saw nothing but open land in all directions. Slowly, he patted his flat pockets. No cash. No phone. No water.

Hayes had put his massive palms on Cesar's temples and pushed with great strength as he threatened to crush Cesar's head. Was that why the relentless pounding between his temples felt like his head might explode now?

Cesar was tempted to lie down again and return to oblivion. If he did, he might never wake up again.

In the moment, he welcomed death.

Death couldn't possibly feel any worse, surely.

Cesar had read that death from dehydration was relatively painless. It could take ten days or more.

He'd feel thirsty, lightheaded, experience muscle cramps and weakness. Nausea and vomiting, too, but that wouldn't last long.

Rapid heartbeat and rapid breathing would be uncomfortable, but less so than the other symptoms.

Could he stay out here for ten days, baking in the sun, becoming dryer and dryer until his body resembled nothing remotely human?

Why didn't Hayes just kill him and get it over with?

Cesar seemed to remember the man's answer to that question. What was it he'd said?

"I could easily kill you. But unlike what you did to Maria Greer, I'll give you a chance."

That's right.

He'd mentioned Maria Greer.

So he must have some connection to her.

She lived like a hermit. She was a single woman with no children. Cesar couldn't imagine Maria Greer and Hayes had been lovers.

So what was the connection? Cesar couldn't think of any.

"If you make it to the Red House Ranch, maybe they'll take pity on you," Hayes had said. "Tell them who you are. The rich and powerful Cesar Baez. They're indebted to you. You've been stashing undocumented migrants there for years. Promise them half your fortune if they let you live. See how that goes."

Cesar tried to breathe. The air was hot and dry and hurt his lungs. But as long as he was still breathing, as Hayes had said, he had a chance.

Briefly, he considered praying for rain. Sometimes storms rolled into this part of Texas. He remembered one particularly bad storm about ten years ago. Lightning and thunder and washouts everywhere from the downpour.

That was when the original red house ranch building had burned to the ground.

Rain could happen.

But Cesar had long ago lost his faith. Prayer wouldn't help him now.

He pushed himself off the ground and staggered to his feet, pausing and shuffling until he could balance well enough to walk.

Cesar scanned the landscape surrounding him. Hayes could have killed him, but he hadn't. Instead, Hayes had dropped him here, in this particular spot, for a reason. Cesar had no idea what that reason could be.

Mostly dry, flat land in every direction. A few oil wells and windmills in the distance. Dark clouds far away in the west suggested rain, maybe. Somewhere.

He noticed a mild west wind, maybe a smidgin cooler, but still too hot to provide much relief.

Cesar had no idea where he was, or which direction would lead him to the Red House Ranch. But he simply couldn't muster the strength to walk west into the wind and toward the blazing sun.

Slowly, painfully, he headed east.

He fell twice before he'd covered half a mile. On the third try, his unsteady gait smoothed a bit, and he remained upright. Momentum carried him away from the blinding glare.

As his limbs continued to function, more or less, Cesar began to wonder if he might hitch a ride.

He'd seen no traffic so far.

But if no one ever drove on this road, there would be no road at all. The road existed. Which had to mean that vehicles used it. At least often enough to justify the construction and maintenance.

The thought buoyed his spirt slightly.

He continued his jerky, uneven trudging eastward to the steady beat of his throbbing head. An observer might think he was drunk. A blood alcohol test would prove otherwise.

Cesar began to consider what excuse he might offer to explain his appearance, should he live to get the chance.

Hayes had pummeled him mercilessly. He had cuts and bruises over most of his body. Sharp pains on both sides of his torso whenever he drew breath suggested at least two cracked ribs. Maybe more.

His face must be terrifying.

He felt like he'd been dumped into the desert from a helicopter. He probably looked even worse.

Avoiding the police was his first concern. But if a cruiser came along, what could he say that would sound more like a stranded traveler and less like a crime victim or worse, a criminal himself?

He'd already rejected Hayes's suggestion that he identify himself. He'd have about a fifty-fifty chance of getting himself arrested or killed that way. The Baez Cartel had been operating in Texas for more than seventy years, making more enemies than friends.

Cesar was so totally preoccupied with the struggle to move his broken body and tame his pounding head that he didn't hear the vehicle approaching behind him until it slowed and swerved around.

The big, growling engine pulled up beside Cesar and stopped inches away.

He felt the heat from the vehicle and stopped walking. Carefully, deliberately, he shaded his eyes with his palm and turned his pounding head to look.

Chapter 51

Tuesday, May 31
Near Echo, Texas

Baez had never hitched a ride of any kind before in his life. The sons of Diego Baez had been chauffeured as young men. When they left for college, they didn't own vehicles because they didn't need them. At Harvard, owning a vehicle would have been simply a nuisance.

Later, Baez had returned to Durango, Mexico, with his wife. The old man settled them into a villa similar to the one they now lived in. The new life came with servants, including a driver for both Cesar and Gabriella.

Despite his lack of hitchhiking experience, he imagined some kind of pecking order in picking up travelers on the road based on a subconscious assessment of risk. An older man offering a ride to a younger girl seemed low risk and most likely.

All of which meant that Baez immediately comprehended his luck.

The odds were heavily against a woman stopping for a bedraggled man, even without his disheveled appearance and the fresh bruises visible on his face.

“Where to?” she called out from the driver’s seat, sounding a bit unsure about the impulse to stop for him.

Of course she was worried. Who wouldn't be?

"Anywhere," he replied, and instantly regretted the words.

It seemed like something an aimless drifter would say. But he didn't know where he was or what civilization lay ahead. If she left him here, he might die before another vehicle came along.

She considered things for a long minute or two. In the end, her humanitarian instincts prevailed over natural self-preservation ones.

"Okay," she said, head ducked down and face tilted up, looking out through the window. "I'm headed south of Echo."

"Perfect," he said through his split lip.

He opened the passenger door and stepped inside. She had the AC running full blast and the leather seat felt like a block of ice under his ass. It was the best feeling he'd had in way too long.

He closed the door, she buzzed the window up, slipped the transmission into drive, and rolled the heavy SUV forward along the pavement.

"Adjust the seat if you want. There's plenty of room," she said, with a quick, nervous glance across the cabin.

"Thank you," he croaked from his dry throat.

As if she could be joking, perhaps, she said, "And don't get any ideas. I've got a gun."

"You don't need to worry," Baez said sincerely. "I'm a wreck. I'm no possible threat to anyone."

She was short and slim and dark-skinned and fine-boned. Her hair was almost jet black. Altogether a small person. Maybe forty years old, give or take.

Mexican, Baez guessed.

She was wearing a simple sleeveless dress of the kind his wife favored. Simple, but expensive. The skin on her arms and legs looked smooth and shiny as if it had been polished.

The scooped neck of her dress revealed a near perfect collarbone. There was a thickened knot there from a healed break. Perhaps she'd fallen off a horse long ago.

She had both hands on the wheel. Her fingers were long and tapered. Her nails were buffed and polished. No rings of any kind.

When she'd accelerated enough to get up to speed, Baez noticed quiet conversation from the backseat. He craned his neck to see two young girls, safely buckled in.

One was maybe sixteen. Wild blond hair. Freckled face. Blue eyes. The other was about seven or eight and the exact picture of what her mother must have been at that age. Small, dark, beautiful.

"My daughters," she said, with pride and a wide smile that revealed her perfect white teeth. "Do you have any children?"

Her accent was purely American. Maybe a slight bit more Californian than Texan. Like the rest of her, the voice was silky and smooth and altogether perfect.

Under different circumstances, Cesar would already be thinking about how to get her into bed. As it was, he simply didn't want to get thrown out of the car.

"Yes. I have four. Two boys and two girls," he replied easily, as if they were talking over dinner in his villa with his family nearby.

"How did you end up on the road back there?" She glanced quickly into her mirrors, as if she expected to see something coming.

Baez had anticipated the question, so he had an answer ready. Sheepishly, he replied, “My brother and I had a fight. He left me and took off.”

“Was he trying to kill you? Because you look like a man who’s gone a dozen rounds in the boxing ring with a heavyweight,” she said. “I almost didn’t pick you up.”

“Why did you?” Baez asked, barely recognizing his own raspy voice. “Pick me up?”

“It seemed like the Christian thing to do.” She paused for a few seconds before she cleared her throat and added, “A long time ago, I lived out here. I know how unforgiving this country can be. Looks like we might get a spot of rain later, but you didn't look like a man who could survive until someone else came along."

"Well, thank you for giving me a ride." Baez turned his head to stare through the window, seeing nothing but flat land on all sides of the SUV.

He glanced in the side mirror and noticed the dark clouds in the west seemed to be moving eastward.

She was rolling along now at about fifty miles an hour.

She reached over and opened the console between the seats. "Want a bottle of water? You look like you're dry as dirt."

Baez stared into the deep console. There was a stack of fresh three-liter water bottles inside.

"Thank you," he croaked as he reached for one, twisted the cap, and poured half the water into his mouth. In that moment, the lukewarm water tasted better than the finest champagne and the best coffee and the most amazing tequila all of his money could buy.

He swished the water around to hydrate the inside of his mouth before he swallowed and then drank the rest. Two gulps and it was gone.

He'd have snatched another bottle from the console, but he didn't want to frighten her. He was beginning to regain some of the strength he'd lost, but he didn't want to test his body against the elements again.

If she kept talking, she might not worry about him so much. So he asked, “You said you were once settled in this area. I haven’t seen any homes. Where did you live?”

She went quiet. Her bottom lip was caught between her teeth and her eyes were narrowed. She was worried about something. Maybe more than one thing. But she seemed to have it under control.

Baez saw that he’d taken a wrong tack with the question, so he didn’t ask another. They continued in silence.

The SUV was big and quiet and cool and at least as comfortable as any motel room around here was likely to be. He was exhausted and hurting all over. Silence suited him perfectly.

Baez relaxed in his seat, leaned his head back, and closed his eyes to rest while he could.

He must have dozed off. After a while, he felt the SUV slow and heard the turn signal indicator's rhythmic beats. When he opened his eyes, he noticed a fairly new barbed wire fence running along the property line ahead.

About half a mile farther along the barbed wire changed to a picket fence on either side of a big wooden gate. The fence and the gate were painted dull red.

She was turning right off the road and onto a well groomed gravel drive.

Baez sat up just as the SUV rolled

under the gate. When he saw the name, he smiled.

“Where are we?” he asked, although he already knew exactly where they were.

“Red House Ranch,” she replied. “I lived here a very long time ago. They’ll have a phone you can use to call your family. You can stay here until someone comes to pick you up.”

“That’s very kind of you,” he said.

“I’m Carmen, by the way. What’s your name?”

He would have given her a nonsense answer, but he was spared the trouble. The two girls began to squeal in the backseat, pointing out the horses grazing in the pasture.

"Girls, we'll only be here about an hour. You can go see the horses. Ellie, you have your phone?" Carmen asked, in the way of all mothers everywhere.

"Yes," Ellie said quietly from the back seat. "We'll come back here as soon as you call."

When she pulled the SUV to a stop in the gravel parking lot out front of the big house, the two girls opened the back doors and ran toward the barns.

"What is it about girls and horses? My daughters love them, too," Cesar said to further soothe Carmen's concerns.

Carmen nodded, preoccupied, and abandoned her question about his name.

Chapter 52

Tuesday, May 31
Presidio, Texas

Kim fastened her four-point harness and settled firmly into the co-pilot's seat. Methodically, Flint completed his preflight weather and flight risk planning while she focused on controlling her queasy stomach.

"Should we just drive? It'll take longer, but at least we'd get there in one piece," Kim said.

She knew the crash statistics. Many a helicopter crash had resulted because the pilot perceived he had no alternate plan and flew the helo when he shouldn't have.

"Looks like we can make it if we keep our speed up. The clouds are moving in fast, but the ceiling is high enough. We can fly below it, at least long enough to get where we're going," Flint explained his plans.

Kim didn't object. She'd fly the helo herself if she had the training. She didn't. He was the expert. Flint said they could make it. So they could. Simple as that.

Like Kim, Flint was alive today because he relied totally on himself. No one else. He'd make the decisions and he'd make them for solid reasons.

She found his hyper focused individualism comforting. Self-reliance made sense to her. She'd lived her entire life that way. Whenever she'd allowed herself to rely on others unnecessarily, they too often let her down.

Lives had been lost because she'd trusted an unworthy partner.

A hard lesson she didn't intend to forget. When she had a choice. Which she didn't have at the moment. What she had was faith in Flint. He'd proven his worth to her more than once.

"Relax, Otto. I've flown in worse weather hundreds of times. I've checked my resources and I've got a good handle on the storm track. It's moving fast, but we can move faster and stay out in front of it," Flint said with a grin, as he readied for the flight. "We might die today, but not because our helo crashes amid the raindrops."

He spooled up the engine and lifted the bird into the gusty air as if the process was as simple as breathing to him. Kim hoped it was.

Flint's concentration on the task at hand was reassuring.

The flight was both longer and shorter than she feared. The storm clouds approached faster than Kim hoped, but Flint pushed the helo and kept ahead of the weather.

A few hearty gusts seemed to shove the helo forward, up, and down, at unpredictable intervals. Kim's clenched jaw and pursed lips kept her stomach contents where they should be.

True to his word, Flint kept the helo aloft.

No rain so far and she hadn't seen any lightning yet. Thunder louder than the deafening noise of the helo's rotors seemed to be chasing them away from Presidio. Fortunately, the helo didn't have a rearview mirror from which she could watch and worry.

The view from the air revealed bleak, brown and tan ground ahead in all directions. There were mesquite trees here and there. Brown grasses. Oil wells and windmills and power lines.

Briefly, she wondered how homes were powered out here. They'd need power for air conditioning. Winters were probably cold enough to require heat, too. Natural gas or propane generators would probably do the job. The power lines suggested there was electricity traveling from somewhere across the open land.

Kim thought about the changing fortunes of people. Only the toughest lived through the ups and downs. People like Rusty Greer.

In photographs, the woman looked like a dried prune wearing a messy red flame on her head. She'd endured the demanding hardships of ranching and she was still standing. Her husband died; her son was murdered. She'd killed at least one man, and that one had sent her to prison.

Rusty Greer had been oil rich fifty years ago. And then the oil dried up. Until changes in technology came along and gave Greer land a whole new life, making her oil rich again.

Rusty Greer had lived through it all. She was a tough old bird with a hard heart. Kim marveled at the woman's strength. What kept her going? From everything Kim had read about her, the answer had to be pure meanness.

Kim noticed a limestone mesa on the west side of the land. Ten years ago, two assassins had died there when they'd tried to kill Reacher.

She shrugged. They should have known better. Reacher fights to win.

Finally, she saw the Red House Ranch in the distance. Flint saw it, too.

Chapter 53

Tuesday, May 31
Echo, Texas

Pilar had been to the Red House Ranch only once before, the night she'd come across the border in Miguel's van. She remembered the absurd picket fence and the way the house and the fence and the barns and the gate were all painted red.

She knew the ranch was south of Stockton, but she'd never have located it on her own. Fortunately, José had programed the route along the back roads into the SUV's navigation system.

On the long drive, Pilar didn't need to worry about taking a wrong turn. Which meant she had plenty of time to consider how she would deal with Baez.

Her first thought had been to kill him immediately.

But José had told him they were coming. Baez would be expecting her. If she got too close to him, he might kill her first. Maybe that's why he wanted her there. If not, he might be tempted when he learned what she'd done to José.

When she was at the ranch before, there had been other people present. Bobby and Rusty Greer. The maid who had been nice to her. And various workers milling about. Pilar hadn't tried to count them all.

Thinking back on it now, maybe there were two dozen people around. Give or take.

Isolating Baez from the others at the ranch might be difficult. She'd need to be alert for the right opportunity. Planning only went so far. After that, she'd make decisions in the moment.

Her self-preservation instincts were strong. They'd served her well. Every reason to rely upon them now.

Pilar followed the guidance, approaching the ranch from the west again.

She turned right onto the long gravel drive and traveled under the big wooden gate. The red house was directly ahead on the right. Several vehicles were parked out front. A black SUV. A couple of pickup trucks. One beat up van.

The horses were in the pasture by the red barns beyond the house. Two youngsters were out there with the horses and a couple of ranch hands. One of the girls was tall and blond and obviously related to Bobby Greer. She looked exactly like him from this distance.

The other girl was small and brown and definitely Mexican. Must belong to one of the ranch workers. Or maybe one of the illegals passing through.

Pilar shook her head. Only in America would two girls as different as that become friends.

Pilar had never made friends with a white person in her life. Nor did she expect she ever would. The few whites she'd come in contact with back in her village had no interest in befriending her, either.

Perhaps her life would be different here, but her imagination couldn't comprehend a world where she'd become friends with girls like that blond in the pasture.

There was rain in the forecast. Dark clouds were fast approaching, and a strong west wind pushed the girls sideways. They were feeding the horses and petting them. The younger girl wanted to ride, so the older one boosted her up and sat her astride a pony.

Pilar spent a couple of minutes watching them. She imagined living here with her mother and sisters. How different her life might have turned out if she'd had a home like this. Horses to ride. People around who took care of her. A normal childhood.

She shook off the melancholy. None of that mattered now. Nothing could be done to change it.

Pilar pressed the accelerator and rolled closer to the house. For a moment, she considered driving the SUV directly into the house and setting the remaining gas in the tank afire. The west wind would blow the flames everywhere to destroy everyone and everything.

She'd watched those vehicles ignite back at the fundraiser after her sedan exploded. If she opened the gas caps for the vehicles parked out there and splashed a bit of fuel around, a quick spark would be enough to get things burning hot and fast.

She could stay inside the vehicle and end her own life at the same time.

The idea was appealing.

But she realized it wouldn't work.

It was Baez she wanted dead. She didn't know for sure that Baez was here.

She could destroy the house and everyone in it, but if Baez didn't die, she'd have failed.

Perhaps she could destroy the house and everyone in it after she dealt with Baez. A warm feeling flooded her body, and she smiled briefly before turning her attention back to the moment.

Pilar took a deep breath to calm her pounding heart before she reversed the SUV and backed into her parking place. The nose of her vehicle pointed straight down the gravel drive to the front gate.

After she killed Baez, she'd be able to get away fast. And go where? California still?

Pilar didn't have anything to unload. Her duffel had burned inside the sedan back in Austin.

José might have a bag of clothes somewhere, but they would be too big for her.

Maybe she could borrow something from the maid. The woman was about Pilar's size.

She had José's phone and the phone he'd given her. She left them both in the passenger seat.

Pilar had only the clothes on her back, the dagger in her pocket, and the pistol. Somehow, that seemed fitting.

She stepped out of the vehicle, dropped the keys into her pocket, and climbed the steps up to the kitchen door. Perhaps the maid would tell Pilar when Baez was scheduled to arrive.

When she climbed the last step and approached the back entrance, she heard arguing from the kitchen.

A man and a woman.

The man was Bobby Greer. Pilar remembered his voice.

She had never heard this woman's voice before.

Bobby shouted angrily, "You think you can come around here making demands, Carmen? Sloop paid you off years ago. We owe you nothing."

"That was then, Bobby. This is now." The woman was just as angry, but more controlled. "Ellie is one of the old man's heirs, just like you are. Her father died before the oil money started gushing in again. She's entitled to her share of his wealth. If Sloop had lived, he'd have made sure she got it."

"We'll see about that," Bobby snarled.

Pilar recognized the next voice, too. The salty old bitch she'd met here before joined the argument with just as much heat as Bobby.

"What do you mean? Maria was the only other heir. She died. That has nothing to do with Ellie. Maria's share comes back to me. And I'm leaving everything to Bobby." Rusty Greer's sharp, scratchy voice halted for a long, ragged breath. "You tricked my son into marrying you and when he died, you got Sloop's money. That's all you're ever going to get, you conniving Mexican whore."

"Think again, Rusty," Carmen said sharply. "Maria left her share to Ellie. She had a valid will. Her lawyer's filed it with the court. Nothing you can do about it."

Bobby exploded into a white-hot rage. "What the hell are you talking about?"

"Too bad for you, Bobby. The lawyer says Ellie will inherit. Maria wanted Ellie to have her share. Guess you didn't know that when you had her killed." Carmen said, standing up to the bully in a way that made Pilar cheer.

"Yes!" Pilar yelled on the porch. "You tell him!"

The conversation halted abruptly.

Heavy footsteps strode to the door and pushed it open, almost knocking Pilar over.

"What the hell are you doing here?" Bobby asked angrily.

"Not expecting me, then?" Pilar replied, sticking her chin forward and pushing her way into the kitchen. "I'm meeting someone. I can't wait in the car. Not with a storm coming."

Rusty let out a raspy cackling laugh. "It's May, little girl. We haven't had a big Spring storm around here in ten years. Maybe more."

"Then I'd say you're due, wouldn't you?" Pilar replied with all the pent-up belligerence she'd been swallowing her entire life.

When Pilar scanned the kitchen. The maid wasn't there.

But the woman Bobby had called Carmen was standing near the doorway. Her beauty stole Pilar's breath away and for a brief moment, she could only stare.

How could such an amazing Mexican woman possibly be connected to these gringo pigs? Turning her gaze from Bobby to Carmen and then back again, Pilar's mind made lightning-fast connections to the two girls she'd seen in the horse pasture.

The big blond girl resembled Bobby. The small, dark one was a mini-Carmen.

The blond girl must be Ellie, the dead brother's daughter.

Who fathered the brown girl?

Pilar understood instantly. Their argument was about money.

Everything always came down to money. Poor people and wealthy people alike were driven by lust for money. No matter how much or how little they had, people seemed to always want more.

Pilar understood the desire. She'd felt it herself, her entire life. Baez had promised her money when she killed Emily Brandon. Liar. Yet another reason to remove the bastard from the earth.

"I'm leaving." Carmen was the first to speak again. "I came to tell you that I'm not the scared young college girl Sloop brought down here all those years ago. Ellie owns a controlling interest in this ranch and all of the Greer holdings now. Rusty's been in prison for ten years and you've had a free hand here, Bobby. But that's over. Ellie's lawyer will be in touch."

As Carmen moved to walk past Bobby and out the door, he grabbed her arm and shoved her down into a chair. He stood over her like a giant guarding a mouse. Carmen was boxed in. No way she could escape.

"You're not going anywhere. Ellie's not taking anything." Bobby's face was flushed so red he looked like he might stroke out on the spot.

His eyes were bright and vicious. Every word snarled from Bobby's fleshy lips. "Sloop should have killed you when he had the chance."

An unnatural silence greeted his words.

“Rusty!” Bobby’s voice roared. “Go get those two brats. Bring them up here.”

“Why? What are you planning to do?” Rusty demanded.

“Stay right there, Rusty!” Carmen shouted back from her chair prison. “You hurt my kids, Bobby, and you’ll never even live to regret it.”

Briefly, Rusty seemed confused. Her fuzzy red hair whipped in all directions. First, to Pilar, then to Carmen, and finally to Bobby.

“Go right this minute,” her son demanded.

Before anyone had a chance to say anything else, Cesar Baez appeared at the top of the stairs.

“Hello, Pilar,” Baez said quietly.

Pilar turned her head and stared. The argument in the kitchen faded to background noise, like a movie soundtrack. Pilar’s total focus was on Baez.

What a bastard he was, Pilar thought, her gaze still glued to the battered, disheveled man at the top of the stairs.

Baez, the considerate lover when she was still a virgin.

Her savior when she’d stabbed that rutting pig at the brothel.

The one who’d ordered José to destroy her.

Chapter 54

Tuesday, May 31
Red House Ranch

"We'll be on the ground shortly. Could be a bit bumpy, so hang on," Flint said through the headset, nodding toward the ranch. "We'll set down on the gravel drive, near where those vehicles are parked."

As the helo descended, Kim saw ranch hands herding the horses from the pasture into the barns to shelter from the coming storm. A small rider atop one horse was being led by a taller girl with wild blond hair trudging against the wind.

Ranch workers were gathering into the outbuildings, closing shutters and doors.

Flint lowered the helo. A couple of times, the gusty wind seemed to lift the wide body up from below, jarring Kim in her harness, before dropping again, sending her stomach into her mouth.

Her grip was already tight enough to choke one of those horses in the pasture. But she tightened both hands on the holds and kept quiet. Flint knew what he was doing. Panic wouldn't help.

Two more hard thumps and Flint managed to set the helo firmly on the gravel. He shut down the engine.

"I'm gonna need to tie this bird down. Quickly. The storm could still pick her up and crash her, but at least she will have a chance," Flint said, unfastening his harness, preparing to slip outside.

"Can I help?"

"Check the house. Get a couple of ranch hands to help me and some extra ropes," Flint said as he climbed out.

Kim pushed the co-pilot's door against the wind to force it open. She slid out to the gravel and ran against the heavy wind toward the house.

The rain began to fall. Big, fat drops landed in slow motion.

She was halfway to the house when a booming clap of thunder sounded in the west, rattling the ground and pushing Kim to run faster.

Standing outside in a thunderstorm was foolish. Lightning strikes produce thunder. And every school kid knows, humans are no match for Mother Nature. Lightning kills.

The wind carried voices from inside and Kim heard the argument before she reached the porch.

"Rusty!" A man's voice roared. "Go get those two brats. Bring them up here."

"Why? What are you planning to do?" An older woman's raspy demand.

"Stay right there, Rusty!" A younger woman shouted. "You hurt my kids and you'll never even live to regret it!"

A moment later, a scrawny woman with wild red hair came bursting through the kitchen door, waving a gun in her hand.

Rusty Greer.

She ran with the wind, faster than Kim thought possible, putting significant distance quickly behind her.

"Ellie! Kara!" Rusty yelled as if her voice would carry all the way to the girls. "Come here! Quick!"

Kim turned to look toward the barn. The two girls she'd seen in the pasture with the horses must have been Ellie and Kara Greer. Carmen's daughters.

Which meant Carmen was the younger woman in the kitchen, arguing with Bobby.

The girls emerged from the barn holding hands. After a few steps, Ellie seemed to recognize Rusty, running toward them, waving the gun.

Ellie stopped, jerking Kara to a halt.

The two girls stood staring at the crazy red-haired woman brandishing her pistol.

"Rusty! Stop!" Kim yelled into the wind.

Kim's quick analysis scanned the angle, the wind, the rain, Rusty holding the pistol and moving toward the girls and closing the distance.

She made the snap decision not to fire her weapon. Too many variables.

Kim dashed toward Rusty, running as fast as she could, attempting to tackle the old woman before she could fire.

She sprinted faster than Kim expected.

Rusty raised the pistol, aiming on the run, preparing to shoot.

Half a moment ahead of the bullets, Ellie dropped into the dirt and pulled Kara down with her.

Rusty fired. Once. Twice.

Both bullets went wild. Would have been a miracle if they'd hit the targets in these conditions.

Rusty kept running erratically toward the kids, waving the pistol, prepared to fire again.

The closer she came, the more successful she was likely to be.

The girls were huddled together on the ground, Ellie shielding Kara with her body.

Rusty's jerky floundering momentum zigzagged across the muddy ground. She slipped a couple of times but managed to right herself without falling.

Kim realized the crazy old woman was dead serious. She would kill those girls if she got the chance.

She was old and frail and crazy. But she was propelled with strength forged by tragedy and pure grit.

Rusty was too close to her targets.

Kim was too far from Rusty.

In that moment, Kim realized two things. Rusty would never give up. The girls were stationary targets Rusty wouldn't miss.

And Kim couldn't catch her soon enough to stop her.

There was only one thing Kim could do.

Quickly, she adjusted her angle of approach. Stopped and drew her weapon. Took aim and prepared to terminate the threat.

Before she had a chance to fire, a shot rang out from somewhere behind Kim.

Rusty took another couple of steps and then stopped, her body swaying. A red bloom spread across her back.

Kim hit the ground, whipping her gaze back and forth, scanning for the shooter through the blinding gravel blowing against her face.

Another shot came quickly and put the old woman down.

Rusty fell face forward into the dirt, half of her head blown away, still holding the pistol with her finger on the trigger.

Kim saw Flint running toward her, crouching low.

When he was within earshot, she yelled, “Did you fire?”

“No. I thought it was you,” he yelled back over the howling wind.

“Cover me,” Kim said, as she pushed herself up and ran toward the girls.

No further gunshots were fired.

Kim pulled Ellie and Kara up off the ground and told them to run toward the barn and stay there. Both girls were sweaty and wild-eyed and probably scared out of their minds.

But Ellie seemed to know what to do. She took off toward the barn, pulling Kara along behind her.

Kim wondered what trauma the kid had endured before to make her so clear-headed in a crisis.

Flint had taken cover behind a battered old pickup truck parked outside the barn. Kim ran to join him.

"See anyone out there?" she asked, still scanning from the house to the barn and the vehicles parked on the gravel between the two.

When she looked back, she saw the dark clouds were rolling in faster than she'd realized. Another loud clap of thunder made talking impossible for a solid minute.

Flint shook his head. “You think Bobby or Carmen shot Rusty?”

“Hitting Rusty like that under these conditions? Just two shots to take her down, both perfectly placed? From that distance?” Kim shook her head. “Nothing I know suggests that either Bobby or Carmen could shoot like that.”

“Then why didn’t they come out of the house when they heard the shots?”

“Maybe they didn’t hear or realize what the noise was. Could have been drowned out by the thunder,” Kim raised her voice enough to be heard over the rushing wind.

Another loud clap of thunder punctuated her sentence.

“Or maybe the shooter’s inside the house with them by now,” Flint replied. “Or he could have circled around to the barn.”

“We need to split up. I’ll take the house,” Kim said. “Can you get into the barn and make sure the girls are okay?”

In the distance, she saw lightning flash from the dark sky to the ground, lighting up the countryside.

How far away was the lightning?

She stopped to count the seconds, waiting for the thunder.

Fifteen seconds. Maybe three miles away and moving in.

Raindrops were falling harder and faster, too. The gusting wind pushed Kim and Flint against the old pickup.

"Ready?" she said.

He nodded.

Kim pushed away from the pickup and ran against the mighty wind into the open yard.

Flint ran the other way, toward the barn.

Just as she reached the porch steps, the skies opened up, dropping a cascade of water. Kim was instantly drenched.

A crack of lightning flashed in the black sky, followed by a series of long rolling thunder coming from the western edge of the Greer property.

Kim's view of the lightning was partially blocked by the house, but the storm was relentlessly advancing.

She took the stairs to the covered porch two at a time and approached the screen door, pausing briefly to listen before she rushed inside.

Another blast of rolling thunder filled the air, each one closer than the last, like a warning of approaching danger.

As the noise of each wave of thunder receded, Kim heard Bobby and Carmen screaming inside the house. She couldn't make out the words.

She drew her weapon, pulled the screen door open, and stepped into the kitchen.

Chapter 55

Tuesday, May 31
Red House Ranch

After Rusty ran out of the kitchen, Pilar tilted her chin to peer at the man at the top of the stairs. Her shocked gaze absorbed Baez's appalling appearance in a single glance. She'd seen better looking beggars on the dusty streets of her village.

The smooth, handsome, persuasively patient lover Pilar had known as a child was unrecognizable. Baez stood awkwardly as if every inch of his body was in agony.

She hoped he was. He deserved eternal agony. She prayed he'd get it.

Baez had been severely beaten. His face and head were bruised and his body battered. One eye was purple and swollen shut. Two front teeth were missing.

His expensive suit hung in filthy rags, as if he'd been tumbling in the dirt. One of his shoes was gone. His left arm hung awkwardly below the elbow inside his sleeve.

Pilar's initial shock lasted only an instant, rapidly replaced by the fury that had propelled her here. She wanted to shriek her outrage while running up the stairs to claw out his remaining eye.

Instead, she clenched her fists at her sides and firmly planted her feet on the floor.

She cleared her throat of all emotion, retrieved the gun from her pocket, pointed it in his direction, and simply replied, "Baez."

Before Pilar could say more, a tiny Asian woman stepped through the screen door and into the kitchen. Pilar hid the gun behind her.

"Who the hell are you?" Bobby Greer turned toward the woman and scowled.

Whoever she was, the woman's entrance provided the distraction Carmen had been waiting for.

She screamed and lifted both booted feet and kicked Bobby Greer's groin with all the power a fiercely protective mother could muster.

Bobby yelled and doubled over, holding his crotch.

Pilar almost cheered again.

Carmen took advantage of Bobby's momentary weakness to jump out of the chair and escape past his looming body.

She dashed toward the Asian woman standing just inside the doorway and shoved her aside.

The Asian woman momentarily lost her footing and stumbled, thumping her head solidly against the open door. She looked stunned.

"Rusty! Leave my kids alone!" Carmen screamed as she ran through the doorway, across the porch, and into the driving rain.

Bobby's rage fueled him past his pain. He limped past the Asian woman, outside, across the porch, and down the steps in hot pursuit.

When he reached the driveway, he pulled a gun from his waistband and fired in Carmen's general direction.

The gunshot startled her, and she slipped on the wet, muddy gravel and fell.

Briefly, Pilar considered shooting Bobby in the back. The moment's hesitation stole her chance. He was already out of range.

Bobby fired again and continued to chase Carmen.

The Asian woman had regained her balance. Quickly, she glanced toward Bobby and Carmen through the doorway and then scanned the room.

"I'm just the maid," Pilar said, trying to look frightened and worried.

"Does Carmen have a weapon?" she asked.

Pilar shrugged.

The Asian woman turned and followed Bobby Greer into the storm.

At least two Greers out there with loaded firearms. Maybe they'd screw up and kill each other. A quick smile stole onto Pilar's face. Talk about justice.

The Greers were not her problem. Baez was.

Pilar swiveled her head back to stare at the empty spot at the top of the stairs where Baez had stood before. He was gone.

“Mierda!”

She’d come too far to find him. She wouldn’t let him escape now.

Pilar pulled the gun from her pocket, dashed to the stairs and ran up, two at a time.

She recalled the general layout of the house. The staircase dead ended at a hallway that ran to bedrooms on the second floor. Each bedroom had its own bathroom.

When she reached the top, she counted four rooms on the right and four more on the left. She squinted in the darkness. There were no windows in the hallway but using the weak ambient light reflecting up the stairway from the kitchen, she confirmed that all the doors were closed.

Which one had Baez chosen?

Pilar started with the closest door on the right.

She turned the handle silently, pushed the door open, and ducked in.

Pilar glanced outside through the large bedroom window. The sky was as black as tarmac.

Rain deluged in thick torrents, limiting visibility to inches in all directions faster than the thirsty ground could absorb it. Large puddles formed in a few seconds as Pilar watched.

Lightning flashed rapidly, cloud-to-cloud, cloud-to-ground, cloud-to-sky. Mother Nature's fireworks.

Followed instantly by the kind of thunder that sounded like bombs were landing in the yard, not fifty feet away.

Baez would be hiding here in the house somewhere. Only a fool would go outside in this weather.

Whatever else Baez was, he was no fool.

Pilar waited for the next lightning flashes to scan the room. The first bedroom and its adjacent bathroom were both unoccupied. She flipped on the light switch for a more thorough look to confirm.

Seven rooms left to check. She turned the lights off in the first room and moved into the hallway again, leaving the door open.

Pilar covered each room methodically, one after another.

Even with the window shades open, the bedrooms were too dark to search thoroughly. She followed the same procedure as the first room. She stood motionless until continuous lightning strikes brightened each interior, scanned, then turned on the lights to ensure that Baez wasn't hiding there.

She continued to leave the doors open as she moved down the hallway, silently stalking Baez under cover of the deafening storm.

Pilar confirmed the four rooms on one side were unoccupied. With the doors open, lightning flashed brightness into the black hallway like an unpredictable strobe.

She completed the first four rooms and moved across the hallway to room number five. Baez was within her reach.

She could almost smell his fear.

Chapter 56

Tuesday, May 31
Red House Ranch

Following Bobby, Kim dashed through the kitchen door, across the decking, down the steps, and into the pounding rain.

Visibility was near zero. Both Carmen and Bobby had disappeared into the raging storm.

Carmen was frantic to protect her girls. She would have run toward her daughters, even as Bobby chased after her.

Kim looked toward the barn as water sluiced across her face, blinding her.

She could not see clearly, even when she swiped her eyes with her free hand.

Inhaling was as impossible as breathing underwater. Short breaths and exhales through her mouth were all she could manage.

Kim kept moving. Her footfalls landed in puddles slow to soak into the dry earth. She'd slipped twice, barely righting herself instead of hitting the mud.

The third time, Kim slid three feet sideways and fell to her knees. She raised her weapon into the air at the last possible moment, saving it from submersion in the mud. She climbed upright and slowed her pace slightly as she trudged forward.

She held her gun by her side, attempting to shield it from the increasing downpour.

The Glock was designed to fire under all sorts of conditions. It should perform in the rain and even underwater.

But Kim had never personally tested her duty weapon in the field under storm conditions. This was no time to fail because she'd submerged the gun in a grimy puddle.

The storm was immediately overhead now. She'd seen photos of storms like this. From a distance, they resembled a mushroom cloud like a nuclear bomb.

Rain blasted straight down from the center.

787 Lone Star Jack

Clouds extended for miles in every direction.

Lightning strikes came fast and furious, one after another, followed almost instantly by the deafening thunder they generated.

Subconsciously, Kim counted seven strikes in less than one minute. Her uncanny memory for facts reminded her that lightning was five times hotter than the sun. A powerful electric charge that destroyed buildings and caused fires and blackouts across entire cities.

People died from lightning strikes every year.

It was crazy to be out here in the storm.

They should all be inside.

They all knew that.

But Carmen was hellbent on protecting her daughters.

Bobby would kill Carmen if he could reach her.

And Kim couldn't let that happen.

But first, she had to find him.

Bobby might have fired his pistol again, but she couldn't distinguish the gunshots from the thunder.

Kim focused her hearing but attempting to block out the noise of the storm was futile.

She wiped her eyes and peered into the pouring rain.

When the next bolt of lightning brightened the sky, she scanned the open yard.

Her attention was focused on finding Bobby.

She didn't notice Rusty's body blocking her path.

Rushing forward as fast as she dared, Kim's boot tripped on Rusty's torso, face down in the mud.

Momentum carried her body forward.

She fell flat on top of the dead woman, landing hard. An oomph of air escaped her lungs, leaving her breathless.

Quickly, she rolled off and scrambled onto her feet again in the slick mud.

Where was Bobby Greer? If he'd left tracks in the mud near his mother, the rain had already washed them away.

And if he'd seen Rusty lying here dead, his rage against Carmen would know no bounds.

Kim stood in the constant rain and closed her eyes to locate the barn from memory using the position of Rusty's body as her orientation point.

The old pickup where she'd left Flint was a second fixed point she could identify.

She made a ninety-degree turn and began to run again, careful now to watch the ground as well as the open areas ahead.

Suddenly, the storm's noise seemed to stop.

An unnatural quiet enveloped the ranch, like the barely perceptible split second a golfer pauses at the top of his backswing before the downswing.

In that brief, silent instant, Kim heard gunshots coming from the direction of the barn. Four shots. Two weapons. Fire and counter fire. Unmistakably.

And then the storm rushed back with full momentum, gathering speed and force seemingly as fast as the speed of light.

Chapter 57

Tuesday, May 31
Red House Ranch

Pilar's methodical search of the bedrooms led her to the closed door directly across from the stairs. Room number six.

Which presented her with a choice.

Should she continue as she had been? Or move directly to the last?

Baez had to be in one of these two rooms. If she chose the wrong one, he could slip out and dash down the stairs while she was inside.

Lights shining into the hallway from the open doorways had flickered in unison several times. The storm could extinguish the power at any moment. She had to find Baez first, while she still had the advantage.

She switched the pistol to her left hand and wiped her sweaty right palm against her pants. She could shoot with either hand, but her aim was better with the right.

Pilar flattened her back against the wall, reached for the doorknob with her left hand, and pushed the door into room number six.

She turtled her head and darted a quick glance into the darkened room. Her silhouette was softly backlit, which wasn't okay. He might see her and attack. But she couldn't find Baez in total darkness, either.

As if her brief thought had summoned the devils, a sharp flash of lightning touched down from the black clouds blocking the window.

The flash illuminated the bedroom for much too long a moment. The cracking, booming thunder followed almost instantly.

Another sharp flash and then heavy pounding.

Then unlucky strike number three.

Bolt.

Boom.

Baez.

There. Back flat against the wall next to the window.

While the flash lasted, Pilar raised her right arm, aimed, and fired.

Baez ducked low and rolled along the floor.

She predicted his trajectory and fired again. Again.

The storm raged fiercely in an all-out attack.

Pilar couldn't hear her own gunshots over the noise. Had she hit him? Where was he?

The fourth lightning strike stole in, pouncing like a prowling tiger.

The blinding bolt speared the bedroom window, breaking the glass.

Thunder boomed immediately like a bomb had landed in the flower beds surrounding the house.

A spark ignited the varnished wood floors pushing an oomph of fire into the room and out the doorway to where Pilar had been standing half a moment before.

The house was filled with combustibles. Linens, pillows, curtains, rugs, and more, caught the flames.

Pilar felt the heat on her face. Where was Baez? Was he dead? Had she killed him?

She tried to peer into the bedroom, but the blinding fire made vision impossible.

The conflagration burned hot and fast. She would be consumed if she didn't move.

Now.

Pilar turned and ran, feeling the fire chasing her all the way.

Down the stairs to the kitchen. The maid was standing at the stove. Pilar grabbed her hand and pulled her toward the screen door, even as the confused woman struggled to stay inside.

"What are you doing?" the maid yelled. "Let me go!"

They reached the screen door and Pilar pushed it open with her right hand, still holding the gun.

She pulled the struggling maid through the door, onto the porch, and out into the muddy yard. Rain was still gushing from the clouds.

At the end of the paving stones, Pilar gave the woman a hard shove forward. Then she pointed toward the house.

“Look!” she screamed.

They both turned to gape at the burning house.

The fire seemed to spread in every direction at once. Flames burned inside every upstairs bedroom. The heat was intense, even through the pounding rain.

As they stared, two upstairs windows blasted outward. Then two more.

The maid ran toward the barn.

Pilar had no idea how many people were still inside the house. Perhaps some of them could be saved.
She reached into her pocket and retrieved José's cell phone. She dialed 911, although she had no idea how firefighters could possibly save the place or the people now.

The call did not go through. She tried twice more before she gave up.

Pilar stared at the flaming building, mesmerized. The fire was soothing. Watching it consume the building calmed her rage, somehow.

Had she managed to kill Baez? She didn't know. But if he wasn't dead before the fire started, he soon would be.

Her work was done here. The thing she needed to do now was save herself.

She hurried to the big SUV she'd parked in the lot when she first arrived. She jumped inside and started the engine.

Pilar slid the transmission into drive, tossed the gun onto the passenger seat, and mashed the accelerator.

She was near the end of the long gravel drive before she looked into the rearview mirror. The house was almost completely engulfed in flames now, burning high into the sky. When the fire finished, there would be only ashes left.

As she watched, an explosion blew off the porch outside the kitchen. A thunderous noise even louder than the storm sent a fireball high into the sky and debris flying in every direction.

She had no idea what caused the explosion, but probably a gas leak of some kind.

Pilar floored the accelerator. At the main road, she turned west, into the storm, because she'd traveled that stretch of road twice before.

"Better the devil you know," she whispered under her breath.

Five miles west of the Red House Ranch, the storm seemed to have spent itself. The clouds had moved east. The rain stopped. She saw no lightning. Heard no thunder.

The strange, hot, dry, quiet returned.

After a few more miles, Pilar could no longer see the smoke from the fire at the Red House Ranch in her rearview mirror.

Pilar reached for the navigation system and punched in **Los Angeles, California**. The route was easy. She had money in her pocket. The SUV was in good shape. She could reach her new home by tomorrow, latest.

She imagined the green lawns and paved sidewalks of California as she'd seen them in all those movies. The ocean on one side, the mountains on the other. Pilar knew how to wait tables. She would find a job in a beach bar. She'd sleep on the sand. Make friends for the first time in her life.

"About time you got a break." She smiled and began to sing a popular song she'd learned in Mexico.

Pavement was dry here, along this stretch, miles from Red House Ranch. The land on either side of the road was dry and dusty. Traffic was non-existent.

She'd driven twenty miles when she noticed her dashboard. The amber low fuel light was on. When had that happened? She didn't know.

The gauge reported enough fuel to travel another thirty miles. Pilar suspected the estimate wasn't very accurate. Best not to rely on it.

She punched the button on the navigation system for local gas stations. The closest was fifty-seven miles ahead.

Pilar backed her foot off the accelerator and slowed the big SUV in an effort to conserve fuel while she thought things through. The thermometer reflected an outside temperature of more than one hundred degrees.

There were no vehicles coming from either direction as far as her eye could see.

She found José's phone again. Maybe she could call a tow truck.

Still no service. She tossed the useless brick onto the passenger seat along with the gun.

Pilar turned off the engine and let the SUV coast to a stop in the travel lane. For a while, she'd leave the doors and windows closed to preserve the cool air inside.

She could turn the engine on again when she got too hot. And it would be dark soon, which would help with the heat.

Sooner or later, someone would come along.

"After all, there would be no road here if no one ever drove on it," Pilar said, to reassure herself.

She stared into the rearview mirror for a few seconds and then looked straight ahead. If she saw another vehicle, she'd turn on her flashers. Surely, someone would stop.

A bit of steam rose from the pavement. The wavy atmosphere distorted her vision. The heat would burn it off fast enough.

Pilar wiped her eyes and turned to look straight behind the SUV.

Was that a truck coming up from the east? It looked like the old, beat-up pickup she'd seen in the yard back at the Red House Ranch.

Pilar retrieved her gun from the passenger seat and shoved it down into her pocket. She grabbed José's phone, too. Then she climbed out of the SUV and stood next to the rear fender, waving her arm, signaling the driver to stop.

He slowed the pickup as he approached.

She didn't recognize the driver when he pulled up alongside her. If he'd been working back at the ranch, she hadn't run into him there.

He lowered the window and leaned toward her with a serious frown.

For a moment, she was nervous about accepting a ride from him. She felt the gun in her pocket for reassurance.

The man was huge. Blond hair. Blue eyes. Hands as big as frozen chickens.

He could snap her in two without even thinking about it.

But what choice did she have? She shrugged.

“I’m out of gas,” she said, opening the passenger door and climbing into the cab of the truck without being asked. “Can you give me a lift?”

Chapter 58

Tuesday, May 31
Red House Ranch

The lightning strikes that hit the house were accompanied by sonic booms and blast waves strong enough to toss Kim off her feet. She slipped in the mud again and landed on her ass.

Kim saw the fire start and spread quickly through the top floors. Was anyone still inside? Surely, they could get each other out of there. She couldn't go back now.

She jumped up quickly and plowed forward as best she could, feeling the heat from the fire across the yard. Maybe rain would extinguish the fire quickly. If not, the whole place could go up in flames.

Kim fought the storm, pushing against the wind, avoiding the lightning, enduring the pounding rain, sliding in the mud, as she moved forward toward the barn.

She still couldn't see the building because of the curtain of water between them.

But if she wasn't moving rapidly, then Bobby and Carmen weren't either.

Carmen had a head start. Maybe she'd already arrived.

But Bobby was armed and dangerous. He'd kill her and her

children without hesitation if he got the chance.

Ten feet before Kim reached the barn, another lightning bolt flashed cloud-to-cloud high overhead. The thunder roared. Frightened horses screamed inside the barn.

With the last quick flash of light, Kim breathed a little easier when she saw what was ahead.

The barn door was closed and secured. The horses and the people inside were probably frightened, but okay.

“Carmen! Open this door!” Bobby Greer stood pounding on the barn with his fist. He was thoroughly soaked, his clothes covered in mud.

He resembled a creature in a horror film. "Carmen! Carmen!"

Kim came up twenty feet behind him, weapon drawn.

"Bobby!" she screamed.

He didn't hear her. His attention was focused on one thing only. He continued to pound on the door and yell for Carmen.

Flint came around the corner from the side door of the barn, weapon ready. He fired a warning shot past Bobby, who didn't even flinch.

Bobby stood back, aimed his gun, and fired repeatedly at the area around the metal door latch. The wood splintered and separated and finally released its hold on the metal.

“I’ve got this,” Kim said to Flint, prepared to fire.

He jerked the door open, waving his gun and screaming, “Carmen! You little whore! Come out here!”

“FBI! Stand down, Bobby Greer! Hold your fire!”

Perhaps he thought she was Carmen. Maybe he was too crazed to think at all.

Bobby turned toward her, gun raised, and pulled the trigger.

His blurry vision or anger or fatigue or all three combined affected his aim.

Even so the first shot came uncomfortably close to Kim’s right leg.

"FBI! Last chance! Drop your weapon!" Kim screamed loudly over the storm and the horses, aiming her weapon so that he couldn't fail to see she was prepared to shoot.

Instead, Bobby glared, more enraged than ever, and raised his arm to fire toward her again.

The world seemed to slow. The storm ceased to exist. Kim took careful aim and fired directly at Bobby Greer.

Three quick shots, all center mass, just like target practice.

Bobby went down onto the barn's dirt floor.

He landed on his back. His head bounced on the hard ground. Right arm flopped, extended out to his right side. Still holding his pistol.

Kim approached carefully, weapon ready, just in case. She kicked Bobby's weapon aside and stood breathing heavily over his prone body.

Bobby Greer's dead eyes quickly confirmed he was no longer a threat to Carmen or her girls or anyone else.

From a dark corner of the barn, Carmen, Ellie, and Kara emerged, shivering from the cold and the trauma, shuffling slowly across the dirt floor. They needed to see for themselves.

Kim took a quick scan of the situation, noting that Carmen and her daughters were unharmed.

The barn's side door opened. Flint had circled back and now hurried inside. He was soaked. Hair plastered to his head.

"First responders are on the way. The house will be a total loss. The rain is helping, but not enough. And it's going to stop soon." Flint nodded toward Bobby Greer. "Anybody else we need to worry about?"

"What about Pilar? And Baez?" Carmen asked, eyes wide, breathing unevenly. "They were inside."

"We can't go back in the house now. Too dangerous." Flint explained patiently to the traumatized woman. “No idea what happened to Baez. We haven’t seen him. Hopefully he got out. Maybe he left with Pilar.”

“Reacher said Baez was the one who hired Maria Greer’s killer,” Carmen whispered, shaking her head wearily. “I didn’t know when I picked him up on the road and brought him to the ranch. Reacher said to be very careful of him. He belongs in prison.”

“How did Reacher know that about Baez, Carmen?” Kim asked.

“He didn’t say. But Reacher’s smart. He knows things. If he said it, I believe it,” Carmen replied softly before she returned to her children.

Kim watched Carmen with the girls. She was so careful with them. Hugging them, holding them as if they were precious treasures.

Kim wondered once again why Reacher had tried to help Carmen, both ten years ago and now. She had loads of questions, but they could wait.

"Cooper's gonna love that." Kim said dryly, stowing her weapon into her holster, and flexing the cramps from her fingers. "The two people who might have been able to shed some light on this whole thing are both missing."

"Two?" Flint said, cocking his head.

"Pilar and Baez," Kim replied.

“Don’t forget Reacher. He’s missing again, too,” Flint said with a single nod.

“Again? He was here? You saw him?” Kim asked.

“He was here with the kids, waiting to turn them over to me after he shot Rusty,” Carmen said. “You handled Bobby before he got the chance. Reacher took off after you shot him.”

“He’s been ahead of you the whole time,” Flint nodded.

“I don’t suppose you could have simply asked him to stick around and debrief me,” Kim said, annoyed. “Or leave a phone number or something.”

Flint grinned. “Why would you think I didn’t ask?”

Slightly mollified, Kim said, “What did he say?”

“Same thing he said to Gaspar. Talking to you is like talking directly to Cooper,” Flint replied. “When he’s ready to do that, he’ll let you know.”

“Did Reacher say why he doesn’t want to talk to Cooper?” she said, recalling that Cooper had implied that Reacher would show up when he learned Cooper was in Texas.

Seemed like Cooper had been right. But then Reacher took off again. Made no sense.

“The guy’s not very chatty,” Flint said with a grin.

Kim nodded toward the corner where Carmen and her girls were talking quietly together. “Your job was to solve Maria Greer’s murder. You figure you’ve done that?”

“Not exactly. My job was to be sure Ellie didn’t get cheated out of what was rightfully hers,” Flint replied.

“With Rusty and Bobby out of the way, I guess that’s likely,” Kim said.

“Ellie will inherit everything the Greers owned. Alice will see to it that she gets it. And that’s as it should be,” Flint said.

“And Baez? Pilar?” Kim said.

“Baez is probably dead. It’ll take a while, but they’ll find his body in the ruins. The Double Death Task Force will follow up on all of that," Flint shrugged. "Nothing more for either one of us to do here."

They walked out into the yard. The old pickup truck was gone.

The fire had almost consumed the entire ranch house. The flames were, in their own way, astonishing.

There were no other buildings close enough to the house to be in immediate danger.

The fire would burn itself out, probably before the firefighters arrived.

Nothing Kim or Flint could do about that, either.

"I've got to get going."

"My assignment is to find Reacher and we know he's not here. I've got no desire to answer a zillion questions from the locals," Kim said after a moment.

"Can I drop you somewhere?"

"Yeah. Less mess for Cooper to cover up if I leave now, too. And I'll need to check in with him," Kim replied, walking with Flint toward the helo.

The storm clouds had moved on and the oppressive heat returned. The mud was still soft but hardening again quickly. Kim's clothes and hair were wet and steamy, but they would dry fast enough.

She looked up, wondering about flying conditions. The sky was clear, and she could even see a few stars. "Where are you headed?"

"Houston," he said as he began to untie the helo and prepare to take off. "It's a long flight and I'll need to refuel at some point. So if there's somewhere you'd rather go, we can make a detour."

Kim helped with the tie downs. Flint checked the aircraft for damage and then carefully covered his preflight check list. Soon, they were in the air again, this time headed north and east.

Chapter 59

Tuesday, May 31
En route to Houston

First order of business was to check in with Cooper. Kim rummaged in her bag until she found the satellite phone and placed the call.

Over the past few months, her communication with Cooper had settled into a familiar rhythm. She called. He didn't pick up. She left him a long message. He'd call back when he felt like it.

The pattern was comforting, somehow. She'd come to rely upon it because she rarely wanted to talk to him anyway. She dropped the phone into her bag and turned her attention to the spectacular view from the helo's windscreen.

The night was clear and calm. The moon rested softly in the correct position. Sun rise was not yet visible off in the distance.

Sometimes flying could be beautiful, Kim supposed. If she ignored everything she knew about the risks and focused only on the aesthetics.

Flint answered a call via the headset, which meant Kim could listen. It was Alice Aaron.

"Hey, Alice. Everything squared away?"

"For us, yeah. We're done," Alice replied. "Cops have a lot of paperwork to do. They'll be spending years unraveling all those cases. But hey, that's the job, right? All in all, they're looking at more than eighty homicides in at least ten states. The joint task force will be busy for a good long while."

"That's good news, I guess. Complete job security for the FBI," Kim said with a smile. "What about Carmen?"

"The Red House Ranch burned to ashes for the second time. Nothing could be saved. She just laughed and laughed. I doubt she'll ever paint anything red for the rest of her life," Alice replied. "But Ellie wants to rebuild and to live there. Kara, too. The girls love horses. And there's no reason they shouldn't have them."

"Well, that's all great. Glad it worked out. I'll tell Scarlett to send you our usual outrageous bill for exemplary services rendered," Flint said with a smile.

"Tell Scarlett I'm glad to pay it," Alice replied. "Seriously. We couldn't have done this without you."

"What about Elana and her baby?" Flint asked.

"Oh, it's a girl. A full-fledged US citizen, for better or worse," Alice replied. "Elana has decided to return home to Mexico and her family. She never wanted to leave. It was Javier who pushed her to go."

Alice disconnected and Kim nodded toward Flint. “So Carmen wasn’t your client. It was Alice, all along.”

Flint grinned. He neither denied nor confirmed.

“What do you think about Baez being a criminal mastermind behind eighty homicides? Seems far-fetched, doesn’t it?” Kim asked. “I never met the guy. Did you?”

“Yeah. Once. A long time ago,” Flint replied.

“Forty murders for hire, and then forty assassins. Over a period of years. Seems unlikely, but possible, I guess.” Kim’s tone was hard. “If Baez isn’t dead, he deserves to be.”

"Can't argue with that," Flint replied as another call came through. He picked up. "Gaspar, don't you ever sleep?"

"Rarely. And not for lack of trying. Otto with you?" Gaspar asked.

"Yeah, Pepe, I'm here. What's up?" Kim replied into the mic.

"Couple of things you'll want to know. First, they found Pilar Mendoza."

"Yeah? Where?"

"On the road to Presidio. She was unconscious on the front seat of a battered old pickup truck registered to Bobby Greer."

Kim and Flint exchanged glances. "How did that happen?"

"She says she was low on gas, and she hitched a ride with the driver. She said she fell asleep in the truck."

"But you don't believe her?" Flint asked.

"Oh, I believe her," Gaspar replied. "But you're right. There are open questions about her story."

Kim said, "Like what?"

"The maid confirmed Pilar left Red House Ranch in an SUV. But when they found her, there was no SUV. Only the truck," Gaspar explained. "And the truck was out of gas. Totally. Couldn't even be started. Beyond that, all four tires were flat."

"So someone wanted to be sure to keep Pilar in place until locals could find her." Kim nodded slowly, thinking things through. "Did she get the name of the guy who picked her up?"

"She didn't have to," Gaspar replied.

"Might have been helpful if she had," Kim said.

"Maybe. But the reason she didn't have to is that we already know." Gaspar paused for a long moment.

Kim smiled. She really missed working with Gaspar. "Okay, Chico. You have my full attention. Give me the punch line."

"I thought you'd never ask," Gaspar replied. "Reacher called me. Told me where she was. Told me to send the sheriff out there to pick her up."

Kim nodded in the darkened cockpit as she watched the stars. “You might have led with that, Chico.”

“That wasn’t all he said,” Gaspar continued.

“Okay. What’s the rest?”

“He says Cesar Baez was definitely the man behind Maria Greer’s death. He said he could prove it. He gave me offshore bank account numbers,” Gaspar said. “I’ve sent them to your secure server. Also passed them along to the FBI task force.”

“Well, that’s helpful,” Kim said thoughtfully. “Did Reacher say anything else?”

Gaspar inhaled a long breath and held it a bit before he replied, “Yeah.

He said Baez's client for the Maria Greer murder was Bobby Greer."

"You two had quite the little chat, didn't you?" Kim replied. "I guess Reacher is traveling in Pilar's SUV, then. Probably syphoned the gas from the truck and then left her with the truck and an empty tank. Anybody trying to find the SUV?"

Gaspar paused for a good long while. Kim knew what he was going to say before he said it.

"Not yet."

Kim let that sink in and decided not to ask further questions about it at the moment.

The longer they waited to report the missing SUV, the more time Reacher had to slide away, melting back into the country and slipping off the grid again.

Until Kim understood why Cooper and Reacher were playing cat and mouse, keeping Reacher out of the hands of the FBI seemed like a good move.

Cooper would find out what she'd done. And he'd be livid.

But plausible deniability was everything. No reason for Cooper to know about Reacher's call to Gaspar. No way he'd find out. Gaspar was too good for that.

Besides, Cooper wouldn't want Reacher located by anyone except her, or maybe, himself.

Sharing the intel that Reacher was driving Pilar's SUV with local law enforcement was something she needed to run by him before they did it. Or at least, that sounded like a good excuse.

"Couple other things," Gaspar said, bringing her thoughts back to the conversation.

"I've got nothing but time for another five hours or so, Chico," Kim replied.

"Kara Greer, Carmen's younger daughter, was probably fathered by Teddy Redstone," Gaspar said. "Carmen certainly has terrible taste in men, if nothing else."

"So that's why Carmen came to the funeral. Because Kara was the old man's granddaughter. I guess that means Kara will never be alone in the world. Not sure whether that's a good thing, especially when Teddy runs for office and his enemies get ahold of the story," Kim said. "How do you know?"

"I don't know for sure. And it's none of my business, so I'm not looking into it any further," Gaspar said. "But the discovery came up in the materials the FBI located after working the riot at the funeral. Which means it's out there, for anyone determined to find it."

"What's the second thing?"

"The second thing?"

"You said you had a couple of things. Kara Greer is one. What's the other?" Kim asked.

Another long pause followed.

“Pepe? You still there?” Kim asked.

“Yeah. Sorry.” He cleared his throat, and she heard his fingers clacking the keyboard. “The second thing is Cooper. They can’t find him. You talk to him lately?”

“Not since Pecos. But that’s not unusual. He never talks to me unless he feels like it,” Kim replied.

“You know who Poppy Redstone is, right?”

“The late senator’s widow. Saw her at the funeral. Stunning woman, by the way,” Kim replied.

“Yeah, well, you should’ve seen her thirty years ago if you think she’s beautiful now.”

Kim nodded, wondering where this was going. “Okay.”

“Oh, come on,” Gaspar said, as if she was just a beat too slow on the uptake. “You never wondered why Cooper was really going to that funeral in the first place, Suzie Wong?”

“Didn’t seem relevant.”

“It’s not, I guess. Strictly speaking.”

“As it happens, I did ask him. He said he thought Reacher would come to the church. Because Reacher had some bad history with the Redstones. And also because Reacher would want to confront Cooper,” Kim said, recalling the gist of the conversation.

Seemed just plausible enough at the time.

“Turns out half of that could be true,” Gaspar said. “But what’s definitely true is that Cooper had a hot and heavy affair with Poppy Redstone long before she married the old senator. Guess Cooper loved her, to the extent he’s capable. She’s the one who got away.”

“And that’s where he’s been?” Kim asked, shaking her head incredulously. “Off the radar with Poppy Redstone?”

Cooper was a lot of things, most of them less than honorable by Kim’s standards. But she’d never have guessed he was a jilted lover carrying a torch for an old flame. Or that he'd prioritize love over work, for any reason.

"You have any proof, Chico? Because that could come in handy at some point," Kim said.

"I'll send you what I have. Be careful what you do with it," Gaspar said, reminding her of things he'd told her before. "Cooper won't like that you know. He's a viper. He'll strike hard and fast and fatally. When you're least expecting it."

Another thought popped into Kim's head. "Cooper said Reacher had history with the Redstones. He implied that Reacher would want revenge on the son, Teddy. Any idea what that's about?"

"The list of people on Reacher's revenge list would fill a city phone book," Gaspar replied with real concern.

Before she had a chance to say more, the signal began to break up. Static interfered and the transmission shut down.

Of course, Gaspar was right. Stepping between Reacher and his enemies would be a disaster of fatal proportions.

Surely Cooper wasn't one of Reacher's enemies. Kim had always assumed they were wary warriors, but ultimately on the same side.

Otherwise, Cooper wouldn't want Reacher for any classified assignment.

For a long time, Kim had wondered whether there was a classified assignment at all.

She'd thought for a while that what Cooper really wanted was Reacher dead.

Now, she believed Cooper's story was at least partially true. There **was** a top-secret job. Cooper actually wanted Reacher on the team to complete the job.

And a top-secret project required a team Cooper could trust.

Which meant, Cooper believed Reacher could be trusted to complete that mission.

Good to know.

ABOUT THE AUTHOR

Diane Capri is an award-winning **New York Times**, **USA Today**, and worldwide bestselling author. She's a recovering lawyer and snowbird who divides her time between Florida and Michigan. An active member of Mystery Writers of America, Author's Guild, International Thriller Writers, Alliance of Independent Authors, Novelists, Inc., and Sisters in Crime, she loves to hear from readers. She is hard at work on her next novel.

Please connect with her online:

DianeCapri.com
Twitter.com/DianeCapri
Facebook.com/Diane.Capri1
Facebook.com/DianeCapriBooks

www.ingramcontent.com/pod-product-compliance
Lightning Source LLC
Chambersburg PA
CBHW020345310726
48979CB00015B/2513/J
9781962769273